Praise for THE ECSTATIC

"LaValle's hero barrels through his comic novel attending beauty pageants, writing horror flicks, corresponding with a political prisoner, and dealing with his super-dysfunctional family. Unlike your typical monocultural tome, we get everything from this novel—Gogol as well as Biggie Smalls. His characters remind one of Chester Himes and Charles Wright, but LaValle is special."   —ISHMAEL REED, author of *Mumbo Jumbo*

"In the majestic tradition of William Faulkner, Victor LaValle has created, with love apparent, a singular cast of crazies, con men, and beauty queens out for their piece of the pie. This quest is a rollicking laugh-out-loud wild ride, but be warned: It is punctuated with stunning grief and mournful beauty. *The Ecstatic* is a jubilant American novel."
     —BINNIE KIRSHENBAUM, author of *Hester Among the Ruins*

"Possessed by Kafka, Carver, and the Notorious B.I.G., this is a tale of the new millennium American experience, grotesquely captured in a prose so crisp that it cuts to the core before you can blink. LaValle exposes our absurdity—clinical and otherwise—with all its hilarity, eroticism, violence, and horrific beauty. "
     —WILLIE PERDOMO, author of *Where a Nickel Costs a Dime*

"LaValle's characters emerge 3-D from the page, formed in masterfully few sentences, lively in the reader's brain from beginning to end, funny, poignant, absurd, profound. This book satisfies in a hundred different ways."   —ANTONYA NELSON, author of *Female Trouble*

"Seldom does one find a young novelist so adept at dark comedy, with an edge to his voice that is at once raw and sophisticated— no easy trick. Céline comes to mind, and the Henry Miller of *Black Spring. The Ecstatic* is a fabulous novel and Victor LaValle is a wonderful writer."
     —NICHOLAS CHRISTOPHER, author of *Franklin Flyer*

"A comic feast, deeply felt and beautifully written. *The Ecstatic* proves that Victor LaValle is a voice to be reckoned with for years to come."
     —ERNESTO QUIÑONEZ, author of *Bodega Dreams*

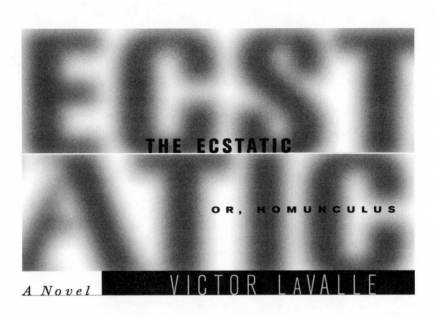

THE ECSTATIC

OR, HOMUNCULUS

A Novel VICTOR LaVALLE

CROWN
Publishers
New York

Published by Crown Publishers, New York, New York.
Member of the Crown Publishing Group, a division of Random House, Inc.
www.randomhouse.com

CROWN is a trademark and the Crown colophon is a registered
trademark of Random House, Inc.

Printed in the United States of America

DESIGN BY BARBARA STURMAN

Library of Congress Cataloging-in-Publication Data
LaValle, Victor D., 1972–
    The ecstatic : a novel / Victor LaValle.— 1st ed.
    1. Young men—Fiction.   2. Uganda—Emigration and
immigration—Fiction.   3. Fatherless families—Fiction.
4. Schizophrenics—Fiction.   5. Grandmothers—Fiction.
I. Title.
    PS3562.A8458 E28   2002
    813'.54—dc21   2002006766

ISBN 0-609-61014-7

10 9 8 7 6 5 4 3 2 1

First Edition

TO VIRGINIA SMITH,

a great writer, editor, and human being.

Who knew anyone could be all three?

Underneath it all I hear pan pipes tooting and a cloven hoof beating time.

—JOHN FAHEY

1 THE WHALE,

They drove a green rented car into central New York State to find me living wild in my apartment. Wearing shattered glasses and my hair a giant cauliflower-shaped afro on my head. I was three hundred and fifteen pounds. I was a mess, but the house was clean. They knocked and when I opened the front door there were three archangels on my stoop. My sister rubbed my ear when I cried. She whispered, – Why don't you go put on clothes?

My family took me home to Queens and kept me in the basement. When I tried to go outside alone, they discouraged it. My sister led me by the hand when walking to the supermarket. Mom cut my meat at the dinner table. They treated me like what some still refer to as a Mongoloid. A few days of this is tenderness, but two weeks seems more like punishment. The spirit of blame stooped in a corner.

Their concern was wonderful, but the condescension was

deadly. And surprising. Before opening the front door to them I really thought my life was full of pepper.

Three weeks after coming back to Rosedale I cooked a big, red breakfast for my family just to prove that I could. Not only to them, but to myself. It was September 25th, 1995. I remember certain dates to organize and understand my disaster. Without them my mind is a mass grave.

It was a red breakfast because I added ketchup to the eggs when scrambling them. And to the bacon as it curled in the pan. Call me tasteless, but ketchup is the only seasoning I need.

I was so nervous that I even dressed up that morning. This bright purple suit that was loose on me and hid my tits. Made me look like a two-hundred-fifty-pound man.

Our oven was so hot I had to watch I didn't sweat into the food. Wiped my forehead with my tie. I pulled butter from the fridge to set next to a plate of toast and if this didn't make them happy then I was out of ideas.

But they didn't appear. I waited a long time.

Even though I heard their beds creak then footsteps on the floor, they never came around the corner. It was like they turned to dust. I prodded the bacon, but without enthusiasm. There was no sizzle yet. With my left hand in my pants pocket I hoped to look cool. I counted numbers to keep from fidgeting.

I turned the gas flames lower. I washed dishes left in the sink overnight and put them in high cabinets. Sunlight addressed the windows.

Worst of all fears is abandonment. Eventually I had to know where they'd gone. The white linoleum tiles ticked against the undersides of my dress shoes.

I was silent in the hallway. There weren't any windows here so the place was dark and the ceiling seemed far. My hands tapping the walls was the echo inside a hollow bomb.

They'd hid in the bathroom. Mom leaned against the sink while Grandma rested on the toilet and my sister, Nabisase, sat on the rim of the tub. Three versions of the same woman—past, present and future—huddled in one room. With the door partway shut I was unseen and apart from them.

Mom whispered, —We should go to him.

—Yes. Grandma agreed, but they stayed there.

My family was afraid of me.

I expected more sympathy, actually, because I sure wasn't the first one in my bloodline to go zipper-lidded. You should've seen when my mother tobogganed naked through Flushing Meadow Park in 1983. Four police carried her to the hospital wrapped in their jackets. Parents on the hill thought Mom was a hump-starved fiend out to abduct their children. Her illness often made her frenzied sexually. Whenever she relapsed the woman was an open womb, but Haldol had stabilized Mom's mind for years.

There was my Uncle Isaac, too, who walked from New York to the Canadian border in 1986, and emptied out his brain pan with a rifle. So when they discovered me in that Ithaca apartment Mom and Grandma recognized the situation. Their boy had become a narwhal.

I pushed in the bathroom door to surprise them, but instead of shuddering they only sighed.

—Good morning, Grandma murmured.

—I made eggs.

Nabisase smiled. —That's very good of you!

She was confused and angry. She was thirteen and thus only partially human when it came to compassion. Call me her older brother, by ten years, but Nabisase practically had to tie me down to cut my hair that first week back. I kept saying that I looked fine. No kid is going to enjoy that. Sarcasm was her mild revenge.

Mom and Grandma were earnestly complimentary; anything I did earned praise. If I'd taken an especially heavy boweling they would have bought me a squeeze toy.

Nabisase asked, — Is the fire oven still on?

— Fire oven?

— The place where you cook, Nabisase explained slowly.

— It might be, I admitted.

They ran past me. Forget that. Right over me. Even Grandma, a ninety-three year old, vaulted my doughy shoulders and sped into the kitchen. Where Mom was turning the burners' dials straight off, to six o'clock.

— I wouldn't have started a fire, I told them.

— How do you know? Nabisase asked.

Neville Chamberlain believed Hitler would be satisfied to taste only a jigger of Czechoslovakia. My family knew I wasn't retarded, but the idea of one more paranoid schizophrenic in our fold fucked with their common sense so much that they never mentioned medication, hospitalization, examination. For what? They wished that I was fragile instead of berserk, so that's what I became. They handled me with cushy mitts.

Grandma's English was slightly twisted. She was from East Africa. Uganda, specifically. My mother had also been born there, but Nabisase and I were from Queens. Grandma said, — Well we should have nice dresses then.

— For breakfast?

Grandma said, — You are wearing a suit. We should put on long pants.

While they changed I finished with the food. I got the frying pans going again; the smell of pig meat warmed my heart. The eggs were solid; not dry, just firm. So much grease on the skillet that they floated pretty as kids in a wading pool. I wasn't fat because of any thyroid condition.

We lived in Rosedale, at the southeastern end of Queens. A

suburb of New York complete with the growls of cars leaving driveways. The sound of engines was pleasant to me.

Grandma came back first wearing a yellow housedress and black flat shoes. She walked down the hallway, into the living room, then sat on the sectional couch waiting to be served. Across the street a husband backed his RV into the yard of a home he shared with his wife. My family was middle class and I liked that.

Then, loud as the Devil in his best pink shoes, my sister attacked my mother. A blitzkrieg; bomb blasts and shouting. Lightning behind Mom's bedroom door.

My mother came down the hallway chased by her daughter, who was swinging a hair dryer and yelling Mom's name. Nabisase hammer-slammed Mom across the back of the skull and the dryer's nozzle shattered into plastic chips around the room. Nabisase took two handfuls of Mom's hair and used them as handles for pulling our mother, face first, to the ground.

Grandma tried to stand, but the couch was shaking too much because Mom had pushed Nabisase backward across it. My mother might even have strangled Nabisase if my sister weren't scratching the skin from Mom's hands.

Nabisase pulled the television from our gray entertainment unit. It would have made a louder crash but my mother's foot stopped the fall. Maybe a toe was broken. I bet my sister wished that was true.

My mother had dabbled with art—dress making and sculpture to name two. The only proof of this was a horrendous statuette on top of our entertainment unit. A tiny bust meant to resemble Sidney Poitier except that both ears were on the same side of the poor man's head. With the television crashing the small bust wobbled about to fall so my mother set it safely on the floor.

Then there was a broom against the wall, so Mom took it and

gave Nabisase two baton shots in the ribs. This put my sister on the floor.

And I was the one with a problem?

Grandma yelled, —Anthony! Come. Anthony! Please.

When I stood between my sister and mother they went around me. My sister threw couch cushions over my head hoping they'd hit Mom. Not to hurt, but to annoy, which was a fine alternative.

Mom whipped a small picture frame under one of my out-stretched arms and it plunked against a wall, chipping the paint. —I'm getting a lock for my bedroom, Mom promised. I'm getting it today.

At which point Grandma raised her voice. The old lady climbed on the couch. —You crazy three bitches! she yelled. You stake my heart!

She fell backward, but caught herself. The yellow housedress hung down between her thighs. With her spindly old arms and legs visible she became a giant wiry spider. Gnashing and screaming and the yellow fabric gathered below her like a dangling silk line. Loom of the dead. She scared us away.

There really were worse situations than mine. Mothers and daughters are war.

Not to seem monomaniacal, but there was still the matter of nine eggs, eight slices of toast, six pats of butter, four glasses of orange juice, two cups of tea, six sausage links and thirteen strips of bacon awaiting an eating. How could they forget that?

My mother and Nabisase went to dress; passed the kitchen like there was no food inside. This is something I couldn't do. I didn't understand how my mother could. She used to be weak like me, but now I was the only one who felt the pantry calling. There are people who love to eat and those who don't. My mother might have changed, but I was still a man who found any complication less daunting after a full plate.

I took our largest salad bowl from one of the cupboards above the kitchen sink and threw in those nine eggs. I added another half-cup of ketchup and a teaspoon of salt.

I mixed the ketchup, eggs, sausages, salt and some syrup with a wooden spoon. Until there was a red-and-yellow soup four inches deep and thicker than sap. The idea was to sour mash this concoction then sink into the basement where I could eat it at leisure on my bed. When anyone decides to tell me I have a problem with food I gesture to the long line of helpful advisors forming a kissing line to the right of my ass.

And I would have made it down if I hadn't gone back for the bacon.

Right at the top of the basement steps I realized the thirteen strips were in a bowl next to the pepper shaker. If I didn't get them now Mom would toss them to thwart her own gluttonous tendencies. I darted into the kitchen, grabbed the bacon, dropped it into my big bowl and was set to sashay merrily away, but before I turned around Mom and my sister were at my sides.

—Oh that's too much food for one, my mother said.

My sister put her arm on my shoulder. —You should put that in the garbage place.

—Garbage place?

Mom didn't dignify Nabisase's goading, but her own tone wasn't much better. The difference was that my mother didn't even know how to spell patronizing, so forget realizing that she was doing it.

She asked, —You don't want to get a stomachache, do you?

I said, —Do you people realize I was the first one in this family to even get to college?

—We've all gone to university, Mom said. Myself, your Uncle. Even Grandma. And we got our degrees.

—But that was in Uganda. I was in the Ivy League for two years.

My sister touched my arm. —The only place you'll graduate from now is McDonald's University.

Mom said, —I'll throw it out for you.

I looked at the brew mournfully. I could have fought with my mother, but why? I unloaded the slop into our garbage bin. This made my mom glad.

She was fifty-three years old with gray stubble on her chin. It was while I was away at college that Mom became beautiful by losing ninety pounds. She was sane and slim now. When I'd been walking around downtown Ithaca with cookie crumbs in my hair, Mom was jogging across Brookville Park. Seeing her again had been the hardest. Before I went to Cornell we were misfits, a pair. We'd finish an entire Louisiana Crunch Cake in twenty minutes; hiding from Nabisase and Grandma in the bathroom.

But do you believe our world is an alchemical comedy? Because I do.

Inside the house I was a twenty-three-year-old college dropout, a girthy goon suffering bouts of dementia, but when I opened the front door I was That Right Young Man Living In An Otherwise Hysterical Home.

New York City Police had been called to our address four different times in the month before I returned. Sister against Mother. Mother against Sister. Once Grandma called cops on both. No one was ever arrested, but there was a quartet of pink police reports on the fridge under a magnet shaped like bananas.

Outside, the ladies were crazy and I was brand new.

I walked down the front steps and pulled our green garbage bin from one side of the house onto the sidewalk. I auditioned for the role of conscientious new director. After putting out the trash I coiled the lawn hose by the driveway.

The man across the street, with the RV, said, —Taking care of a house is never done, is it?

His wife was next to him; we spoke from their yard to mine.
—But we're glad to see someone's over there doing it, she said.

Meanwhile Nabisase and my mother were inside yelling again.

My sister left through the kitchen's black security gate. When she went out she slammed that metal door and a gong sound woke Rosedale's sleeping dogs. It was just seven in the morning and now they barked like it was noon.

When other neighbors peeked they saw me throwing away supermarket circulars as Mom opened the same kitchen door, slammed it even louder, then made the Oldsmobile Firenza's engine bleat by twisting the ignition key too hard.

—You keep it up, both husband and wife told me.

Rosedale really was a lovely place. Trees grew beside great lampposts. The sycamores caught starlings on their bare branches. This neighborhood was for teachers and tax preparers. One supermarket manager. A family who owned their own meat store; the specialty was goat.

Two branch supervisors for Bell Atlantic phones.

Two bus drivers.

Nurses.

I spent the next hour in the front yard holding a trowel while theatrically grunting through light field work. I did that because neighborhoods expect cooperation from every family. I know it's dumb to care about other people's opinions, but I wanted everyone to think highly of me.

At the top of the front steps I checked for mail, but it was too early. My sister had cut my hair to the raw scalp. The cold wind hurt, but I didn't put on a hat.

Even after I opened the front door my left and right foot refused to enter. Who would give up manhood, honestly? With so many benefits. The world defers to me.

—Pull the door closed! Grandma yelled from the couch. She watched the television news and read a copy of *The Globe,* too.

I shut the door then slapped down on the standing ironing board.

When Grandma grumbled I apologized.

I remember when she turned around in the green rented car. That whole trip from Ithaca my grandmother only spoke once. She was in the front seat, taking tissues from her bra and handing them to my mother. It was September 3, 1995. Grandma turned to me and said, — We will be fixing you.

2

They were surprised when I turned down a family cookout. They wanted to celebrate my return, but by cookout they only meant four of us in the backyard turning franks on a tiny grill. In that scenario Mom would be pre-chewing my rice the whole afternoon. No thanks. I demanded guests.

—Who? Nabisase asked.

—These other buildings have people in them, you know.

—Bring neighbors!? Grandma yelled.

Mom walked to the front window just to pull down the shade. —Why would we tell people you were back?

I said, —They won't ask.

Other folks must have it easier when they're throwing parties. Invite people and watch them come. But I tried to be objective about my family; we'd have to offer a bribe. I printed flyers and put them on car windows, in mailboxes. I taped them to trees. The two biggest words were the ones that worked: 'Free' and 'Food.'

Even with charcoal blackening the beef and unthreatening soul music on a portable radio, guests wouldn't enter our yard. I was in the basement waiting to make an entrance when my sister came down the stairs. She said, —They're on the sidewalk.

—Then open the gate.

—They just keep asking to see you.

Nabisase was Old-Testament-beautiful; wrathful, privileged loveliness. A short girl with long legs and big thighs. Her face was mostly lips and chin. She'd been to forty beauty pageants in thirteen years, but never won or placed. My sister didn't take them seriously enough to try, just to attend. There were plenty of participation sashes in a suitcase under her bed. She was one of those good-looking women who can be so carefree about their natural splendor that you only want to kick them in the forehead.

Next to her I would have felt insignificant if I wasn't wearing my purple suit. I'd bought it with my savings. I didn't have much, but the suit wasn't worth much. The material was wrinkle-proof. There were washing-machine instructions inside the jacket.

But still I wore the slacks, tie, shoes, everything, because a suit explains a man to his world. It organizes him in a respectable compartment. This formal outfit wasn't camouflage, it was an announcement.

On the drive back, from Ithaca, Nabisase showed me card tricks. She was practicing for a pageant in November. Even long after getting bored Nabisase flicked face cards around the car just to keep me from becoming maudlin.

More maudlin.

—They want to greet the man of the house formally, I said.

Nabisase nodded. —I'll send Mom.

Neighbors were on the sidewalk honking at each other informally.

I pulled our gate open, they walked in.

This was on a Saturday, October 7th. A clear day, but chilly because it was winter. People wore coats, scarves, dickeys.

One woman passed me, then two. Like that. Women. Women. All these women and me.

Nabisase tapped my shoulder. —You couldn't invite shorties? she asked.

—I don't think there are any other men in this neighborhood.

—What about those two? I can go tell them right now.

Before she could talk I put my hand on her mouth. —They look busy, I said.

The pair of guys were about my age and only twenty feet away, relaxing on a stoop next door. One was muscular and the other was thin, so you can guess why I ignored them. I believed in market dominance, not competition. They waved, but I didn't. I pulled my sister to the backyard; I had the only 'y' chromosome around.

It had been three parched years for me. I don't mean three years since I had sex; I mean thirty-six months since a friendly handshake. I'd been reduced to brushing past women on crowded elevators; I was that man in the subway car who enjoys overcrowding way too much. When I made it to the back the crowd called my name.

—Anthony! they hailed instinctively.

They didn't question what I'd done in the world. College, work, armed forces, whatever.

My hands uplifted, they encircled me; the planets continuing their heliocentricity.

I knew what I needed and that was a woman, but my mother had her ideas. After the great greeting I had an appetite, so I went to the tables. We had plastic plates, knives, forks and spoons.

There was a bowl of off-white sweet potatoes, a flat pan of fried chapati which are these flat bread disks originally from India that my mother loved since childhood. A pot of oxtail soup. A pot of chicken in salty brown gravy. A pot of meatballs hand-rolled by Grandma, then fried before being simmered in tomato sauce. A dish of brown rice and another of white. When I list these things it's to say which items I sampled first. There were nine others that I'd touch on the second round.

When I sat on one of the cheap chairs we'd rented for the party Mom propped herself next to me. —That's quite a calorie base you've made.

It was a diet tip. Mom was full of them, but because I was feeling so special and wearing my purple suit I had thought she was complimenting me on choosing foods well.

—But do you know what's just as filling as those meatballs?

—The crawfish?

—Broccoli.

What a stupid person. What a colossal wingnut. —No plant tastes as good as meat.

—You've never had a shiitake mushroom, then.

I couldn't lift the first forkful to my lips, though I tried. This seemed odd until I realized my mother was holding my left hand down.

—Eating healthy doesn't just help you lose weight. It can change your complexion. Your blood pressure improves. So many of your problems could be solved.

She was referring to my mind of course; as if lentils were a natural antipsychotic. Though she'd been on a number of medications she wasn't pushing them on me. I'm sure Mom gave more credit for her wellness to leeks and various tubers.

—I'm not asking you to become a vegetarian.

I looked at her strangely; I hadn't realized I was talking out loud. That happened to me occasionally; the blinds between thoughts and words drawn up.

—Then what are you telling me to do?

—You remember when I was 270 pounds? Mom asked.

—1981–1990.

—You don't have to be that specific. Was it really for so long? Now I can't remember.

—We used to sneak whole bags of cookies.

—It was never that much, she said.

One of us was lying.

I thought: If my mother doesn't let me swallow some ox I'm going to fall into a coma right in the grass. I'm telling you this even though I'm not proud of it.

—I'll start tomorrow, I promised, though I didn't mean it.

—You don't mean it, she said.

I covered my forehead so she wouldn't also see the sexual frustration I had gathered inside.

—Start today, she said. I'm talking about a whole change. You won't believe how much of a difference it makes.

Imagine that everywhere you went some sprightly guy follows you; a train, an elevator, in the shower. Now this guy isn't so bad; he doesn't hit you. He just plays an accordion loudly and right into your ear. This goes on so long that it's no longer exactly noticeable, but the sound is wearing you down. You become irritated and try to make him stop, but when you try to grab his throat he takes a tiny step just out of reach. And keeps playing. It's no longer music or even separate chords, but a constant buzzing just behind you. It keeps you awake for days until exhaustion makes the stupid acts seem sensible. I'd been walking around my apartment naked on the day my family found me only because wearing clothes in the house felt too confining, I'm sure that lots of people do it. The problem is that when I opened the door I was just too haggard to get dressed. Though they must have thought I went outside like that all the time.

I gave my mother the plate of food then she took it to the trash. While Mom felt sure that this would save me, I had my own idea.

Walked up to a seventy-year-old woman with a face like warm pie crust, soft and dimpled. I took her hand and kissed it.

While pouring a dumpling-shaped teenager some fruit punch I told her: —Cornell's architecture program is one of the best. You should let me see if I can get you in.

She shrugged then went back to her chair, somberly chewing potato chips. She was expressionless, her face amorphous, but I was so horny that she charmed me.

None of my lines worked, but then neither did straight conversation.

There was a lady leaning against one side of our house with her hair pulled back under a bright scarf, face in some book. I tiptoed closer because if I'd had any luck in the world it was with literate women. But this one was only checking the horoscopes in the back of her *TV Guide*.

Though she did smell like cocoa butter, which was nice.

Mom came around again checking if I'd loaded a new plate, but I hadn't. The backyard was only about twenty feet by twenty, so where could I go to nibble mashed potatoes undetected? Since I couldn't fulfill one hunger I tried the other; applying my smile to more women regardless of age or infirmity. One old woman had no voice box thanks to cigarettes, so she used that electric wand against her throat. As a girl she said she'd loved to sing, but no one listened since her operation. She wasn't bad looking or at least I tried to be objective about myself here; I had no room to discriminate. She told me she'd sing two Jim Reeves songs, but if that was English I didn't understand. Every word she sang was just a long or short variation on a sound, –zzz– or –zzzzzz– and occasionally, –zuh–. I held her hand gently, but it was clear that sex was long past her. So when Mom went inside to get napkins I ran to the meal tables and stole a chicken leg.

I crept to the side of the house then waited next to our Oldsmobile Firenza; even bent over like I was checking the hubcaps. Until I heard Mom out back again.

—You're Anthony.

A man behind me spoke before I could eat so I turned with more than a soupçon of agitation asking, —What? What?!

—Nothing to worry about, my man. Your mother told me about the party. She told me about you.

He was taller than me. His suit was tailored tight to make him seem even longer. From a block away he'd look six foot three, but closer it was an even six.

—What did she say? I may have sounded agitated. All I needed was for Mom to ruin me with the neighbors, by telling them I was touched in the head.

This guy smiled, saying, —Hey now. No problems.

He said, —Ishkabibble.

—S'l'm aleikoum, I answered, unsure if this was right.

He asked, —You a Muslim?

—No, I thought you were. What did you say?

—My name. Ishkabibble. I helped your grandmother get the paper she needed for this house.

—She couldn't do it on her own?

—I'm better than the banks, he said. I am the U.S. Treasury to half this neighborhood.

Ishkabibble had a doofy tooth. One of his front teeth was doofy. White and fully grown, but twisted about twenty degrees abnormal. He could sip a straw without opening his mouth. Would it be rude, I wondered, to suck the marrow out of a chicken bone right now.

He said, —I understand that you're ready to enter the world.

—I bought brand new clothes and everything.

He nodded, then smiled. —Of course. I'm not trying to down you. Your mother just told me you were gone.

—That's what it was.

—So now you come back to help them out?

—That's what it is.

What I didn't want to do was act greedy. —She's in the back if you're looking for her, I said.

Go ahead out back and let me feed, that's what I actually meant.

—Your mother? I'll speak with her later, Ishkabibble said. Right now I want to talk with you. Young man comes home and starts to work, he needs a way to get around.

—I'll get a bus pass.

He slapped my shoulder lightly. —Are women putting out for bus transfers these days? Let me tell you, a nice car gives any man a polishing.

—You think I need one?

—Who doesn't?

This guy was good. If he'd had a contract I'd have signed it without reading.

We were at my open front gate. —There's five cars on this block that I helped with. Come see what we can do.

I had the chicken leg palmed so that the meaty top was hidden in my hand while the bone was up against my wrist, obscured by the sleeve of my suit jacket.

My neighbor's garbage bin had been tackled in his yard. A big mess, there was a splash of yellow rice, egg shells and diapers across their front steps. A spoiled wave lapping at the shore. Before I could figure what made the mess a tiny dog ran out from behind the garbage can, leapt the neighbor's low fence and attacked Ishkabibble's skinny leg.

Rosedale was used to this. I hate to admit. Yes it was a middle-class outfit, from the mid-price cars to the Catholic schools nearby. A neighborhood of well-kept homes. But it was still common to find feral dogs hopping from yard to yard; so starved that their ribs showed through. Where had they come from? Children. Stupid, stupid kids. Who lost their dogs or set them free. Or even some who let their dogs hump in the park just to laugh at the sticking motion. This is how five loose dogs becomes fifteen. Then forty. Besides the domesticated house pets and yard guards, some frenzied crossbreeds terrorized the neighborhood. Daily there was shit on many stoops, torn garbage bags in driveways. At night they bayed from Brookville Park or street corners or under our windows.

But now there was the mutt trying to eviscerate Ishkabibble. It was a mix of Pug and Pekingnese; with a face so flat it might have been concave. A short-haired body, but a fluffy tail.

The man looked to me for help, but what did he expect? That I would drive my hands into the maw to pry his pant leg free? I turned to get my sister, the tough one.

Ishkabibble said, —Throw him the chicken leg.

—Why should I?

—What?!

The skin was reddish and greasy. Now he wanted me to give it away?

He kicked stiffly at me, but moved off-balance like a marionette.

—Okay, I said to Ishkabibble. I'll help.

But not right away. I picked at the chicken tenderly.

To his credit Ishkabibble checked the dog in the jaw with his heel.

When it barked Ishkabibble got free and tried to shut the gate, but soon as he pushed it the dog stuffed its charged face in between and there wasn't enough room to throw down the little metal clasp.

—What the fuck are you doing? he yelled.

—I'm just taking the skin, I said. Let me get the skin at least.

The man actually spat on me.

On the lapel of my jacket.

I stopped tearing at the meat then threw it to the road.

As the food went over its head the dog disengaged from Ishka-bibble. It caught the morsel in the air then made a choking noise as it swallowed the bone then broke it under the teeth. And chewed. I watched the Peking-pug do that for a whole five minutes.

Until Ishkabibble asked me, —Are you crying?

There was a fight in the backyard, but I was in the basement so it had no effect on me. After four hours with the guests I felt I'd made the strongest impression I could. Strategically speaking, retreat was victory.

In the basement, beside my bed, were the ten boxes of books I'd brought home. Each one smelled like vanilla because Grandma sprayed them with air freshener that morning.

My mother was outside, saying, —Just come out and tell me what he said.

A woman answered. —You told him I was old!

—I just told him you looked older than me!

Any book would do. I wanted to read quietly for an hour. Growing up with lunacy means learning to allow the skirmishes. Other people don't understand and think: look how badly your mother was acting. But one fight was nothing. You can't imagine how much worse it used to be.

My learning wasn't remarkable. When I was enrolled at Cornell I read enough to pass, but couldn't remember much of it now. Only after the expulsion did learning start to seem important.

—I don't want you coming onto my block now, I heard the woman tell my mother.

—Well then get your husband to stop driving down mine!

Through the basement windows I saw partygoer legs, but not bodies. The shins had gathered into a circle around Mom and the married woman. Maybe it was true that Mom had slept with the lady's husband. Though she was on Haldol there were other explanations for that kind of behavior. After losing weight Mom became bitter. It must have been the fat times, decades of being treated like a burlap sack by men and women. Now that she was dazzling Mom used her beauty as a shiv.

—Please, Mom! My sister yelled out there. Mrs. Hattamurdy, please!

That's when I should have gone upstairs, but I'd already chosen the collected stories of Algernon Blackwood. The book was in my hand. They were supernatural tales which, like Edgar Allan Poe's, were ripping good until the last few pages.

I might still have helped my sister. She was yelling my name. She was forced to be referee at her own mother's cockfight. I stayed below. Soon, Grandma came with me.

Down the basement stairs as I was reading Blackwood's "The Man Who Was Milligan," a dumb story that I still wanted to finish.

—Your mother has trouble, Grandma said.

—I don't really want to go up.

—No?

I made room for her. —Sit down here, Grandma.

—I will, she whispered.

She was wearing yellow rubber gloves. —You've been doing the dishes? I asked.

—Who else?

—I would.

The ceiling in the basement was lower than on the first floor.

Eight feet instead of eleven. The room felt crowded amid Grandma, our cowardice, and I.

—A woman says your mother has had friendship with her husband.

—Did she call it friendship?

—No she did not.

I shut the book then put it in my lap. My breath smelled bad even though I'd brushed my teeth this morning, so I tried not to breathe on her but then remembered that this was my grandmother; not every woman was a potential partner.

—I'm always glad to see how much you like books, she said.

—How do you stay so thin, Grandma?

She sighed. —You know I have always wanted more weight. They called me skinny names when I was young.

—I would give you some of mine if I could.

—I have always been trapped between small and smallest. She put up two threadlike hands to show the parameters.

—People expect me to stay somewhere between bigger and bigger forever.

—Maybe your sister will stop the fight, Grandma said.

—She'll learn how. I did.

—Your mother has been doing so well for a long time.

—Yes?

—I just don't want her to now make new problems. My sadness comes from your pain.

—I like the way my boxes smell. Thank-you.

Grandma nodded. —I will spray them every day.

She took the book from my lap then set it facedown on my pillow. The cover showed a hazy painting of children wearing grotesque masks. She didn't think much of the subject matter, I guess, but then all she read was tabloids. —Will you get a job? Grandma asked.

—I'll apply for some tomorrow.

—A safe one.

—I want to move furniture.

—Oh, you will break your back.

—I worked even after I stopped going to school, Grandma. I cleaned houses in Ithaca.

—Why don't you do that here? That's no danger.

—Moving is like cleaning. I like to see things get organized.

—How long did you work like that. Houses in Cornell?

—The last two years.

—Two years! Such time. Why didn't we know?

—Because I didn't tell you.

—We believed in your letters. You wrote us about classes.

—But you never asked to see my grades. I touched my knees. What made you come up in September? I asked.

—Your sister begged us to take the time.

Of the noises outside Grandma and I ignored most of them. I was an expert at it and she was the grandmaster.

—Being a moving man is hard, she said.

—I could get an easier job, but it won't pay any better.

—Not easy, she said. You should labor. So much of your problem would be solved. Your grandfather toiled harder when he was sick and it always healed him.

I nodded. There were many suggestions. Everyone wanted to make me better, but we couldn't even name the problem.

3

I met Lorraine on the 6 train when it was between 14th Street and 23rd. We were in a tunnel, but I choose to remember this as meeting when it was dark.

Sunday, October 8th, my mother woke with bruises on her cheeks because the married Haitian woman was a better fighter.

That morning we sat nearly together in the living room, with Mom, Grandma and I on the sectional couch. Nabisase on the floor eating cereal from a yellow bowl in her lap.

My mother and sister talked, but I was quiet just like Grandma. When anyone's tea was finished I made more. Grandma convinced Nabisase to let her comb and braid her hair. In this way we hoped to apologize to Nabisase and even Mom.

My mother and grandmother were foreigners, essentially, so they had an alien's attitude about forgiveness. Mom apologized and expected that all bad feeling was soothed. But, being Americans, my sister and I expected contrition. Saying sorry was fine, but tears were better. This is a country of moral failures, not simple mistakes.

But Mom only said, —I didn't mean to fight. Forgive me.

That's it.

Then she and Grandma left to clean the bathroom, mow the yard, keep living.

Leaving my sister and I as mystified as a Baptist with a Buddhist groom.

Our living room was painted red, but in the low register. Nearly crimson. It was a serious little chamber; only more so with my sister in it.

—This family needs church, my sister said.

—Awww. I groaned, ground my teeth, gripped the couch cushion then collapsed.

—Let's get dressed, Nabisase commanded.

—You should at least ask me.

—Wear a suit, she said.

—I've only got one and it's dirty.

Mom and Grandma weren't going. —We did our time in that institution, Mom insisted.

When I hid in the boiler room I hoped my dithering would make us miss the preacher's call, but Nabisase appeared carrying my shoes and black socks. I ducked into Grandma's closet and my sister brought me a tie. A thirteen-year-old girl haunted me.

This had nothing to do with religion; if this had been Saturday she'd insist we go join a synagogue. On Monday it would be to attend a school board meeting for Community School District 29. A teenager's natural talent is for blending tedium with enmity.

Unfortunately in Queens it was possible to indulge this impulse for Holy Ghosts or Holy Rollers at any time. I couldn't delay us out of a sermon. There were seven churches in a one-mile radius from our home; even one that operated from midnight to six A.M.

Storefronts, trailers on the side of the road, established brick venues with gabled rooftops and parking lots. Christ was here. I later discovered that Queens was much like the South. Places where there is one God and he tolls for thee.

There was a church three blocks away. Close enough that Nabisase and I walked even though I didn't want to.

On the corner of 229th Street and 147th Avenue there was a small brick building that might have been mistaken for a speakeasy rather than a church. It had no windows and only one gray metal door in front. The sign on the gate that surrounded the church read: Apostolic Church of Christ. A Church with Old Time Powers.

—These people actually believe in God, I told her. Do you understand that?

I didn't want to attend a service just to hear my sister rant to the pastor afterwards. Screaming about how much she hated Mom's corrupt behavior at the picnic.

Nabisase would do that because she believed the church was here to serve her, not the other way round. If she knew that self-centeredness was a sin she'd never have gone inside. Airing family distress seemed like the wrong reason to attend anyway and, more to the point, embarrassing. I really wanted to avoid that kind of thing in Rosedale. I thought I came off pretty well at the cookout so I wanted to make more good impressions, not fewer.

As my sister opened the church door I ran away. Slowly. Two blocks to the bus stop.

I went to the subway via a gypsy van to Jamaica then an E train from Parsons Boulevard. Since it was Sunday and I couldn't look for work, I'd decided to buy a second suit. They were only $100 for everything. Not including shoes and socks. I transferred at Lexington Avenue to the 6. Where I met Lorraine. A little shredded paperback in her hands.

I sat next to her so I could be sure she wasn't reading a hair pamphlet or a cosmetics catalog or a douche brochure. I don't know.

Where we sat the train car smelled pleasantly like cinnamon because of two small girls whose hands and cheeks were iced and sticky from pastries. That seemed like a good omen for a fat man. Even better when the cover of her book showed the words, Translated from the Russian by Andrew R. MacAndrew.

— How do you like the story? I asked her.

Lorraine turned her face to me, but not her body.

I don't want to make too much of her; Lorraine was on her way to being as heavy as me. We had the same shape. Just she was six inches shorter. Her face was nearly lost in these frizzy hairs that dangled from the sides of her head. She lurched forward so much as she sat that her nipples nearly touched her belly button. Lorraine was a shlump and tremendously glamorous. I wanted to cry over her feet because I was so thankful that she'd turned around. More so when she kept listening to me.

She was reading a book of stories by Nikolai Gogol so I told her about his novel, *Dead Souls*.

That when he'd finished the first third his mind began to twist, instead of just being a good story he was convinced that his book was meant to save the Russian people. When he realized this was nonsense he burned the unpublished pages, most of the second third, then starved himself to death in a religious fervor. The year was 1852.

Lorraine didn't find the tale very compelling, but she liked the fact that I knew it. Most of the guys she dealt with divided their time between PlayStation games and good weed. I couldn't tell a woman with that kind of bias that I'd rather be discussing ghost stories. My freshman lit class had taught me enough to approximate erudition.

We spoke on the telephone most evenings. Lorraine was a college student and in class during the day. I was never allowed to ring her because she had a volatile roommate studying to be a veterinarian. A guy. She said she lived in the dorms, but I sure didn't believe her. Because I didn't have her phone number I felt powerless. Whenever she chose Lorraine could stop calling, then where would I be?

Every conversation I asked her to spend the night with me. For two weeks she waffled, but why else were we talking.

Two weeks to wear her down.

She suggested this motel with a view of the Cross Bronx Expressway.

Snug between a furniture warehouse and an abandoned furniture warehouse Red Penny Motel looked positively high-toned. Seventy-five rooms, but only two lights were on. Twenty-six cars in the parking lot. The night was so cold that my nose had numbed and I didn't get to smell this rich city.

I walked into the parking lot. Probably the first person over the age of sixteen who'd ever done such a thing. The bus stop was seven blocks away, and calling a gypsy cab would have been a waste.

The lobby entrance was cramped down by the giant penny slung above the doors. Eight feet across with a large Abe Lincoln whose nose was misshaped long and had a pointed beard, more Devil than the long-interred emancipator. Maybe the crazy black Hebrew Israelites had gone into the hospitality industry after realizing there was no profit in broadswords.

I went into the lobby to get keys for a room then waited on a bench across from a pair of old women. I had never seen such love as theirs. They held hands absently, but firm; one set of fingers like kudzu, the other like dirt. It was the kind of friendship earned after forty years. I doubted they were renting a room; the motel clerk was letting them rest some warmth back into their bodies. If they had shelter I wouldn't know it; how they made money I can't surmise.

After ten minutes our quartet had, involuntarily, synchronized our breathing. A tiny gasp around the room and then a silence deeper than the fields of space.

The first woman wore sandals even though it was October 21st. Her toes were exposed. Her heels were calloused into stiff yellowed skin that I wanted to caress between my thumbs.

I missed women very much.

I was wearing a dark green suit that was ugly, but I got good service at the store. It was fitting that I wore it to see Lorraine again since I'd been on my way to buy it when I met her. The Egyptian guy who owned the place in midtown Manhattan even recognized me when I visited. He came from behind the counter screaming, Big Man! I have the jacket for you! You know famous rapper Mr. Notorious B.I.G.? I make you look as good as that.

The suits were worn at home and at work. I'd started moving furniture a week ago.

I stood and smoothed my clothes the best that I could when an old Cadillac arrived; it had commercial license plates and darkened gypsy cab windows. My hands were shaking.

Out stepped Lorraine. She paid the driver a twenty.

As I led Lorraine to our room I felt the pulse of nature on the stairs. My arms and legs trembled so much I thought they were going to tear.

The room had a double bed and that's it. Not even a night table. The telephone was on the floor. There was space for a dresser or chiffonier, but those starving animals had been sold off by the farmer. I would have made a joke about the decor, but was too afraid that Lorriane only needed one excuse to leave.

—I'm glad to know that, Lorraine said.

I had that feeling again, of my mind being read.

—Your smile, she clarified. I'm glad to know you can smile.

She was nervous. She was.

If I sound surprised that's because I was surprised. To me women were like the perfect model of government: paving the roads and protecting the weak. Omnipotent.

Boys without fathers say that kind of thing a lot. About their mothers. About their wives. Comparing ladies to goddesses and gold. But still I think we hate women even more than the average guy.

My hands were on her shoulders. I reminded myself that we weren't in love. Be fun, I told myself. Don't get weird. She only wants to play.

A man walked across the second floor landing right outside our room. The curtains were drawn so I only heard his boots on the concrete in drowsy cadence. He stopped by our door.

Lorraine wasn't listening, but I was.

She touched my neck to tell me that we could kiss, but I wanted to hear the man outside go mosey off. I tried to think of some excuse for checking the door, but didn't want to look like the cheating husband afraid that he was being followed. Or worse, a nut.

Lorraine made my skin tin again. When she squeezed warm hands around my cheeks they curved and shaped easily. I wanted to enjoy it, but hardly could because the outline of a man was still visible through the window when our curtains shifted.

Don't think I'm being too spectral here, I wasn't afraid that the guy was a ghost; it was a push-in robbery that worried me.

—There's some things I've got to take care of anyway, Lorraine said, then dropped her bookbag on the floor.

I was agitated by the guy standing outside then by the fact that my hesitation had curdled our mood. —Why don't you forget about that? I suggested. What is that?

—My books, she said. I have to write a paper.

Insulted, I went to the bathroom. Who brings homework to a rendezvous?

Of course, geek that I am, outrage gave way to a fantasy of she and I doing naked research on the bed. How erotic it would be to write up the bibliography with her bare thighs pressed against my back. Then when I walked out again Lorraine was packing.

—We have to move, she said.

—What the hell are you talking about?

—There's no working phone and I need one.

Lorraine had unscrewed the mouthpiece from the handset to find that inside it someone had lumped ten or twelve pieces of gum.

—What do you want the phone for? I can help you.

—Please, she scoffed.

I got angry that she didn't want my sexy research assistance. —You know these rooms are usually hourly, I said.

—It took you almost an hour just get up those stairs.

I sat on the bed and stifled any cracks about her own fat back because Lorraine seemed an insult away from running home.

—It's not so hard. You go down and tell them the room's not how you want it.

I was so annoyed that I forgot about the spook by my door until I was out there with little of Lorraine to protect me. But I did still have the perfect clean smell of the woman, which seemed to be enough because the man out there had gone.

This new room was like the other one except that we had a night-stand which Lorraine used as a desk. While she chatted with class-mates on the working phone I sat on the floor, horseshit insane for pussy.

When another half hour passed I walked over to see that she was writing her essay in bubble letter handwriting, like a junior-high-school girl. Plus the book she used for reference was wrong, mostly because she used only one. Lorraine was writing, in part, about Lee Iacocca's relationship with Henry Ford II and what caused Iacocca to finally leave Ford. But she used only Iacocca's autobiography for the facts!

When I get bored my favorite pastime is to catalogue the stupidity of others.

—I thought you were supposed to hang up a jacket so it wouldn't wrinkle, she said just then.

—Uh, this is wrinkle-proof.

—Nothing natural is wrinkle-proof.

She laughed, but I wondered why she had to be so shitty. Maybe she'd seen me sneering at her two-inch-wide margins. I felt my face warming and didn't want the ridicule. If we'd been having sex already this wouldn't come up.

My mother might think a diet was going to save me and Grandma feel the same about hard work, but what I truly needed was to release this hydroelectric dam—sized nut then the lesser problems like debilitating psychiatric disorders could be swiftly fixed.

But my outburst only made Lorraine less horny, imagine that. Instead of shredding off her underthings she asked me some questions that I didn't understand.

—Do you think Ahmed Abdel deserves another trial? she repeated.

I shrugged, I stalled, I had no idea who this guy was but wanted to sound well informed. Maybe he was a singer who'd killed his wife while on drugs. William Burroughs never went to jail, so why should this guy?

—That's not what happened at all, she yelled. What do you do with your time?

Lorraine drained a pamphlet from her bookbag. His name was Ahmed Abdel and he'd gone to jail for exploding a police car while two cops sat inside. He swore he hadn't been involved. That he was a journalist, not a jingoist. This was on the first page of the pamphlet.

—My friends are making time for his campaign. What about you?

I didn't like her tone; it sounded like a dare. —I'm afraid I'd get lost in the crowd.

—You are the crowd, she said.

I think my hesitation rubbed her rawest parts. She was in college, a time of optimistic fascism when it seems that all the world needs is one more rally.

—I'm not sure we'd ever be good friends, I told her.

—Is that why we're here?

—Well.

—You keep that. Getting involved can change your entire life. Make you a better person.

She pointed to the pamphlet and wouldn't relent until I'd put the ten-page document in my jacket pocket. I was on the bed and so was she, but we faced dissimilar walls.

Two hours past midnight Lorraine said, —You've been quiet.

—I've been looking at you.

She had a faint mustache over her upper lip. It didn't make her ugly or masculine. Right then it was the most beautifully feminine thing that I could stand.

I crept toward her. Dim light was the best special effect; it made me appear graceful. My knees were in some of her papers; my palms ground down on the books. She put one hand out to push me back, but I was fawning over her and she liked that as much as everyone does.

She got into bed under the comforter. I dug in there to find one of her feet.

Lorraine squirmed, but I pulled her down toward me. I touched the back of my hand against the top of her wide foot.

I took her clothes off without getting to see her naked. Pulling the socks, jeans, shirt, panties even, while the covers stayed up to her neck. It was nice. Like she was stripping, but I only got to see the layers once they were removed. Her body, under there, became more real the harder I imagined.

In the bathroom I ran a washcloth under hot water and motel soap then sat near her again and pulled the covers away from her thighs. I massaged the cloth into her leg until one was slick with bubbles. Under the knees. On her shins. Until the cloth was dry.

Wet the hand towel again. Soap again.

Lifted her other short thick leg onto my shoulder, pressed the red cloth against the back of her thigh. Wrapped the cloth over my pointed finger and touched it to where leg greets pelvis, where her skin shifted from one shade to one darker.

Did this steadily until her hips matched the rhythm of the wet cloth and my hand. As she pushed against me lather wept down her leg.

I squeezed the little towel until the soapy water uttered into a puddle in my hand then I rested my palm against her pussy. When she rubbed against me the slight tickle of her hair played up my forearm into my elbow. Moved my hand until the foam spread across us then I touched my hand to my own neck, to my mouth.

The look on Lorraine's face might have been mine. With her eyes shut she seemed far away. I wondered where. I doubt she was even focusing on Ahmed Abdel or that guy she lived with. She had reclined into that calm state people only find when alone.

I rubbed the top of my head on the lips of her pussy just to spread her scent on me.

I thumped her knees lightly with my fingertips.

What sounds? If the curtain hadn't been so thin there would have been that kind of total quiet when there's no light. We had a sackcloth warmth in the room.

I wanted to ask her everything.

If she genuinely cared about Ahmed Abdel's cause. Why she had started college late. If she had children. If she'd ever been out of the country. If she was in love with me.

—Why won't you give me your phone number?

She answered sluggishly. —A woman keeps power however she can.

—Why does that prisoner mean so much to you?

—Because his mind is such a powerful tool.

—Could you imagine feeling that way about me?

I asked, but she didn't answer. Only breathed.

—What are you that I don't know you are?

Without hesitation Lorraine replied, —The hero.

Two hours later Lorraine could sleep, but not me. I was pretty naked except for my T-shirt and boxers that I wore the whole evening because even in the dark I was self-conscious. I took them off since she was tuned out, then ran naked around the motel, three times.

Okay I felt like doing that, but if I really had it would have been an act of joy, not madness, though it might have appeared otherwise to the average person.

I did have trouble sleeping though, so I spent time in the bathroom wishing there was a television above the tub. I hadn't even brought a book because I'd had this fantasy of Lorraine and I sexing each other for eleven hours, which is the kind of thing one comes to believe in when years pass between layovers. I forgot that people and parts get exhausted.

Eventually I was so bored that I tried to wake Lorraine again, but her eyes were soldered shut. This led me to that paper she wrote. Just to do something. The one on the nightstand, the one that I took. I shut myself inside the bathroom and corrected the work.

I didn't mean to be snotty when I wrote questions in the margins like, Are you sure Ford was a 'toad of a man'? and, Should you really describe Lee Iacocca as having 'the business sense of a god'? and, Do gods really have business sense? Which one? Mammon? Ayizan?

My suggestions left a terrible smell. Instead of running off tonight I wanted to have sex with her in the morning. I wanted to wake her by gliding my tongue up the crack of her ass. I wanted to do that many times in the coming weeks, but that wouldn't happen if she found this cutjob. So I rewrote the paper, making the corrections I could, but without rearranging her ideas entirely. It was so much fun. I would have made a good English teacher, except that I hate kids.

After I was done I wrote a note on another sheet of paper apologizing for having spilled water on her notebook, so that was why I had to do it over by hand. Then I tore her version, the one with my critiques, and flushed the scraps away.

Fingers of my left hand were cramped from writing awkwardly; sitting on the toilet using my crossed leg as a desktop. After I put the notebook back on the nightstand I ran warm water over my hand, but I heard Lorraine mutter around so I thought she was waking up and I turned off the light in the bathroom. This was the first moment in an hour when I wasn't doing anything wrong, but I wanted to feel good alone.

I shut the bathroom door then locked it. The water was running into the sink, but the faucet made another sound, too. Like a gas oven burner when the dial's been turned halfway, but the flame hasn't yet been lit. A —hisss— that was soothing not sinister. I couldn't see myself in the mirror, only the outline of me since the light came faint through a small window near the ceiling. I couldn't go outside and do it, but in here I took off my clothes to prance around the little room; I shook my naked ass celebrating an end to one long dry season.

4

Lorraine and I parted the next morning. Sunday, October 22nd. I never saw her again. She stopped calling. Her number had come up as 'Unavailable' on the caller i.d. box every time.

But I wasn't sad then. We didn't talk about getting together again, but yes I'd expected it. Now it's like there are two versions of me. The one who knows that she left and the one who doesn't. My longing clouds the portrait of him, but his delight remains with me.

I was overjoyed that day. So much I skipped in the parking lot then down the block to the bus stop. I just about popped.

If I'd wanted I could have taken an express train rush through the Bronx and upper Manhattan, but back in Rosedale, this being Sunday, my sister was undoubtedly strapping on her church shoes.

Nabisase'd been so angry two Sundays earlier when I first ran off and met Lorraine on the 6 that she made me promise to come the next weekend, but that was the first time the movers had work for me, overtime pay, so I swore to go this weekend, but then Lorraine again.

I made the two-hour commute home last three. Passed four magazine stalls on various subway platforms; bought a Watchamacallit at each one. When I opened the kitchen door Grandma nearly pounced on my shoulders. —Where were you! she demanded. He's here, she called.

—Where did you go, Mom asked, coming up from the basement. Where did you get to?

—I met a friend.

—You must call, Grandma told me. She was using a bucket and mop on the kitchen floor. Though she was ninety-three, Grandma still sewed, did the laundry, walked to the supermarket and carried groceries on her own.

—Or else we wonder, Mom said. Tell us you won't do this again.

—An oath, Grandma whispered.

—I promise, I swear, I pledge and I vow. Am I going to have to go to church, too?

—You missed Nabisase, Grandma said.

Am I crazy then, for expecting I'd avoided lecturing, hectoring? Mom even agreed.

—You don't need church, she said from the kitchen table where she was preparing a breakfast of asparagus spears and weak tea.

Mom took my hand. —I know what can help you.

I said, —Great.

Every realm has its capitol and for Southern Queens that's Jamaica. Sanctuary of discount shoppers. 99¢ stores and used cars sold along Hillside Avenue.

Mom drove up Merrick Boulevard. It wasn't congested at noon, but by one o'clock all the churches freed the faithful. You wouldn't imagine how many believers there are until you see them filling the roads.

I kept the car window down because I had the smell from between Lorraine's legs still drying on my chin; no mother wants to smell pussy on her son's face.

—You're right about that! Mom laughed and slapped the dashboard.

I was embarrassed for what she might have heard. I put my hands around my forehead.

—Did I say something?

—Never mind that. You're a grown man I guess.

An admission I'd appreciate on any other afternoon, but this time it made me feel oily.

—Reach in that dash, she said.

Gladly. I went into the glove compartment elbow deep pulling out every item asking Mom if that's what she wanted. What about this? In one movie I liked, *Little Tricks,* a man hides his monstrous, deformed brother under the car's dashboard; the creature eats unsuspecting prostitutes one digit at a time.

—One of the music tapes! Stop playing, Mom said. It has your name on it.

The tape with my name on it was so old that the plastic outer shells were held together with Krazy Glue that had gone gummy brown in the cracks. While the tape began reeling I took off my shoes. I wanted to sleep. I would have, but then my mother asked me a question.

—How old are you today?

Her voice sounded strange because it was playing through our two car speakers. Then my answer was funny, because I squeaked.

—I'm ten years old.

—You keep these in the car? I asked over the recorded conversation.

—Not always. Just recently.

If I was ten on the tape then it was from 1982. She'd been taking photos, home movies and even these cassette tracks since I was five. Whenever she was institutionalized I sent her the tapes of Nabisase and I to comfort her.

—How do you like your new little sister? My mother asked a ten-year-old Anthony.

—She's fine, he answered.

—Is that all you can say about her?

—My sister is always making BM's!

That's how the dialogue went; I was underwhelmed, but my mother was marooned. She was back there now, in 1982, without need of rescue.

She said, —Do you remember when you were that little boy?

—You taped us a thousand times.

The rest of the way she and I were quiet while Mom and Anthony spoke. They were funny, sometimes bland, but I enjoyed the time capsule, too.

We parked on Linden Boulevard then walked around the corner onto Merrick. Two of the four corners at the intersection were occupied by gas stations, the third was a hair salon and fourth the Hillman Christian School.

Hillman A.M.E. was the grandest landowner in Southern Queens; its elders ran the school and other businesses. The church itself, two blocks from this intersection, was one hundred thousand square feet. It looked like a massive clam, a wooden quahog, surrounded by flood lights. A house of worship constantly lit for a Hollywood premiere.

This Hillman church consortium ran for-profit businesses like the Christian School along Merrick Boulevard. Hillman Neighborhood Care Team, Hillman Christian School Early Childhood Learning & Development Center, Hillman Home Improvement Association. Hillman Federal Credit Union.

They placed caregivers with the homebound elderly.

Ran small-business seminars.

They were even buying back homes from the Arabs and Jews who'd been overcharging the largely working-class black renters for two decades. There was much applause for this in local black papers because it was still two years until Hillman A.M.E. raised the rents to prices neither type of Semite would have ever dared.

—How many more of those tapes do you have? I asked her.

—Plenty. Of you. You and your sister. Your sister and I. A couple of Grandma. Isaac.

—We're all saved, I said.

The long corridor that is Merrick Boulevard pushed sounds up into the ceiling so that car horns and bus horns and truck horns, the music of Queens, floated away. And underneath them I heard the cheerful wind of birds flirting.

I was constantly surprised by how many trees there were on every block out here. Is that a stupid thing to say? When I was at Cornell, Ithaca's ponds, the foliage, made me forget what my city was really like. When friends who weren't from New York would call it mechanical and unnatural I agreed. Pretty soon I was describing the piss in building staircases or heaps of trash ten feet high because I thought it made me tougher to come from a hard place. But I didn't tell enough about Flushing Meadow Park's scarlet maples. The white-rumped sandpipers of Jamaica Bay.

—I want you to drive with us to a pageant in November. You know I can't stay awake more than two hours in a car.

I didn't believe her. Not about the contest, but why she wanted my participation. —You just don't want to leave me alone in the house for a weekend.

One of the stores on this Hillman-owned block was our destination. —Anyway, she said, here we go. Mom held the door.

I looked up to read the silver letters above the entrance. Hillman Halfway House, it read.

—I'm not going in there.

Mom pulled my arm forcefully. —What's the problem?

—A halfway house? You want to put me in a hospital, just take me there.

She read the sign out loud then laughed. —I'm not thinking that way. You've got the wrong idea.

—How do you mistake the words Halfway and House?

—It's a saying of ours. 'Once you step inside you're halfway to your goal.'

—And what's my goal?

—To be healthy.

—Healthy?

—To be lean.

—This is a weight-loss clinic?

—It's a Diet Center.

My mother had to follow me back around the corner to Linden Boulevard, because I walked away.

—What are you doing, Mom? This isn't going to make things better.

—It's not? When did you become a doctor?

—Oatmeal in the morning won't fix me!

She put a few of her nails into my hand. —Worked for me.

I couldn't deny that she looked force majeure, but this solution was as idealistic as Grandma's. Labor was not a balm. At a job in the Bronx I'd tried to pick up a couch by myself a day ago and strained my shoulders.

—Maybe you should just get me some of your Haldol. I'll take it if that means you'll all stop trying to save my life.

—I'm telling you that's wrong, Mom said. I stopped taking it a year ago. And look at me.

Reflected in the glass panels of the hair salon on the corner Mom and I looked like a married couple. I was wearing a cheap suit plus my fat added twenty years. I looked forty-three. And Mom, fetching, sinewy, wearing a red rabbit fur scarf, seemed thirty-five at best.

— So what do you use for . . . I tapped my right temple twice.

— I used to have faith in doctoring. But the doctor's had no faith in me. They don't want you well just wasted.

The stinging odor of hair dye made it out to the street. Along with it came the vinegar odor of straightening treatments, the cloying dreadlock butter. We walked back.

— Why is a church running a fat camp? How do they make a profit on it?

— It's in Hillman's honor.

— Hillman A.M.E., that's a real guy?

— Bartholomew Hillman was a slave in New York in 1787. He had a weight problem.

— The church is named for a fat slave?

— I wouldn't say it that way.

We reached the Halfway House again.

— How could someone be a fat slave? Did he work in the master's house?

— No, she said. He worked in the field. They think it was a glandular problem.

Inside, the reception area was a mix of purple and cream. The carpet, the chairs, the walls were these two swirled hues. It was like standing inside a bruised sky. Heaven as a lounge.

At the back of the room there was a narrow door and a wide one. A lacquered wood desk with a receptionist behind it; the receptionist was the lady who walked over to greet my mother with a robust hug.

— And this is my son.

— You're halfway there, the receptionist said to me in a quiet voice, cleared her throat then said louder, You're halfway there.

I don't know how my mother found the clothes hooks on the wall. They were part of the misted background, indiscernible as each water particle in a cloud. Mom's long brown coat floated nearby as she offered to take mine.

— I'll wear it a little longer.

Mom didn't fight me. She wore a thin white sweater with silver sparkles on the shoulders as epaulets. Her boots must have been part of the outfit sale at Rainbow Shop because they had sparkles too, on the three-inch heels. My mother was beautiful despite her general tackiness.

There was a buzzing noise because the receptionist was pressing a button, though I couldn't see where it would be on her desk. My mother walked to the narrow door and pointed to the other one. I didn't want to go, but it was the only one I'd fit through. The big door was four feet wide, of gray steel, heavier than terror.

— You go right in there, said the woman at the desk.

— You'll be happy. Mom cried.

The room was in a gloom worse than the Bronx Zoo's World of Darkness. I could see only because light came through a pane of one-way glass in the wall to my left. We could see out, but the people on the other side didn't have to look in.

There was space for twenty normal-sized people, but ten of us filled the room to capacity. I thought there were nine big ladies with me but as my eyes adjusted I realized there were only five. The rest were men like me, curvaceous.

A high-pitched groan played in the room. When I shut the metal door the notes bounced around, above and beneath me. Eventually I recognized it as whale song. I suppose it was meant to be soothing, but did it have to be so loud? I thought the damn mammals were floating inside this tiny room.

I pushed past hefty legs, but there wasn't much room so people had to stand or shift in their seats. This is when I realized that wasn't whale music cooing from ceiling to floor, but nine poor metal chairs groaning. When I settled in I added a tenth.

For ventilation there was only a grill the size of a steel wool pad in the ceiling; every person was sweating over his clothes. I undid my tie then the top two buttons of my shirt.

Our freight-entrance door was locked from outside.

We faced the glass.

There were two rooms, ours and the other. Where this one was cramped, in shadows, theirs had floor space and an enormous skylight. A column of sun came down as one thick finger of an approving god.

My mother was with him.

I walked right to the large pane and pressed my face against it. Envy was the climate in our room.

Lorraine's friend Ahmed Abdel was a Japanese man who'd converted to Islam while incarcerated. He was supported by black and Latino college students; also white celebrities. I thought of his romantically gaunt figure from his pamphlet photograph as I mashed myself against the one-way mirror. Each day that it became clearer she wasn't going to call me I read that nattering tract because it was all I had. Pathetically, yes, I thought that if I got into his struggle, joined that righteous rigamarole, I'd find my way back to her as an attractively conscientious man. I looked at his photo ten times a day, jealous that it stirred the blood of spoon-eyed revolutionaries like Lorraine. Envy.

—You're hurting our eyes with that glow-in-the-dark suit so sit down!

—Who said that? I asked.

Nothing's uglier than unattractive dieters. Even if they lose the weight their faces are still half-Wookie. The grim little pudge who'd yelled at me pointed toward the back of the room. When I returned to my seat it made the whimper of a humpback whale again.

—Oh shut up, I told it.

In the other room seven trim women and men were doing routine tasks while we watched them. Opening letters. A pair danced in a friendly way. One tall man climbed a seven-foot ladder and then came back down. After thirty seconds he went up again.

My mother sat on a wooden footstool lacing up her sneakers. When the right and left foot were done she pulled both strings out to start again.

— See, they don't need food every minute of the day.

To my right the outline of a man's large head shifted as he spoke to me. My eyes had adjusted enough to see the mound of his face, but not the features.

—Thanks, I said, because I'd been confused as to what the hell we were doing.

His stomach was even bigger than mine. That was comforting. He wasn't actually short, but because his thighs were so thick his feet didn't touch the ground while sitting. When he introduced himself I repeated the name three times because I couldn't believe it.

— Ledric?

— Ledric.

— Ledric!

— Yes! he yelled at last. Ledric Mayo, he said.

I thought of a war chest of jokes, but before submitting the first one the beetle-faced man who'd mocked my bright green suit yelled, —I can't concentrate with that jibber-jabber going on back there!

This was an isolation tank, not a meeting room.

— How long does it take to get on that other side? I asked.

— You've got some time, Ledric said.

Yeah.

After an hour the seven fetching men and women over there had gone through so many different tasks I forgot my own name.

Besides those lacing boots and climbing a ladder there were others filling out credit card applications. They'd actually fill in the name, address, home-phone-number business and press the completed paper against the glass. There weren't any subliminal messages playing. It was a hard sell with a soft touch.

For sixty minutes.

Without any other stimulus.

One hundred twenty minutes and my big pink walnut of a brain kept wandering no matter how much I agreed with their weight loss training. I marveled as the others in the room nodded like they were learning something new; as if it had never occurred to them that they could play catch without hot dogs in their mouths.

When my family came to get me from Cornell I tried to act like I was fine. After we'd packed my essential books and clothes I took them for a tour of the campus. For ten seconds I pretended that they were wrong, I was still going to school and doing fine. They would have humored me if I'd wished, but being patronized is worse than straight failing. I showed them Olin Library, where I could have studied. Potential classrooms in Uris Hall. They were happy to see such tidy facilities.

I was an English major before leaving school. One of those squishy guys who make up a third of any college campus. Weasels in glasses. I took my family past Day Hall to the Arts and Sciences quad; even inside Goldwin Smith because it was left open on the weekends. Up to the second floor; the English Department's locked wooden doors; we posed for twenty pictures in front of them. That evening I rented two movies, *Camera Furio* and *Chilly Grave.* I thought they'd want to see how I passed my free time in Ithaca, but horror films were too depressing considering their mood. I enjoyed the pictures when they slept.

I'd stayed in Ithaca for two years after getting expelled because off-campus rooms were cheap. I worked a lot. Cleaning houses and offices, mostly. They were satisfying jobs; I feel calm once I put messes in order. When snow packed onto Ithaca's hills during the long winters I pretended my apartment was a ski chalet. This time was so much fun for me that I hardly slept. I didn't want a moment to pass without me. My living room clogged with Arthur Machen, Joe R. Lansdale and the *Dictionary of the Supernatural. Twenty Years of Congress* by James G. Blaine just because I thought the title was a funny fucking pun. The most uninspired life can seem charming to a twenty-one year old. Sitting next to Beebe Lake on Cornell's North Campus, reading Lord Dunsany's awfully over-blown prose, I had a laughing fit because I was so blessed.

Without a warning Ledric opened a plastic container that emitted a smell bad as bunion paste. To my right, there he was, with the plastic container balanced on his serving tray of a stomach. His face was so greasy that it reflected light.

—What are you doing? I asked him. What is that?

Ledric breathed heavier than lust. —There's salmon and some perch in here. Pike too.

—That's fish?

It looked too old to be fish. Maybe the rumor of fish. A fable of fish.

—Not that bad, Ledric answered. I let this sit out for twenty-three days, he said.

The salmon wasn't even that appealing bright pink anymore. Just a gray custard saturated with orange oil.

—I'll go get you some KFC, I offered. Anything's got to be better than that.

He shook his head. —You don't understand.

—Just put the fish down and I'll take you out for some pizza.

Instead he mashed the stuff around with his spoon. Some delicate grayish-white bones stuck out of the meat. The food made squelching sounds when he touched it.

Ledric looked at me. —I can't wait ten years to get skinny. I can't do it. Not no more.

—That's diet food? I think you could find better stuff through Weight Watchers.

But Ledric would not be stopped.

The guy who'd given me lip before started banging on our metal door.

A woman stood so fast that the chair stuck to her ass while she went to the glass and yelled.

Ever see that film *The Thing*? John Carpenter's version. The people in here were like the dogs that had been shut off in a cage with the alien. The canines scratched, yelped, barked to get out because they were encountering an unnatural terror. A creature so hideous that it would destroy them. A Magogdamn terrible sight.

—There's cestodes in here, Anthony. Ledric enjoyed the drama. He dug two fingers into the pulp then pulled out a wad of chaw. He swabbed a dollop of rotten fish between his lower lip and gum, then chewed.

A guy at the door begged. —I need some air! I need some air.

—Cestodiasis, Ledric said to me.

—Why did they lock us in here? I yelled as the thin people ran from their section.

—Whenever we get a new guy they block the door so you can't leave, Ledric explained.

I heard the key go in and twist.

—What are you doing?! I screamed at Ledric.

—Tapeworms, he said.

5

I quit my moving job after falling down a flight of stairs. We were taking an old Quaker woman from Brooklyn to Pennsylvania so she'd be closer to her friends. Books were already boxed when we got there, with categories written on the side. History, Literature, Geography, Religion-West, Religion-East.

A framed letter from Lyndon Johnson was still on the wall. In it the departed President thanked the Quaker's deceased husband for his speechwriting work. I told her I didn't know why Kennedy got sole credit for helping out black people when it was Johnson who signed the Civil Rights Act.

—He was a locomotive with a little boy at the engine, she said.

Holding an armful of books I walked from the third floor of her house to the second when this asscrack of a man, another mover, dropped his box on top of mine. Said he needed water but before I could tell him to set his load at the top of the stairs he laid it on me; I shut my mouth to get the work done faster.

Four hundred and fifteen pounds going down makes more noise than a subway car derailing. Three hundred and fifteen pounds of me lay on the landing next to one box called 'Architecture' and the other, 'Divine.'

I tried not to vomit while the Quaker woman did what Quakers apparently do best. She brought me a cool cloth compress for my forehead; she brought Band-Aids though I wasn't bleeding. She disappeared.

Moving furniture wasn't for me. For days I'd been pretending my chest didn't hurt dramatically at the end of each strenuous job. That everyone gets light-headed from taking a small lamp up two flights of stairs. I liked the idea of being a mover more than the work. Cleaning houses had calmed me, but really I was only washing dishes, rearranging the living room: small acts of tidiness. I'd thought that packing, lifting, moving whole homes would be exponentially easeful. Instead it felt like I'd flattened a few disks in my spine.

The Armenian foreman, who was also the driver of our truck, asked me if I was going to be okay, but as he asked lifted 'Architecture,' and his question trailed off down the stairs toward the sidewalk. Leaving me sweating, staring at the box of 'Divine.'

Later the foreman butted one chubby forearm into my gut as a friendly gesture. He spoke a melted English; only half of each word was actually spoken. —You're not so bad, right? he asked. You're a big guy, shake it up.

How could I ask to go to the hospital when the company didn't have insurance? Their business sign at the main office on 138th Street and Amsterdam was written on posterboard in black marker. Every two weeks they discarded one company name then made up something new. No paychecks, always bills, none larger than a twenty.

I was compensated for the seven-hour shift, $42. Then the Armenian put me in a cab to Rosedale which cost as much as I did for a whole day. My only regret about leaving early was the tip the Quaker would give. Probably $20 a man if the foreman didn't pocket much.

Better to go home, though, because I couldn't think properly the rest of the afternoon. I poured soda in a soup bowl. Grandma rubbed mentholated cream on my back and made me rest in bed all evening.

It was Grandma who woke me the next morning because Mom and Nabisase had left for work and school. If they fought that morning I didn't know it. I tried to go get some bandages Mom kept in her room, but she had actually installed a new lock on the door, as threatened. One that used a key. I twisted the knob for a few minutes, strenuously. Stubborn sturdy mechanism. I pressed my nose to the door crack trying to smell my mother's secrets. I listened patiently, but her room offered no sound.

I was actually doing well enough that standing, bending, working was possible and I would have felt childish pretending with my grandmother. She expected people to act maturely. She was glad I woke up early. She rubbed the mentholated cream on my back again and gave me a card for a job advertised on the posterboard over in the Associated Supermarket on 228th Street.

The company was nearby. Twenty-minute walk; ten minutes on the Q85. Just past Green Acres Mall, which meant that it was actually in Long Island. The mall and the company were on Sunrise Highway, the expressway that started near my home at the ass end of Queens, then ran like a long intestine to the tip of Long Island where, seasonally, waste was stored in the great colon known as the Hamptons. (Thus I strike a blow for the masses! How's that Ahmed Abdel? Lorraine?)

They hired semi-temporary laborers. Do badly and get fired the same day. Do better and they'd keep you on. It was a husband and wife from Baldwin, Long Island. Men so rarely applied that the office manager thought I'd read the ad wrong. Clean Houses—Get Paid, that's easy. The owners were a middle-aged couple who, like most people, never left the era of their bloom. Curtis Mayfield on the office stereo. Otis Redding, like that. And they called the business Sparkle.

Even after opening her front door to me the woman was suspicious, because I wasn't wearing my uniform. I wore the Bing cherry red baseball cap with ten thousand glitter bits spelling Sparkle on the brim, so who needs the jumpsuit? It didn't fit me anyway. She only opened the door a stitch.

—Sparkle ma'am. I'm here to make your home shine.

If I didn't say the motto then, according to our rules, she didn't have to tip me. Not that she was going to anyway. Blacks and old Jews were cheaper than Chinese food when it came to gratuities. I don't want to complain. The money could be better, but I liked the work.

The woman at the front door of this Rochdale Village home finally let me inside and I followed her down the hall. She wore the dark slacks, jacket and belly of a bus driver. There were no photos on the walls, but prayer plaques.

She said, —My husband is going to stay here today, he's sick. I wrote a list for you so leave him alone. He's going to be in bed.

There were four gold rings on three fat fingers of her right hand.

She took me around, but her house was weak; it could barely hold me up. The tiled floor dipped in the middle of the kitchen, moaned when I walked across it.

—Under the sink we keep the cleaners, and this closet has mops. Do you need gloves?

I tapped my coat pocket. —I've got.

Outside, in one of the company's K cars, I had my own vacuum, towels, cleaning chemicals, sponges. But homeowners took issue with the equipment. This was true at nearly every cleaning job I had. And Sparkle's was as raggedy as the rest; the vacuum only worked if run for twenty minutes first.

Her list was under a magnet shaped like a fridge that was stuck to their fridge.

—This is what needs doing on one floor and the rest on the second.

—No basement?

She grabbed my arm. —We couldn't pay you enough to fix that place up.

That made me like her because few of the homes I'd cleaned had owners with any objective sense. This lady was the first in a while to admit her family had made too big a mess to ask for help. I considered going down there and doing the job for free.

She called upstairs before leaving.

No answer, so I thought he was still asleep. I hoped I wouldn't have to wash out bedpans.

The front door shut then maybe eleven seconds passed and I heard the husband's feet on the stairs. They were faint footsteps pattering above my head. Then this skinny guy comes down dressed sharp enough to cut. Wearing a gray, thin suit as cheap as one of my own. The lapels looked about as thick as wax paper. He was breathing heavy from running.

—You're not no girl, he pointed out.

He stood in the living room watching me at the kitchen sink. I'd been planning to sit a moment, but washed dishes to seem busy.

—No I'm not.

—I thought they was going to send some girl.

The man was crestfallen; he was dressed for a funeral and now he had the proper face. He came into the kitchen and poured a drink while I finished the breakfast dishes.

—You got to do the laundry.

—That's not on her list, I said.

—Well it's on mine.

—Yes.

—We got machines in the basement. You can turn them on and go back to the rest.

I walked into the living room and he followed me. He sat on the couch because I was about to move it. Instead I pulled their big round table to a corner after I unplugged a lamp.

Finished with the orange juice, the master of the house put his cup down on the carpet.

—You could put that in the kitchen now. He pointed below him.

He retied his dress shoes by pulling the black laces hard. A young boy ready for chapel.

I took up the cup into the kitchen where the floor announced its weakness for me with another moan. —Oh shut up, I muttered.

This house would have been silent if not for the oven clock, light bulbs. The rechargeable battery case worked constantly. Three hundred years earlier the background noise would have been wind through the crops, Jameco Indians in the dirt. I lifted the blind from one kitchen window where Englishmen in frock coats and breeches once walked. In the back slaves collected salt hay to feed the animals. Three centuries and now I stood in a kitchen filling a bucket with hot water. It was hard to imagine I was even the same species as any of them. Their lives must have been so difficult and now mine was easy. I know some people long for bygone days, but not me.

—Well then, the bus driver's husband said from the threshold of the living room. Guess I'm going out.

I untangled the phone cord wrapped around a chair leg in the kitchen. Kept to busy work around him so he'd believe I knew my profession. If he even suspected I was an amateur he'd lecture me about how to sweep to his specifications. Everyone thinks they've invented the best way to wipe down a fridge. With this guy, just looking at him, I'd have had an embolism if he took a professorial tone while mispronouncing words like 'ammonia' and 'broom.'

— How long you'll need? he asked when I didn't answer.

— Seven hours?

— Seven hours?! He yelled it. How much you think we got to do here? Shit. She didn't tell you to do the basement too, did she?

— No.

— Then what you talking all this seven hours mess? I'll be back in four and that's what I'm paying you.

He made for the door then turned back. — And what the hell you wearing a suit for?

To appear professional.

When the man got gone I ran back to the kitchen to call Ledric. He didn't pick up for twenty-three rings.

— Who's this? He breathed heavily through his mouth.

— How's your disease coming? I asked.

— Tapeworm's not a disease, it's an infestation.

— How's your infestation coming?

— I lost weight already.

— It's only been eleven days!

— So? I bet I lost eight pounds by now.

— You told your family about all this?

— It's only my mother and father out in Chicago. But my long-distance got shut off.

— When's the last time you spoke?

— I sent them some bootleg videos for Christmas.

— Last year?

— Why are you bothering me about all that?

— I'm not trying to down you, I told him. You're not feeling sick?

— Of course not, he said.

I was committed to Ledric because, well, wouldn't you be?
Also, what if it worked?

After seeing him so desperate to lose a few hundred inches
that he'd actually ingest bugs, refraining from my usual three—Big
Mac snack-attack seemed hardly a sacrifice at all. And what if it
worked?

— It's not bugs, he said on the phone.

— Bugs, worms, insects, whatever. I don't think the fish had to
be rotten to get tapeworms.

His faith would not be shaken. —I didn't want to take any
chances about that.

After hanging up I set the two dirtiest pots in soapy hot water to
let them soak last night's meat loose. I went to the car for my tools.

In the living room I ran the vacuum. I lifted the couch on its
side and left it there.

People don't want to return to a neat house. They want to
enter fifteen minutes before the finish, when the rooms are still a
little disarrayed. If they see no proof that work's been done they
quibble about hours, swear that the appliances were that shiny
before I got there. They cut even cheaper with the tip and I'm not
talking about generous clientele to begin with. It's necessary to let
people think they're seeing backstage at the theater minutes
before the show. They want to be the producers, not the audience.

I mopped the kitchen floor quickly and let it dry while I wiped
down the living room surfaces. The second time I mopped the
kitchen I did it slower. We were supposed to use only one bucket of
water per house, but I was alone so the policy faced revision.
Water, water everywhere.

Washed those two stubborn pots.

Washed the utensils.

Washed the washcloths too.

Why didn't anyone admit that work was fun?

To touch things and move them and lift them and clean them.

The constant activity pacified my mind; my body became a device.

I worked for one hundred and thirty minutes. Laundry had been easy since it was already gathered in bags down by the basement. There were some pillowcases in the dryer when I went down there, still warm; I touched one to my chin. Lorraine's strong hands on my face.

Lorraine was sweet, and fat.

What should have taken me three and a half hours was done in about two.

It's not that I was efficient, just I needed to slow down. I was working so quickly that I'd sweated big patches under my arms and between my thighs. I felt great, but a headache grew. I sat on the living room stairs before going back to the second floor.

I took a while to catch my breath and wiped my sweaty forehead against a wall.

My chest felt plugged with wires that ran from every socket in the room.

I took that stupid pamphlet out of my wallet. Yes, I had it with me constantly. In the photo Ahmed Abdel's narrow handsome face was fringed by enormous black dreadlocks. I could never grow mine into such a pretty mess as this Japanese guy had.

In the pamphlet there was an interview with him conducted by a law student from BU. Ahmed Abdel went on about the anti-immigrant bias of the Boston courts then lambasted the U.S. entirely; condemned Leif Ericson and Eric the Red. But when asked about Japan's own imperial way Mr. Abdel dismissed it. He became mawkish instead. He mentioned the tony gardens of his father's home. (My grandfather would describe a boyhood of public tours through Kyoto Palace in 1928, one of Abdel's answers read. He told the law student, I always drew terrible pictures of the

Kitayama cedars. They looked more like a row of spears than trees!)

I mildly hated this man. How was I going to contend? Kyoto played musically on an American girl's eardrum while Southeastern Queens was a bum note. We have aluminum-sided homes, not fortresses.

With an hour and a half until the husband returned I shut my eyes on the stairs and reclined. The carpeted steps were firm, but plush against my sore back end.

Eventually the boredom would have made me a fridge pillager, but I remembered that there was a video store around the corner. I'd seen it when finding this address.

A place with a Lotto machine by the register; a beeper sales booth near the front door. And, usually, a broad selection of the best action, comedy and horror films.

I left the front door of the house propped slightly open by stuffing a rag in the jamb. At these low-end stores a video membership cost only five dollars. The tape was three bucks for three nights. I rented one then ran back feeling amped. An errand that would have been twenty minutes finished in five.

Other guys would've picked a porno. Rub one out while getting paid. My preferences come with a different kind of warning label. Not frank depiction of sexual situations, but blatant use of gore.

We Like Monsters, released in 1993. It was seventy-five minutes; I might see the whole story while the little master was out. Their TV and VCR were upstairs in the bedroom.

Above their bed a set of knives were nailed to the wall, but only for decoration not defense. They had great black handles. Some spikes on the hilt. I sat on their bed to watch the movie, but couldn't stop imagining a blade falling loose and right through my neck.

The floor was comfortable, too. I felt so good that I had to take my shoes off.

It was a terrible movie. About a guy named Ziff who so wishes to be famous that he disfigures himself in the background of a morning show newscast by pouring an unspecific acid on his face. He becomes famous, but the same stunt that propelled him to stardom is what's killing him now. The acid is still burning under his skin. A 'scientist doctor' explains this seemingly impossible fact. Ziff is disintegrating.

I don't want to explain any more, because this is the moment when the film turns to standard fare. Ziff's skin melts, his skeleton shrivels, until he's just this sniffing meaty creature that goes killing everyone 'for revenge.' But what revenge? He kills a businesswoman who's said to have created the acid, but it's more likely that the stuff was mustered in a lab. He kills another woman said to be his ex-wife, but at the start of the film Ziff laments that he's never been married.

These films mattered more to me than I should say. I sat, half-depressed, as the tape neared its end. Only stubbornness propelled me through to the foolish conclusion.

Okay, by the end Ziff has gone to the home of the reporter who first interviewed him. Ziff asks that his death be broadcast live. The reporter calls over a crew. The scene is arranged for vulgar effect as Ziff reclines on a white bed in a white bedroom; suddenly the reporter is wearing a white contamination suit; this is so that each time Ziff moves the surfaces are flecked with ruddy goop.

Ziff is asked why he did this. The acid on his body. The murders. The actor pronounced some treacle about 'wanting to matter in this world' and I nearly put my foot through one of the bus driver's bedroom walls. I stopped the tape, popped it out and would have stumped it underfoot, but I'd given my real name on the membership form. $80 fine for lost tapes.

What shit me about the finale was that these creatures always have an explanation. The Devil. An alien. A terrible childhood. Why did the virus in *Small Evil* cross the European continent only to ravage a small town outside of Budapest (on the Pest side of the placid Danube)? Because a Roma musician placed a curse on the land where his young daughter was beaten to death by Magyar police.

There's always a reason for monsters. Human beings need rationales.

The machines in the basement had finished thumping so I took the mass of fabric out of the dryer then folded it into separate pieces. I worked quickly because, bad movie or not, the far end of the crowded basement began to seem creepy. There were thirty big cardboard boxes laying around, some open and some taped shut.

Their dining room was smaller than it had been one hour ago. Now the glass dishware cabinet rose seven stories high. The plates inside it rattled when I walked by, which was because of my weight, yes. But what made them shake again as I stood in the kitchen?

In the living room I'd been surprised to find a bookshelf, if only because most of the homes I'd worked could fit all their books in a sandwich bag. I didn't like the man, so I credited his wife, the bus driver, with the library. It's elitist, but I always check the spines on people's bookshelves to find which ones are for status and which ones are a pleasure.

I was impressed because they had *The Seven League Boots* by Albert Murray, but when I opened it the covers cracked audibly; there was the rubber gum smell that wafts off unread pages.

I'd cleaned for black people and Jewish, an Italian family, Latinos, too. Stupid people had a few authors in common: Sidney Sheldon, Judith Krantz, Danielle Steel. What nonsense. Such dreck. How about H.P. Lovecraft, just once. Disposable income was wasted on the dumb.

I closed my eyes. I took one of their trade paperbacks off the shelf. Opened it randomly and spat on the paper. I mean a real goober. Shut the first then went to another.

I did that in their romances, the generational dramas. Thrillers, war stories and immigrant boo-hoos. When my mouth went dry I drank water.

A mirror hung over their living room couch. As I was about to hock into Alex Haley's *Queenie* I noticed the mirror reflecting me.

My pants had ridden up between my thighs and bunched over the hump of my great big ass.

My shirt had risen over the belt line so that my stretch marks showed.

My shoulders were massive, but soft.

My God just look at that thing.

2

MISS INNOCENCE,

6

Ishkabibble was on a cigarette but still managed to say, — You walk slower than my old Aunt.

I nodded because he was right, but why tell me.

— I'm not trying to down you or nothing, he added.

We were on 147th Avenue, only two lanes but respectably wide. Nabisase's church was on the corner, one block away. By the third time I'd disappointed my sister she stopped asking me along. Grandma and Mom, too. Nabisase left at 9 on Sunday mornings and stayed longer every week. That first time, on the 8th, it was only for an hour. One month later service lasted three. In half a year she'd be living there in a state of constant worship.

Ishkabibble gave the last of that cigarette such a pull I thought he'd eat the filter.

When I'd gone out that Thursday afternoon, November 9th, for a constitutional, Ishkabibble hadn't been what I was looking for, but he's who I met. I was walking by Brookville Park's half-hearted playground. A place for kids to swing in the afternoon and teenagers to drink at night. The grounds had seemed deserted, but then Ishkabibble stepped out from behind a water fountain. I'd been alone and then I wasn't. He found me.

At the corner of 230th Street Ishkabibble led me into the Get Right launderette. I was talking, had been for twenty minutes; he didn't tell me to keep quiet, just to follow him as we spoke. He, for one, didn't treat me like a dolt.

Behind the counter of the launderette was the matriarch of a Jamaican family who owned the store. She kept watch against people trying to dry their sneakers in the machines. She wasn't happy to see us, but I blame Ishkabibble. A man whose own mother was probably repaying one of his high-interest home loans.

—Miss Rose.

—Yes, she said, but it wasn't a question, like Yes may I help you?, or even, Yes that's who I am.

I really think I smelled the small black microwave oven behind her before I saw it. Or it might have been the tasty snack she sold. Alongside washers and dryers, this laundromat had food. So many of the smallest businesses around here had to diversify for profit. The owners of the low-budget cab service next door, Fast Fast Car, sold sneakers at the back of the store.

—Beef patty? Ishkabibble asked me.

Of course there was meat in a beef patty and beef is healthy, right? Forget that herbivore routine. How bad would it be to have just one because beef patties are so good when the meat inside is seasoned spicy and the yellow-brown shell is crisp. Maybe she also had coco bread.

Nineteen days since I'd been to Halfway House and seen Ledric's extreme dieting technique. I'd been trying to keep myself to a reasonable five thousand calories a day, but faced with a good beef patty I faltered.

The woman rose, shuffled to the microwave. —You're not eating? I asked Ishkabibble.

—I'm one of those people without much of an appetite.

—Lucky man, I said.

While the microwave carousel rotated for three minutes the Jamaican woman got her checkbook. She set it down; she hadn't spoken; she didn't ask Ishkabibble how much was owed. She knew exactly.

After that she went to the tiny black oven where there was, my delight, coco bread. She heated it separately then put bread and patty together. I was going to ask her for my favorite other ingredient, mayonnaise slathered on the patty's skin, but I didn't. I count this as marvelous restraint.

—How much? I asked.

She hadn't looked at me not once and didn't do it now. She asked Ishkabibble. —How much?

—He's a friend of mine.

Then she waved her hand. —Take. Take, she said to me.

Outside again I talked to him after I'd finished the food. I ate fast though the meat was hot because Mom might drive down 147th Avenue and see me. Maybe Hillman had a satellite in synchronous orbit over Queens smoking photos of its members when we cheated. At times I felt a power must be keeping track of me.

Ishkabibble was an ideal salesman because he had the knack for listening. Anyone else would've rushed me while I explained the shortcomings of *We Like Monsters* and movies like it. *Evening of the Hatchet*, *Crematorious*. I went on for fifteen minutes about how stories of the eerie, August Derleth let's say, usually let me down. The creatures turned out to be paper dolls and the characters were thin.

—Maybe most people like it when the movie gets all gross, Ishkabibble suggested.

—They can be bloody, but they don't have to be dumb, I said.

When I talked passionately about this with Mom and Nabisase they politely answered, Oh yes? and Ah-hmm, but nothing more. To be fair I understand that a twenty-three-year-old man getting agitated over B-movies casts a certain dummy-colored glow.

On two occasions we crossed the street when loose dogs threatened us.

As we walked Ishkabibble looked back down the block. He did it every ten feet, but I didn't think it was only the wild canines he feared.

—You not too popular or something? I asked. Kennedy Airport wasn't far behind us now. A person could walk to his departure terminal from here if he had a little chipperness in the bones.

I was out of breath. —Can we stop a second?

He laughed, but not as viciously as it seemed to me then. —We only walked five blocks, he said.

—I know what it was!

—Okay. I'm not trying to down you.

I only needed half a minute to get some wind. I tell you it's exhausting being so big.

—You not too popular? I asked again when he wouldn't stop glancing around.

—I'm popular when I bring people the money, just not as much when I ask for it back.

—My mother told me you charge nine percent above the prime rate!

—A man comes to me making twenty-nine thousand dollars a year and wants to drive a forty-thousand dollar car, whose fault is that?

—But you're black and doing this to black people!

—I work with Hispanics, too.

—What's that on your neck? I asked, to change the subject.

There was a large red patch of welts on the nap at the back of his head.

—I fell asleep in a tanning machine.

—You tan?

I wasn't surprised that a black man would go under bulbs, but that even with the help Ishkabibble was still so yellow. I mean the man made me look like a cloudless night.

—I trusted one of my customers. He promised me a free ten-minute trial. I helped him buy that business! Some Italian over across the park. He turned the alarm off, so I fell asleep in there for half an hour.

—You're not popular at all, I said.

Ishkabibble was annoyed; when he sighed the breath was a kazoo toot as it filtered through his skewed incisor. —You've got a funny way of asking me for a favor.

—Was I trying to get one?

—You just haven't realized it yet.

I'd thought I was just babbling, but a good peddler hears the plea.

We had breezes blowing gasoline fumes; across the street a harried man uncapped his yellow Freightliner truck, which was parked in the driveway of his home. One of his young daughters was using a hose on the headlights as he pulled a second, muddy girl from getting into the sleeper.

—You want to make a monster movie, he said.

—I don't think that's it.

—Why else would you be talking so much about that. And with me?

—No one in my family would listen.

—Big Man, you are not about to act like we're tight.

—Well what kind of monster would it be? I asked.

—Godzilla movies only cost as much as the rubber suit. I can get you some nice distribution if we make a tape and sell it through barbershops in Queens.

—There's a great one where Godzilla fights a robot Godzilla and at first you can't figure out how there could be two, but it's aliens who created the fake, I said. Some others aliens show up in another Godzilla film controlling Monster Zero, also known as King Ghidrah.

—Anthony. No need to convince me. I believe in your dreams and I can help you finance them. It's already underway. That's my business.

7

The next day Mom rented a Dodge Neon for our trip to Maryland.

Brand new. It was a thing. New York was settling into winter so a trip five states south was exciting. I didn't know my geography as well as I should, so anyplace below New Jersey was Alabama to me.

The trunk of the Dodge was bigger than our Oldsmobile Firenza's; even when we'd stowed every suitcase there was room for more. This astonished us.

—What else could we bring? Grandma asked as we stood together looking in.

—Let's pack more clothes, Mom offered.

This makes us sound idiotic, I know, and maybe we were acting like senseless early hominids, but really it was no different than cooing over a baby; we enjoyed a wonderful invention.

A telephone ring woke us from our daze as we stood with hands on varied parts of the car. Just touching. Nabisase went inside as Mom showed Grandma and I the demure –mumm– of the engine even when her foot was pressed to the gas. Nabisase called my name four times. But when I went inside she was talking on the phone and I was angry she called me away from the demonstration. I watched Mom pull out the driveway to take Grandma once around.

Nabisase said to the phone. —I just told you my name. Now tell me yours.

—Who is it? I whispered.

—You just heard me ask didn't you? No, she told the caller. That was Anthony.

—He wants to talk to you, she said.

—Ishkabibble?

—If you don't tell me your name I won't let you talk to him.

I tried to grab the receiver out of her hand. —Is it Lorraine? She has a deep voice, I said.

My sister ignored me. —That's a stupid name, she said to the caller. Ledric is just not normal.

—No, she corrected him a moment later. Nabisase isn't crazy, it's African.

After giving me the device I waited until she'd gone to her own room to finish packing.

—Why didn't you just ask for me?

He heaved and sighed and spoke. —I heard a girl so I had to know who she was.

—She's my sister. She's thirteen, too.

—I only got her name.

—That's more than you needed.

Mom and Grandma returned; the sound of the Neon's doors shutting once they stepped out was a soft-shoe routine compared to our Oldsmobile, that rattletrap.

—Is it working? I asked.

—You sound more desperate than me! Ledric laughed.

—Is it?

—No.

—How do you know?

—I had a pizza yesterday and I'm still feeling stuffed today so I know them tapeworms didn't eat the whole pie inside me.

—That's not how it works, I said.

—You going to tell me about what you haven't done?

—You don't sound good, I told him. He really didn't, but even before the tapeworms Ledric had to be a heavy breather.

—I got another jar of that fish so I'm going to try one more time, but you got to come over here if something happens to me.

—We're going away for the weekend though. Wait till we get back.

He cleared his throat. —Where you going? He sounded bewildered. As if he'd never realized I lived a life independent of his own.

—Maryland, I said. A beauty pageant.

—For your mother?

—My sister, I whispered, because I didn't want to admit this to him.

—Your sister looks that good?

—Don't ask me that question again, I said.

He forced a laugh, but I wasn't convinced. —You're nineteen and she's thirteen, I reminded him.

—Hey, come on. You're my boy. I'm not thinking about her. By the time you get back Sunday I'ma be ready for my own modeling show, forget anyone else.

Packing was easy for me; I just folded three suits, changes of underwear into a duffel bag. Moving my mother's things into the car was even easier for me because she had a manservant.

He walked through the front door as I got off the phone with Ledric. That skinny guy who lived next door.

—Who's this? I said when he walked inside.

A second man walked in. Much bigger, overwhelmed by muscles. An upper-body so big it looked inconvenient.

The slim one said, —I'm a friend of your mother's.

—You're my age.

—She's young at heart.

This could have been a big fight; what the skinny one said was already enough for me to break his jaw. Theoretically. The last thing I'd snapped was a KitKat bar. Worse than letting him sully my mother's name though would've been to get beat down in my own living room.

—How come you didn't invite no men to your party last month? the big one asked.

—I don't even know your names.

But I did know now and had then, it was Pinch. That's what he was called, but fuck this third-rate Tony Atlas. He was the king of security guards at a high school in Brooklyn; drove an amplified Honda CrX. Sure, I recognized him.

—I didn't see you, I explained.

My mother's friend said, —You looked right at us! I waved at you from my stoop.

The skinny guy, Candan, lived in the brick one-story house just to the right of ours. He stayed there with his mother and father. He did air-conditioner repair. Domestic and industrial. Finding a couple of generations at one address was normal; for Rosedale, as for much of the world, the worst thing a child could do was move away.

—When did you meet my mother? I asked. Candan, Pinch and I were the only people here.

Candan said, —We've been talking on and off since last year.

—Talking about what?

—We've talked about you, he said.

Candan's ears were as small as quarters. So little I bet he

couldn't wear sunglasses in the summertime. When I noticed them his dominance was subdivided. I even smiled.

Pinch said, —I bet it's going to be a long ride. You driving, Anthony?

—Yeah. My mother can't stay awake more than a couple hours at night.

—Oh yes she does, Candan said.

—That's all! Pinch yelled.

I was relieved to see the man could be tamed. Maybe not by me, but someone.

Candan pointed beyond me, down the hall, to the back. —Anyway, she asked me to get her bags from her room.

—She's got a lock on the door.

It was my first response; not why you? Or why did she ask you? Or even why the fuck did she fucking ask fucking you, fuck?

—Your mother gave me the key.

He walked by me. Pinch asked for a glass of water. I took him into the kitchen.

Pinch wore a sweatshirt, but the fabric was stretched at the shoulders, along the arms, his back, oh everywhere. I wondered if he was one of those guys who had nothing else, no brains within, or maybe he'd been bullied as a child. I disparaged all physical discipline as the pastime of the witless. I certainly wasn't going to admit that he looked nice.

—Do you know what my mother told Candan about me? Anything?

Pinch stared earnestly at the bottom of the glass as he drank.

I heard the door to my mother's room open. As soon as Pinch was done I washed his cup three times, until I heard Candan come out of Mom's bedroom.

I stepped into the hall and turned on the light so it'd be less gloomy. He locked the door. I heard him. When he turned around, with a small bag in his hand, I asked, — Can I see what she's hiding in there?

—Tell me why I should?

—I'm her son, I said.

The hallway, the living room, the front door. Candan walked down the front steps, reached my mother and playfully stepped on the toe of her shoe. She brushed him on the shoulder and held him there. He propped the bag between them and they pressed against it from two sides.

Pinch was as ashamed as anyone by the exhibit. He leaned on our gate, looked away, down the block. Nabisase sat in the driver's seat with Grandma as her passenger. When Mom and Candan started playing my sister pulled the lever near her foot and popped the trunk. Harder to see the couple through the rearview mirror that way.

I walked over and asked, — Did you tell this guy about me?

—I don't want you getting angry, Anthony, my mother said. She dropped Candan's hand as if she'd remembered herself. Would you like if I got angry at you for the smallest things?

—You going to answer her? Candan didn't touch my mother, he touched me. A finger at my chest, pressing.

—C.D.! What are you doing? You know you hear me!

The security doors on all our homes make a pneumatic hiss when opening. The sound came after the call of Candan's father, an artifact at their front door.

—I told you to stay in the house! Candan yelled back.

Candan's father was known as the President, though if this was meant respectfully I can't say; his own son might have started the nickname and Candan wouldn't mean it kindly. The President and his wife had a tiny retirement fund; Candan was their sponsor. I'd learned this because my folks carried gossip just like all you others. My family thought an unflattering photo of Janet Jackson was the apex of investigative reporting.

—I need you over to the backyard, the President said.

Candan returned the silver key to my mother; she smiled and watched him walk out our yard into his own next door, then to the front door where his father waited.

—What do you need so bad? Candan asked too loudly.

—I don't want you over there all on that woman, the President said.

Through the leafless hedge separating their house from ours Mom, Pinch, Nabisase, Grandma and I saw Candan push his father back inside their home. One hand against his dad's back and the other squeezing the President's neck.

Grandma stepped out the side door of our home carrying her handbag with two hands, so that the straps hung in front of her thighs and the pouch bumped against both knees. Nabisase followed with a duffel bag over one shoulder; her three gowns were already in the trunk. Mom stood next to the Dodge and tapped the roof with her free hand.

Daylight flattered them. They were good-looking women.

I went inside to get my wallet from my bed in the basement. Upstairs again I turned off the hallway light; the kitchen's, too. Went to the living room to check if anyone had left the iron burning and Ishkabibble was sitting a foot away from me, on our couch.

I screamed his name two times. With such volume that people heard me outside.

—Shhhh! He slapped my leg hard. Shhh! he said again.

—This is breaking and entering, I told him.

—Until the mortgage is paid this house is mine.

—What if it was my grandmother who found you instead of me? She would've died.

He stood up. —Ma'am's tougher than you think. I didn't know you scared so easily.

—Don't make fun of me.

Ishkabibble put both hands up, palms facing me. —I'm not trying to down you or nothing.

—Did you climb through one of the windows? I thought the doors were shut.

—I'm in every house on this block.

—How's your neck? I countered.

—Skin's still peeling, he said. Your movie is on.

—I haven't even had an idea yet.

—Make something up over the weekend. When you come back I'll have a package for you. Very reasonable rates, I swear.

I walked closer to him; maybe my mother had been beeping the car horn a while or maybe it had just started. —It's that easy?

—As far as I'm concerned, the movie's already made.

We shook hands. We hugged. Someone was thumping against the side door.

—I heard his name, Mom yelled.

—I heard it too, Nabisase agreed.

—Ishkabibble! My mother screamed.

—You better turn into a bat and get away before my family sees you, I told him. They don't like to pay you and they sure don't want you inside.

He smiled as though the threat was minimal, but clearly he'd never seen my sister throw a punch. There were other voices though. Pinch. Candan. The President, too. On the stairs at the side of our house. My mother's keys unlocked the door.

When Pinch and Candan came in through the side, Ishkabibble opened the front door. Those two were fast, I swore they had him.

—Get that nigga! Candan yelled.

—Anthony, hold that nigga! Pinch came through.

Ishkabibble went down the front stairs and over my four-foot gate gliding. Then up 229th Street in the direction of 147th Avenue where he might get a bus headed toward Far Rockaway.

Pinch pointed at me. —You shouldn't be talking with him.

—I can talk to whoever I want.

I said it then regretted this. Pinch stood massive in front of me. His breath smelled like menthol cigarettes. That disappointed me. I mean, to work out so much and then be a smoker.

—You're cool with him now? Candan yelled over Pinch's shoulder. Maybe you want to try and repossess my car for him?

Pinch exhaled. He tapped my shoulder. —I'm just letting you know you don't want to mess with him. He tries to take advantage and it really makes me mad when he does it to people who can't really take care of themselves.

—Who are you talking about? My grandmother?

Pinch wouldn't look at me. —Ishkabibble just comes in here and feeds off of us. That's what I'm saying. He's getting rich while we're living like slaves.

I nodded. Pinch and Candan ran out. They got in Candan's car, a burgundy '95 Toyota Camry that had a spoiler shaped like a shark's fin on the hood. As the car moved there wasn't that slow acceleration. Instead it had the gas turbine vim of a jet.

8

My sister was enrolled in a beauty pageant for virgins, a contest I thought she could win. She was cute enough, but also, how many teenage hymens were left in America anymore? Even the emu-faced girls had been initiated by twelve. Fewer contestants fueled better odds.

— You might actually win, I told Nabisase.

— I'm glad that this surprises you, she said.

— Don't take it like that. I drove away from our block and toward the Belt Parkway.

— How come Ledric said he met you in prison? my sister asked.

— He was telling a joke, I said.

— Where did you meet him really?

— Halfway House.

New Jersey plays the ass too much. There are so many jokes about the industrial cloud hovering inches above the state and it's true along I-95, where there's an odor of pancreatic tumor, but not the New Jersey of I-78.

The interstate was bracketed by great umber concrete slats that defended our path between the throngs of elm and red oak, which pressed so close to the road that they leaned over the dividers and wailed terribly when strong winds shook them alive.

I was content though. Mom had given the driving to me. With this vehicle I had possession over one of the four miracles of the modern age: automated destruction. Another was the unapologetic enjoyment of sweet sloppy cunnilingus.

One hour out of New York we passed a farmhouse with a fenced lot holding two brown foals. They dropped their heads into the grass, but were too shaky on their legs to eat. Foal. I knew the word for an unweaned horse but had never seen one. To me horses were like tropical fruit; I thought they couldn't be grown in the tri-state area. It never registered that horses pull those carriages through Central Park; I'd thought those were mules. They might as well have been okapi for what I knew. Even in Ithaca I'd willfully ignored the world beyond my rented room.

We passed a graveyard settled off the highway. Nabisase crossed herself at the four stations, but I didn't believe in her new faith. It can't just happen like that. One day she's hitting our mother with a crockpot the next she's receiving the Eucharist? This was just another way of aggravating the rest of us. She carried a plastic rosary, but the Apostolic Church of Christ wasn't nearly Catholic. I'll bet I knew a Hail Mary better.

My sister and I turned out such heathens I'm surprised we didn't bubble when baptized. I observed crossing signals with more orthodoxy than the laws God gave unto Moses. Still, if Nabisase knew about my skepticism she didn't show it. From the front passenger seat she made the sign of the cross watching the bronze and granite grave markers reflect sunlight, a field of gem-stones glittering all day.

On US-22 one sign read, Pennsylvania Welcomes You.

Getting to it felt like an accomplishment. We tapped each other's shoulders and knees, saying, —We're in Pennsylvania. We're in Pennsylvania.

On our right and left fields of corn took the place of vacant grass lots. I actually pulled off the road because I was so confused. I feared that we had traveled one thousand miles in a blink and asked, —Are we still in Pennsylvania?

Mom looked out the window. I looked at her in my rearview. She had been sleeping, but was roused enough to panic.

—We're in Pennsylvania, Nabisase said. Just look at the markers.

Thirty yards ahead there was a small black-and-white metal marker for US-22 off the shoulder. Grandma wanted to know why we stopped; Mom did too. They both asked if I was feeling sick; they asked me fourteen times. Enough that they sounded more concerned for their own safety than mine.

I drove again and never explained; it was because I thought corn was only grown in the Midwest. That in the East it came out of cans. I was just a simple, small-time city boy. A rube.

We reached Baltimore. —What exit? I asked my mother.

—None.

—I thought we were going to Maryland.

—Virginia. You don't listen.

I had been to Baltimore once, that bipolar city. On one block was the moderately regal Penn Station, then four blocks over a quadrant of desiccated row houses. The neighborhoods went like mood swings, good to bad, horrendous to opulent, without warning.

I had been to Baltimore when an old friend was getting married.

The night before his wedding his uncles drove us to a small strip club called Eldorado's. Even with the wonderful nudity I spent that night glum for gaining so much weight and for failing out of school. For wearing the same clothes four days straight and not showering quite as daily as people should.

One of my friends paid a woman to stand on a platform the same level as my chest and shake her ass at me for twenty minutes; a party favor. She was sweaty from working too long and her butt was cold, icy even.

She cheered me up, something she couldn't have noticed because her back was to me the whole time. I might have started speaking to her if she'd turned around, and I guarantee she wasn't in the mood for one more vapid compliment.

While she shook I clapped my hands right onto her ass cheeks. I put a five-dollar bill in her stocking, that kept her around. The groom-to-be had a lady upside down on his chest with her pussy dangling inches below his chin; he was so strong that when he stood up he held her there, wearing the stripper as a locket.

Eventually my dancer got wigged out by me because I didn't caress her butt or smack it lightly or try to reach for her tits or move. I was there with my hands against her backside with my eyes closed so it looked like I was crying. I might have been.

So how bad do you have to act to make a stripper twitch? Well 'bad' is the wrong word because 'bad' is common. I could have torn her hair and she'd have understood that more; it would be well within the spectrum of a drunken male's aggression. She got uncomfortable because sad men in strip clubs are always pathetic. It's just that I'd seen the money in her G-string and mistook it for a collection plate. I thought I knew where I was.

—You were looking in the wrong place for that kind of thing, my mother said glumly.

The oblong sun cast daylight vigorously. I hoped she was speaking to my sister. I tried, surreptitiously, to glance at my family, but they were all watching me.

Quiet car.

Quiet car.

9

We were going to be late for the Miss Innocence pageant because Mom was collecting dog figurines on I-78. This trip was turning her young.

— Rest stop! Mom called.

At a Maryland gas station she bought a yellow scarf to tie around her neck. Twice already we'd watched her flirt with gas station attendants; Grandma sucked her teeth while my sister rested her limp face against the window. In warmer country Mom didn't have to wear a dumpy coat over her airtight figure.

— Rest stop! Mom yelled again.

I parked the car and Nabisase helped Grandma walk to the bathrooms. In a minute my mother would go foraging through the rest stop gift shop for any statuette with canine features.

In the trunk we already carried a few stuffed toy dogs, a cast iron German Shepherd, a basset hound made of anthracite. Blame me for her newfound interest; I'd made the mistake of going on about how, when I was a child, I wanted a dog so much. I brought it up when the car ride went hush after my Baltimore story. I mentioned the dog idea only to blot out words like 'stripper,' 'backside,' and 'me.' I didn't expect my mother to get frenzied. But she heard me blaming her for a parenting failure.

Mom stayed in the backseat while Grandma and Nabisase walked away; I touched the steering wheel where it was still cool. My mother and I were in the car looking out through the windshield.

—We've got enough by now, I told her gently, diplomatically.

—You said what you wanted, so I'm getting it for you.

—I was just mentioning that. To pass time, not for you to get all serious.

—I heard you. She deepened her voice, Dog! she said.

—How many words do I say in an hour? For you to focus on that one?

—You can't have me buying you all these nice things and then get angry because I did, she said.

This rest stop was flying three flags: of the United States, Maryland and POW-MIA.

Could there still be Americans in Vietnam? I wondered if I even had the right to wonder. Those black flags with hangdog silhouette were memorials that anyone alive could own, but what good were they doing the phantoms in Cambodian cells. It's the living who don't release the dead. My Uncle Isaac might as well have been on this trip with us, there was room; Mom and Grandma left a space between them in the back seat.

—Again? Nabisase cried as she leaned forward to see the car clock.

My sister had been feigning nonchalance about these stops, but now this was our seventh. Nabisase was nearly hysterical, squirming like she was churning doo-doo butter in the seat.

—I have to register, Nabisase whined. And try on my dresses.

—I know, Mom said.

—And I'll need sleep, Nabisase continued. I probably should go to church in the morning.

When we parked only my mother left the car.

Grandma, Nabisase and I stayed. I craned my neck to rub the top of my head against the ceiling fabric. The noise it made was soothing.

Grandma reached forward and touched my sister's neck. —We have all seen Mom acting like this before.

Nabisase slouched, half-alive. —Anthony, if you drove off now we wouldn't mind.

I nodded to show my kinship, but knew my sister didn't mean it. How many terrible things do people say.

At 8:30 PM we crossed the Mason-Dixon line. We were the South's problem now.

10

By the ninth rest stop Grandma, Nabisase and I had been defeated; Mom held control. She saw the exit and directed me off. Up a sloping ramp. We all got out because my mother told us to. Excitable people lead.

But instead of an empty rest area, there was a crowd surrounding the McDonald's.

College-age kids were throwing rancid meat at the public, protesting chemically treated beef. It was night, but we could see clearly. The rest stop lamps were on and a film crew had set up floodlights too. A small globe of starshine on the hill.

The college students had parked a long yellow school bus across the outgoing truck and car lanes. Drivers arrived, but couldn't leave. The parking spaces were full. Minivans were up on the grass. I drove as close as possible, but this was still a logjam.

A white banner was tied up against the yellow hide of the bus, it read: Pretty Damn Mad.

Myself, Grandma, Nabisase and Mom walked toward the commotion because they couldn't walk away. I wanted to get in the Dodge Neon, drive backward down the ramp and try to get onto the interstate again. But my family was raised on tabloids and enjoyed the habit. They wanted to get closer and see.

Inside the McDonald's restaurant another thirty-odd customers pressed against the glass, looking out. The manager stood at the door opening it to let a few of the normal folks inside, but he couldn't have us all. That left many middle-aged men and women trapped out here; they wore comfortable slacks and white running shoes.

The college students didn't run right up to the McDonald's doors. They wouldn't go more than ten feet from the bus. It showed their age. They were courageous only in numbers. I'd been like that in school, willing to commit to a sit-in with a hundred other boys and girls, but stridently polite on my own.

—No meat, it's murder! Don't eat, that burger!

My family was as close as possible now. A lot of families were watching from their parked cars. While the mass of protestors were a bold ball in front of the McDonald's individual kids walked around giving out flyers.

I was so close to the front door of the restaurant that I could see the shake machine being used inside and started to salivate. A chubby girl wearing platform sneakers interrupted my strawberry-smoothie reverie to hand my sister and I the facts about beef production. The horrid truth was printed on magenta paper.

Grandma held on to my left arm; she was so light I could have carried her on my head. She might have been safer then.

Besides a gas-station and the McDonald's under siege there wasn't much to this rest stop. There was a second parking lot, but the way the protestor's bus was situated no cars could get to it. The street lamps over there weren't even on. My only proof that it existed were the faint white parking-space stripes on the ground.

After Nabisase and I threw our flyers on the ground the chubby girl returned, making a round, picking up the many discarded sheets. She didn't look at us, but her lips were moving.

Mom, Grandma, Nabisase and I were stuck by then. Between McDonald's and the people behind me. I'm not talking about the protestors, just other families. As more of us walked close to the scene, it emboldened the ones still in their cars.

Even amongst the loud demonstrators one woman distinguished herself. She was long, as in tall, and black, unlike most of the vegan kids. Sometimes she went along with the murder/burger chant. At other times she made less sense. — Anchorage! she cried. Where is Anchorage?

—Alaska, I whispered involuntarily.

The McDonald's manager came outside yelling, —Police are coming!

The tall woman answered, —You told us already.

—You stay out of this AnnEstelle!

—These kids are just visiting Claude, but I see people eating your poison every day. Where's Anchorage?!

I didn't know who she was asking about, but the manager seemed to understand. —Don't you bring that thing around here again, AnnEstelle.

The film crew was there for the college kids. Four men with cameras, another recording sound and a colossal gentlemen, seven feet I bet. He wore a quality suit and was taking notes.

—I recognize that man, my mother said.

Right now my family was closer than we'd been in years. Four people squeezed into room for two. Nabisase and Grandma had practically climbed on top of me.

Nabisase said, —He's been on TV. She pointed at the gigantic man, but I couldn't place him. It was the suit that captivated me. A muted brown number. And he had the vest. Oh my, that was tasteful.

My movie could be about a homicidal mob of vegans.

Yeah, well. I'd have other ideas.

Then AnnEstelle threw animal bones in front of the McDonald's entrance. Femurs actually. Which are big.

Like she was emptying a laundry sack AnnEstelle turned her bag over. The harsh lights of the film crew made my face warm. Claude, the McDonald's manager, locked the door again. The bones were still covered in blood; a liquid, like mucus, glowed on them.

I was aware that even the other protestors cooed because they were surprised by the bones. Many of them dropped their handbills. One spindly boy ran back into the yellow bus.

A woman next to me, in her fifties, wearing white jeans and high heels, said, —Well, I'll be goddamned.

The man with her had too much facial hair. I mean seven helpings of beard and mustache. If he actually had cheeks I couldn't see them. —I've never liked Maryland, he said.

The only sound I remember was a hollow —bloop— as the banner flapped against the yellow bus.

Everyone, everyone, everyone ran.

I couldn't have kept my family close even if I'd been so inclined. A centrifuge is less effective at separating elements. One hundred and some—odd people went in as many directions. Trampling is a hazard for elephant trainers and anyone in my way. I know Grandma got knocked down, it might even have been by me.

While others tried to get inside McDonald's and many more went toward the parked cars, I found my way to the back parking lot. I was the only one.

Where the lot lamps were out. An outline of hills listed back to the horizon. A space so remote I thought it had been sacrificed back to the land. And the noise of shouting, car engines, police sirens didn't follow me. It was replaced by the heavy breath of night. A snorting sound, actually.

In front of me a cow was running toward a parked truck.

—Hey, I said, but the cow kept moving.

—Hey cow.

It stopped, but didn't look at me. The truck was one hundred yards away, closer to the hills than to us. The cow was even more enormous than me.

—Keep quiet, it whispered.

Talk about making money. If I actually had encountered a cow using human speech I knew we could sell the story. Forget the *Enquirer* or the *Star,* those were only celebrity gossip magazines now. The *National Examiner* or the hearty *Globe* instead. I wish I didn't know these distinctions, but I do. Mom and Grandma had subscriptions.

It was a relief though to find a short woman on its other side leading the cow on a leash. I lost the article, but kept my senses. She was five feet tall and wearing duck boots. —That your cow? I asked.

—My family's, she said.

I had on my suit so I should have seemed authoritative, but she was unintimidated. The small woman shook a hand through her brown hair; she reminded me of a cockatiel, looking at me sideways.

—I'm going to put Anchorage up. If you don't mind I just need you to be quiet.

—Let me help you and I will. Is this Anchorage? What can I do? Push?

—It's not a shopping cart, she said.

—I'm just asking you. I don't know.

—Go open the truck and pull down the ramp.

—What if I yell?

—Then the cops will come here and take my animal from me.

Even as I walked to the rear of the truck's cabin I looked back at Anchorage. It's head was as big as my chest.

—I think that other lady was looking for this, I said again.

—Anchorage isn't hers to have.

—Is she yours?

—She's our father's.

—You mean God?

—Mine and AnnEstelle's.

—AnnEstelle is that loud woman.

—AnnEstelle is my sister. I'm Fane.

She touched the cow near the hind legs to urge it up the ramp. Anchorage walked two feet closer to the truck, which was nearly enough.

Over the top of the McDonald's I could see that police lights had arrived. They were red and flashing, from the ground and up into the sky.

—I have a family, I said as an excuse to go. We still had two hours of driving till Virginia. It was 9:00 PM. Why'd they hold the rally so late?

—It's only a stopover for those kids. This isn't their last desti-nation. But my sister heard they were here, so she had to come on out and get them started.

—Will the cops arrest AnnEstelle?

—They'll bring her back home to me anyhow. In a few hours.

She went up to the head of the monster. That's what Anchor-age was to me. If I'd seen it on a deserted strip of land I'd have shot the devil down. Fane brushed its ears which made Anchorage pull back. Fane whispered, or more like hummed, into the side of Anchorage's face. I felt like there was dirt in my nose; so grainy that I squeezed my nostrils together, but that only drove the muddy smell up behind my eyes.

I didn't actually touch the skin, but held my hand an inch away from it then scanned my palm along the wealthy body. That was pretty close for me. I wouldn't have bothered for any better, but I noticed this discolored patch, a circle little bigger than my fist, between a pair of ribs. I touched this and when I did yelped so loud I bet the Grand Tetons heard me.

—Shut up! Did she clip you?

—Your cow is made of plastic, I said. Did you know that?

She laughed even before reaching me which made my face flush; I put my hands over my mouth less out of surprise than a need to conceal my shame. I didn't know what else to say to her; there was a fist-sized black plastic cap in the cow's side.

—That's what I mean, I said when she stood next to me. I snapped one knuckle against the little plastic disk. Then Fane unscrewed it.

It came out of the animal like a gas cap from a car. I moved my hands from my mouth to cover my eyes because I thought blood or the acids of four stomachs would shoot out. She said, —Don't be scared.

With the top pulled out, this eighty thousand pound mammal stood calmly in the parking lot; there was an open tunnel leading inside.

—Did you do that to her? I asked.

—I didn't, but I would have.

—Don't you like Anchorage?

—I love our animals.

—How many do you have?

—Six more Holsteins. Two sow.

—Do they all have that plastic tube in them?

—Of course not. The other cows produce milk fine. Anchorage is the one who can't. It was to help her. We can put a hand in there to make sure she's digesting her food. We thought that might be the problem.

—Let me put my hand in there?

—What do you think is going to happen?

I felt an urge toward honesty. —Magic?

I should have been wearing a long glove before putting my hand in there, that's what Fane told me. I took off my jacket, rolled the sleeve. The way this worked was to push my hand through the opening. There were a few inches of plastic like the inside of a straw. When my arm went in to the elbow I'd reached a wet stomach; I rubbed my fingers against the walls. I wanted to find a bar of gold inside.

—AnnEstelle does that as a trick sometimes. When she's causing a stir in front of restaurants. She pulls a doll's head the size of a baseball out of Anchorage's stomach and she waves it at the people watching. It's to make them think about what they're eating.

—Does it work?

—It makes people vomit.

—Right into their laps? I asked. Disgusted, but excited to imagine that.

—Then I have to come get Anchorage because the police usually collect my sister.

I tried to reach deeper into the cow. I wanted to touch the other side of her wide stomach just so I'd know it was there. Without grazing that far point my hand only felt like it was floating in humid weather.

—How long have you been cleaning up after her?

—I can't remember when I didn't.

When living in Ithaca only I suffered my messes. An unwashed body or the brass-band argument I had with a Wegman's supermarket manager about sneaking one box of soda crackers down my pants.

—AnnEstelle apologizes all the time, Fane explained.

—Is that good enough for you?

—Depends on what she put me through the day before.

Nabisase was probably waiting at the car with arms crossed and very little confidence in me. I have the keys, I thought. I should go and let her in.

11

Our car entered the city limits of Lumpkin, Virginia, at one in the morning with the four of us asleep inside. I certainly wasn't driving, just keeping the steering wheel warm. Our seven-hour trip had lasted ten. At least, while our eyes were closed, there were fewer complications to life.

When settlers were first tracking across the American Midwest they'd discard big furniture like dressers or great wooden headboards when their horses were near death. When settlers stopped believing they'd reach their destination the littered frontier trails became furniture showrooms. Other travelers following after must have wondered why'd they leave this here and not twenty yards farther; why not ten miles back? What reason?

This was sort of how we reached Lumpkin. Like many explorers before us we stopped when our vehicle went off the plotted path.

Luckily I was in the slow lane of I-81 so we just listed right onto the grassy shoulder. The new white car was one of those rounded models with no real corners or edges and must have looked like a giant commode from far away. I woke when the bumpy earth shook our car. As I drove over to the actual interstate exit I felt like everyone in the world was asleep but me.

—That was dangerous, my sister whispered.

Lumpkin was an acorn-shaped town of 20,000. The only hotels were just off the interstate at the rounded bottom end. It was the Comfort Inn for the Miss Innocence contestants and two family members. A relaxed, two-story affair shaped like the letter U. While my family registered at the front desk I pack-muled the suitcases and gowns into the lobby.

Pageant rules stipulated that I stay in a different hotel. Fathers were the only men allowed. They were very serious about keeping virtue in the Miss Innocence pageant. So much so that they wanted my sister to sign a contract.

Nabisase might have liked Mom to read it over, but Mom was carrying Grandma to the elevator because she couldn't walk on her own.

Grandma took a squashing at that McDonald's riot. Underfoot as my arm was in a cow. Her hip popped audibly when she tried to walk from the car into the Comfort Inn.

I suggested a hospital, but Grandma wanted the pain. Used it.

—If we had not been making stops I would not be harmed, she'd said in the last stretch before Lumpkin.

—Let us reach town so the granddaughter can get to bed.

To atone Mom hefted Grandma from the car into the Comfort Inn and to the elevator and their room. We fastened my grandmother to my mother's back by using my jacket like a tourniquet; tied together at the middle.

Mom didn't talk after we had escaped the rest stop chaos. She was so quiet that I kept looking in the rearview and asking, — Are you there? Mom? Still there?

I was kidding, but that only made her fainter. The sound of her breathing even disappeared for the rest of the drive. At the Comfort Inn, even as Mom got into the elevator with Grandma, she didn't say good-bye.

My sister sat down on one of the brown lobby couches. Late as we were other girls were still arriving.

Nabisase looked most like a thirteen year old as she read the Miss Innocence contract; running a finger under each line; reading aloud.

The Miss Innocence pageant portrayed virginity as something sacred and I don't feel like mocking them for it. I remember one of my freshman scholarships at Cornell demanded that I remain patriotic all the years until I died. In my own way I was trying.

How were they going to check and see if she was telling the truth about her hymen?

—They would trust me, Nabisase said, too serious for a child.

—I'm not trying to down you, I assured her.

This Comfort Inn was excited to host the pageant hopefuls. There were balloons of every color and clipped dogwood flowers in bowls. The lobby smelled like lemon rinds; from another part of the first floor I heard the thrum of a floor buffer on wood.

—Are you actually a virgin?

—Sure I am, she said.

—I thought you'd be insulted.

—No, it's all right.

—Does it say in the contract that you can't ever have done anything? Like with your hands on a boy or anything else?

—What could 'anything else' mean? she asked coyly. My feet?

—Never mind. Let me look at the paper.

She put it behind her back. —You can't say that word? I'll help you. It starts with a B.

—I'm not going to talk to you like that.

—You just asked me if I ever used my hands!

—Come on.

I tried to go around the side, but only managed to nip her elbow. She stood. She walked backward toward the exit doors.

—I'm trying to help here, I said. Just let me read it. Contracts are made to cheat you. They might have fines listed in the small print. $100 dollars for every French kiss you ever gave.

—How would they find that out? She laughed because her older brother was squirming.

—You're like a nun now, church girl, you'll probably tell them. Let me see it.

She held the contract up to one of the ceiling lights. —There's a word you won't say, but maybe it's in here. Bl. Blo. Blow.

—Shhhh!

The desk clerk bestowed electronic key cards upon a father and mother as their daughters slapped at the buttons of elevators to make them race.

—Maybe I should ask Ledric to help me? she asked.

—He can only help you plan a big meal.

She said, —'Blow job' isn't the worst thing you could say to me.

I covered my ears. —If I was a judge and heard you say that word it'd be automatic disqualification.

—You shouldn't worry about girls acting dirty, she said. That's not the meaning of Innocence.

12

The Hampton Inn was accepting the other men; brothers, cousins, uncles, pals. For all the stridency about separating us Comfort Inn was on the same street, eighty-five feet away. There wasn't a fence or even a line of trees. If there had been a natural barrier then at least wickedness would have to be an act of imagination, but boys could look out their windows and see right into any chaste girl's room.

Besides the American and Virginian flags the blue and white Hampton Inn banner was stuck up on a pole in the parking lot. They charged $49 a night.

I wanted a shower, but first I walked across the street to the large twenty-four-hour convenience mart inside Sheetz gas station, where I found a bag of caramels to lull me through the night. When I went back to the Hampton Inn I found room 603 to be quiet except for the heater in the corner burbling in a deep voice.

There were two handbills under my door. I picked them up. I

turned the shower on and took off my shoes; while I sat in the armchair beside the room's single window the sound of hot water slapped softly against the shower walls.

'Goodness Girls' the flyer said. Those were the two biggest words, right across the top. Then there was a picture of a tiara, the diamonds in it badly oversized. A hand-drawing. Under the image there was a question, 'Haven't you always wanted to win?'

My love of horror movies, I can't say how far back it started, but the books came first. I never read fantasy, my personality was more terrestrial. Misty marshes; deserted backwoods; an apartment closet that, whenever opened, exhales a sepulchral breath.

A muffled trumpet woke me at four that morning. Not a genuine instrument, but a children's toy. The sound was from the hallway outside my room door. This was at four o'clock, the hour of grand regrets. I heard shuffling but was too tired to make sense of it. I looked at the time again. Four-twenty.

My curtains were open; I was sitting in the armchair. I could see there was still a lot of night to go before dawn. Maybe someone's dumb kid was playing reveille in his sleep. One flyer was in my lap and the other was on the floor. The one that had fallen was water-stained.

My room was much hotter than it should have been even with the heater running through the night. Steam was coming out of my bathroom in bellows. Everywhere the carpet was wet.

Outside the room I heard sticks knocking together. I looked at the bed hoping Lorraine would be there. Still wearing my socks, my green suit, I walked on the wet carpet.

The shower must have been going three hours now; forget puddles, there were pools. I must have passed out sitting up; the bed was made.

Panic less, I told myself. Be calm. Go get more towels from the front desk.

I opened the hallway door. There was the idea of driving back to Queens but I'd given my real name and home phone number when checking in. Why hadn't I thought ahead and used an alias; I wished I had a criminal mind.

The power was out in the hallway, which really started me shivering because I couldn't ever work off a debt the size of a hotel-wide electrical failure. I touched the light switch in my room, but current wasn't running. Had I blown the whole floor? Could I have destroyed an entire town while sleeping? My eyes adjusted in the darkness until I saw clearly that the hallway was full of dead soldiers.

—What?

I just stood in the hall asking, —What? What?

Four-foot-tall Confederate soldiers in those distinct gray uniforms. In the darkness I saw twelve. Shadows were shawls over their faces.

I said, —No thank you.

But they were children, not dead men. And far down the hall stood one grownup.

Just twelve boys dressed as Rebel forces and six more sat on the ground wearing Union blue. Some knocking short thin sticks together. One carrying a play trumpet. Half a dozen of the standing boys turned then shrank from me.

—We're practicing, said the grown man when he reached me. He was slim, bearded and talked to me dispassionately. I thought, This guy has never been scared in his life. He wore a striped buttoned shirt and Hagar slacks. It wasn't that he seemed tough, just easy.

—I didn't know they used kids for wars anymore.

He smiled politely. The kindest way to deal with any stupid tourist's questions. —We're in the pageant this weekend.

—Miss Innocence? My sister's a contestant. I didn't know they'd have a marching group at the show, I said. Usually it's just music.

—Yeah. There's a band, but our boys show out at just about anything. They'd march before every baseball game if we let them.

He had a black baseball cap in his left hand and slapped it patiently against his thigh.

—What are they commemorating? I asked.

The boys were bored already. I think they were ten years old and without a vigilant chaperone they got frisky; punching arms, mushing foreheads.

—We're up early because they've been forgetting their drills. It's our historical society that sponsors them. I've got a newsletter on me. You can take it. Hey now, said the guy to the boys. Hey now!

They stopped, stood calmly.

Through the picture window at the far end of the hall I could see the bright sign for Sheetz gas station still alight. This was more comforting than it should have been; it proved I hadn't short-circuited the town. Anyway, a little neon always makes me feel like I'm near people I understand.

The imperturbable man in Hagar slacks, probably a size thirty-two, walked close enough to shake hands. That's when his shoes made a —squish— noise on the soaked carpet. My leaky shower had made all the way out the room door into the hall.

—I had a problem in the bathroom, I admitted.

He jumped back, yelled, —It's not piss, damn it?

—It's just water. His raised voice surprised me so much that I even wondered if it was pee.

He looked at it for some time; I wondered if urine made a different discoloration in cheap carpeting; if he could detect such a thing it was the strangest kind of survival training I could imagine.

—That would have been a lot, he finally decided. He grinned, but stood outside the ring of moisture.

—Go get towels from downstairs, he said to the boys who had

stopped bothering with historical accuracy and stood together regardless of uniform.

—How many? two asked in unison.

The coach walked into my room then poked his head back. —Much as you can carry.

The tiny replica war veterans tore off; happy to help, but gladder for the fun of running. After swaddling my floor in blankets they were sent to their rooms by 5:30 AM. I thanked the man another dozen times then put on my shoes. I spent the earliest hours of November 11th reclining in the passenger seat of our Dodge Neon. When I woke up a few hours later a dozen 'Goodness Girls' handbills had materialized on the windshield of my car and every other.

13

'Disheveled' is a generous adjective to qualify my appearance at the family breakfast in conference room C at the Comfort Inn on Saturday morning. I was early since the insistent sun woke me at eight in the car. Afraid to go to my room at Hampton Inn, even into the lobby, I walked to the Comfort Inn and used their main-floor's bathroom to wash my face. My body would have to wait.

In the largest conference room tables were already made. Instead of fifty small round places there were four long rows, cafeteria style. On each was a white table cloth. More dogwoods again, but they'd been left in the palms of small ceramic angel figurines. There were three to each table, twelve altogether in the room. A dozen kneeling baby boys, their wings tucked under rumps, hands held open on the thighs.

The ceilings were twenty feet high and since I was alone in the room I started jumping up and down. Do you ever do that when you're alone? How high could I get, that was the game and it was miserable. I'd have to count my leaps in millimeters. It was silly to do that in some conference room, but it made my nature rise; circulating blood throughout my body. I felt pretty good.

At the other end of the conference room a microphone and podium were just in front of an enormous white screen hanging from the ceiling. I wondered if they'd show slides of pageants past, diagrams of acceptable hemlines. I walked closer just to see if the microphone was on, but when I tapped the mesh end for feedback it didn't.

A server leaned out a doorway. —I can turn it on for you.

—Thanks, I said, though I wasn't planning on singing.

The difference between a waiter and a server is that the former gets tipped, but the latter doesn't have to stand around blithely waiting to take orders.

We misunderstood each other, that server and I; voltage wasn't funneled to the microphone. It was the colossal hanging screen instead. That thing started speaking so loudly it surprised me. I shuffled down the earth tone carpet to get away. It was playing cable news.

The volume of the news was then turned lower. I sat at a table, halfway between the pictures and the exit. There were remote shots from Bosnia and Newt Gingrich. There was footage of a mouse with a human ear on its back.

The mouse story might have been two weeks old, but I was still hard pressed to turn away. Even without the grotesque accessory the red hairless mouse was grisly. It shivered and limped and its eyes were moist.

The anesthesiologist who'd done this breakthrough work hadn't simply stuffed a human ear down some rodent's hole. He'd twisted a polyester fabric into the shape of a human ear then went under the mouse's skin and attached it to the body. The polyester ear had been dosed with human cartilage cells that survived like a parasite, living off of the mouse. As the polyester decayed the human cartilage cells grew to take its place until a human ear was generated where there had been an artificial one. After that the new human ear could be removed to be used in cosmetic surgery while the mouse lived on unhazed.

Why these games the reporter wanted to know as he interviewed the scientists. Build a better ear? A bigger one? Different colors? Would each have a corporate logo and bar code? Would this turn into another dumb fashion craze? The reporter was snide throughout the interview.

Then those researchers explained that some kids are born without ears; terrible car accidents occur that split faces to bits; a young boy lost his nose to a neighbor's champing mutt; a girl fell from a fifth floor window and her ear was crushed. Because of this spiny mouse many people could be fixed.

I'd like to tell you about when my Uncle Isaac taught me how to organize Japanese honeysuckle in a basket. He really did. At the time I thought his bouquets made a Thanksgiving day table warmer than any fireplace could. I'm afraid that I've never let him go. Purgatory might be the place a soul goes until everyone stops needing him in any way. A second life that penalizes the well-known or loved.

By 9:15 AM the conference room should have been filled; if not then how about 9:30? The television was on, but I'd stopped watching. I wished I was a smoker to pass time. I wanted to ask the server if I'd come to the wrong room, but that guy was gone.

I walked out to the front desk, but the clerk must have been in the bathroom because I heard water running from behind a door marked 'Employees Only.' I waited, but after the water stopped going there was nine minutes' silence and nothing more.

I took a pen from the front and walked back to the conference room; the television screening had been turned off. Breakfast was still warming at the rear. I made a plate of eggs and one banana. A cup of apple juice, too.

Besides the flyer that had survived the flooding in my room I had ten others, taken off my car. They said the same thing, only their colors changed. 'Goodness Girls.' 'Haven't you always wanted to win?'

Lumpkin wasn't hosting one beauty pageant, but two. Miss Innocence was regional, but the other was a local show. If the Miss Innocence festivities didn't start until this evening there was still a place for young ladies to compete. And there was no fee to participate. 'Come down this afternoon and get involved.' 'Reputable Prizes.'

On Braddock St. In downtown Lumpkin. The typewritten instructions at the bottom of the handbill were very easy to understand. I would even have offered to take Nabisase, but I had a movie to write. I used the blank backs of each handout.

I tried to scribble out a screenplay in twenty minutes. Apparently it takes longer than that. Everything I wrote was counterfeit. Just versions of movies I'd already seen, but in mine the characters were black or from Queens. A guy in a hockey mask killing geeks of the Ivy League. A demon possesses a girl in Southeast Queens and a troubled young minister has to cast the evil out. That's how badly it went.

Eventually I gave up on creating something new and wrote down capsule synopses of monster movies I'd seen. So I'd know what to avoid. Pretty quickly I understood I had no talent for invention, but a decent memory instead. I recalled actors, directors, approximate running times and even the production companies. Soon I had pages of these catalog entries.

Gurgle Freaks

Feldspar Pictures American, 1985; 64 minutes
Director: Herman Shipley
Starring: Veronica Groober, Paige Pelham, Joe Stat

Veronica Groober stars as the villainess, a saleswoman of cosmetics who kills housewives by filling the throats of her victims with a bilious liquid which she regurgitates into their mouths. The special effects are actually quite gruesome. The villainess is on the prowl because she was disfigured in a boating accident and has, ever since, borne a terrible hatred against all fair females upon whom fate has shined.

Jains, Jains, Jains

Montu Films, 1986; 83 minutes
Director: Ezra Washington
Starring: Manfred Owens, Manil Oswati,
Helena and Bascom Hughes

Jains, Jains, Jains, despite the title and subject matter, is an American-made film. A Jain priest's (a *yati*'s) dead body is mistakenly delivered to America to a quiet, decent childless family. (Helena and Bascom Huz). The woman pries the box open while her husband is at work and when she removes a shroud from his face the *yati* is brought back from the dead. The *yati* grants her one wish. (This has nothing to do with any aspect of the Jain religion.) She wishes her husband would return to the amorous ways of their youth. Then the *yati* kills her.

He commences slaughtering many of the neighborhood wives as the day continues and as he does he frees their many pets. Dogs, birds, turtles; the *yati* releases them all. The final murder is of the local cat lady who keeps about a hundred.

At the end of the film the viewer is supposed to understand, *accept* might be the better word, that this Jain priest has come to America to kill its unrighteous human beings and leave the nation to its holier, more innocent, creatures.

The final shot is of the unnamed *yati* (who is played by an obvious black American, Owens, who doesn't even try an accent—this when there is actually an Indian cast member, Oswati, whose sole job is to explain why Jains are a threat to the United

States) getting on a Greyhound bus in only his white robe and coming, presumably, to your town next.

This film might have been underwritten by the People for the Ethical Treatment of Animals or, perhaps, Pakistan.

After two hours I had nine of these on the table, but still no good ideas of my own.

I never saw another diner while I had my head down working, but when I stopped writing there were 199 plates on the tables, the remains of breakfast on most. Fingerprint-smudged glasses of juice beside them. I got lonely, so I left.

At one of the tan in-house phones I tried Mom and Grandma's room, but there was no answer. My sister was staying on a separate floor for contestants, but that number was blocked. Each time I dialed her room the phone buzzed defensively. A person couldn't even speak to those girls. Corruption entering through the ear.

As I left the Comfort Inn I passed the front desk, where a clerk's dark brown blazer had been placed on top of the service bell. I didn't bother to ring it because I expected no help.

14

The nut-shaped town of Lumpkin was broken into thirds and in ascending order. Starting low, between I-81 and Pleasant Valley Road; near the Hampton and Comfort Inns and Chili's restaurant; the only movie theater; the Asian eateries. A tourist quadrant. European toilets aren't like American, did you know that? I didn't until I read about it. They're designed so the shit doesn't fall right in the water, but gets caught on a little shelf until you flush it away. That layout saves gallons of water, but the human surplus just sits there to be seen. Lumpkin's tourist section resembled a European toilet; we were left there near the bottom to stew until the day we dropped and departed on the rushing interstate.

Four-lane Pleasant Valley Road split the tourists from downtown Lumpkin, the center of local business and historic landmarks. Some of the one-family private homes here suffered leans. Downtown was the fulcrum of this city's poor, because every agency to feed or clothe the broke was there on Cameron Street.

And at Fairmont Avenue I reached the final checkpoint between downtown and uptown; this third was as nice as Jamaica Estates. The houses were larger than in the poorer section, but not by that much. The real difference was in architectural flourish. Porticos; Doric columns like a bastard.

Walking from my hotel to Fairmont Avenue at the other end of Lumpkin took only thirty minutes, and my pace was tame. There were gates around the homes in the poorer section, but in the nicest part of town there were none.

I spent a while on the sidewalks, but how long I couldn't say. My armpits and stomach itched because I hadn't showered yet. Sometimes I stood still in front of a home, but I was only thinking of how to reach my family, who weren't in their rooms. The forsaken quality of the Comfort Inn had saturated the town; I didn't pass any human beings.

I walked into a little ripple of a coffee store even though no one was inside. I opened the door and tried the pay phone before I realized the place should've been locked up. My calls to Mom's room went unanswered. It wasn't that the store was closed: the lights were on and the coffee machine brewed quietly. More like the owner had stepped out the room, maybe quick around the corner.

I poured myself some apple cider from the jug in a fridge behind the counter. To relax I untied my shoes, took them off. My feet appreciated the gesture. I allowed Ahmed Abdel into my life once again.

Even I was mildly worried about how much this guy bothered me. It wasn't just for Lorraine. My freedom seemed constricted compared to the expansive life offered him through incarceration. On page two of the pamphlet there was a brief question-and-answer conducted by the same windswept young journalist at BU.

Q: What is the greatest threat to freedom today, Mr. Abdel?
A: The elite business oligarchies of the Western World.

Q: What question would you like the people who read this to consider?

A: We know who watches us. The police. The military. The mediacracy. But ask yourself who watches the watchmen?

What a twit. What an ultramaroon. This was the man Lorraine would get arrested for? A guy who quoted comic books? With a pen, notepad and my stationary anger I wrote the guy a letter on my last Goodness Girls flyer.

Mr. Abdel,

How is prison? They call it the gray bar hotel sometimes. A friend gave me the pamphlet with your photo on the back with your interview. You have a lot of admirers.

From your 'watchmen' comment I think you have been reading the funnies well into adulthood. Socialism's over-rated anyway. I'll bet you couldn't spell Muhammad before starting your prison bid.

I noticed that you wear dreadlocks, but you are Japanese. Is it that you think you're black? Do you wish that you were black? It's silly to use the name you do. Why is it that other minorities pretend they're black to fight the system? You aren't black.

Yours,

Anthony

I signed only my first name, but put the full return address at the top. Of course I wanted a response; that's why I wrote it. Short, quick and sure to sting. Cracked my toes and set my feet flat to enjoy the cold store floor through my thin socks.

After resting I looked at the clock, but the time was wrong. —It's three? I asked myself.

—It took me two hours to do this little bit?

Which made me think of the work I'd done in the conference room. I lay the sheets on my table in the coffee shop. Read the movie entries so quickly that I had time to do it again. Read them out loud. If I compare the feeling with anything it would be to my mother when she was listening to the tapes of our family speaking into a microphone. Both were just a form of preservation.

I touched the pages gently to my fingertips and considered the next month, the next year. They were in my lousy handwriting; that made them more cherishable. I needed to think impartially about my family and myself. Where the others had been stricken, how would I survive. The first time my mother didn't recognize me I remember I was ten. It lasted a week and the whole time she was trapped on a hospital bed. When Uncle Isaac refused to go to sleep for so many days that he only got rest when he fainted.

In a way it was good luck that I'd sat there so long feeling sorry for myself. If I hadn't I might have put on my shoes and walked out of the coffee store. If I walked out I might have left Piccadilly Road. And if I left Piccadilly Road I wouldn't have seen Nabisase and Grandma running away.

They had fashioned a papoose like the one we'd made with my jacket the night before. Theirs was made of bed sheets. My sister carried Grandma on her back. A thirteen-year-old girl tottering down the road holding her ninety-three-year-old grandmother in a satchel.

They went down Piccadilly, past where I could see them from my chair, so I put on my shoes, left four dollars on the register and one dollar in the tip cup. Followed them with my eyes until they reached a big library two blocks down. My sister made a right.

I walked to Braddock Street, where Nabisase had gone. On the corner there was a marble library too flamboyant for this modest town; a man wearing crisp, new overall dungarees and a nice white long-sleeved shirt washed scuff marks off the fronts steps. He looked spiffier than I did and I was wearing my brown suit.

Judging by numbers the town's missing populace was all on Braddock Street. Though it was a crowd they seemed to take up less space than the same number of people would in New York. Eventually I realized this was because no one was dramatically announcing their hurry with sighs or pushing.

Three circus tents were pitched in the road; each was as tall as the surrounding two-story homes. They were staggered, one tent after the next, and swaying to the right or left depending on the impulse of the wind.

That first tent had teenage girls inside. I saw a few walk in, but not my sister.

Yellow balloons were tied to sedentary objects. To light posts, to trees, car antennas and front gates. A boy in a wheelchair had five tied to his handlebars. This old woman, sitting in a lawn chair on the sidewalk, wore balloons looped around each ear. Her jewelry bobbing up above her hair.

A traveling band was at the far end of the block and when they reached the corner of Braddock, at Louden, turned right to make a circuit through the downtown area. It was brassy music except for one bass drum.

People wandered down the block, mixing around the three tents. Middle-aged women stood together in U-shaped groups, each one's children visible constantly this way.

Christianity was common. I bet my sister was pretending she fit right in. I watched as a minister and two preachers were greeted sweetly; each one mingling on his own. Old women that I passed sang absently of Jesus.

There were black people and white, but I was confused by both. Being from New York, I was used to telling the difference between the two with only my sense of sound. It was just disconcerting to hear a man drawling sweetly with his wife and when I looked the guy was as likely to be blond as he was a brother. I was disoriented watching so many people act politely across the races. In New York there was no courtesy, only parallel worlds. We worked hard at ignoring each other. But down here black people and white people shook hands, greeted each other, and generally hid their mutual contempt.

Women sold meat they'd prepared at home from folding tables set on the sidewalk; pork and a lot of chicken. Besides the booths others walked around with Tupperware serving trays of Brown Betty's, pumpkin pie and malapees (warm walnut cookies dipped in honey then powdered with brown sugar; the woman who sold them told me the recipe, belched and apologized many times). I bought ten for three dollars ate four and put the others in my jacket pocket. I needed the energy. Oh, shut up.

I tried to walk into the first tent with the teenage girls inside, but a small woman wouldn't let me through. She smoked and checked her watch. Since she was shorter than me I looked in, but that was no way to find Nabisase.

At least thirty girls were in there. A Polaroid flashed in the back, many many times.

—You go to the second tent and sit, said the woman in front of me, but I wasn't listening.

—Nabisase! I yelled.

Maybe four of the girls looked at me, but the rest were too busy. About a third of the girls were in scuffed jeans and boring T-shirts. The rest wore long dresses and makeup. I assumed that I knew which ones were involved in this pageant, but found out later that I was wrong.

—You go to the second tent and sit, the woman said one last time, cigarette out of her mouth. She spoke firmly once her slab of husband had joined us.

I looked him up, down, all around, trying to decide if I should rush past him.

At the entrance of the second tent I ate two more malapees. Undid my jacket to straighten my ocher tie. A small boy was there holding a plastic jar, collecting money for another boy who'd been burned plenty. There was a picture taped to the jar. Talk about veal cutlets. I gave a dollar.

I wasn't the only one going into the second tent and I sure hadn't been the first. One hundred folding chairs were filled and many other people already stood along the sides of the tent. But it was still cool inside. Not only because it was November, but a pair of oscillating fans at the far end.

They were propped at both ends of a small elevated stage. In the foreground of the stage there was a standing microphone, but no speaker yet.

I tried to get out of the entranceway, but it was hard. Soon people would have to sneak up under the flaps of the tent, along the sides, if they were going to get a view. If they did who cared? There wasn't any entry charge.

When a tiny Negro walked onto the stage I knew we had begun. I know the word 'Negro' doesn't fit anymore, but he was transported in from a previous century. Dressed like a buggy driver in weathered tails and white spats. The man even wore a derby. If he'd been holding a tiny lantern he might have found work on many lawns.

He was as light as wheat, but obviously black, and half the people here knew him. A few called out when he appeared, —Hey Uncle! or, Yes now, Uncle!

The ones who yelled were the most enthusiastic. Four guys who stood and clapped.

No one else applauded, not the black or the white, the fat or the chubby. Other than his cheering quartet most people just casually watched.

The little man touched the microphone with his thumb so the first microphone broadcast was of a nail scratched across the equipment. The second was his voice, squeaky as a bee sting.

— Dis is many mo' folks dan I eber hoped ta see, yes suh.

That made us applaud if only for the vague way he seemed to be saying something positive about us.

I'll say it, his dialect sure stymied me. Slaves of the antebellum South would have mocked his poor English.

— Why ar we heah? he asked. Why ar we heah?! he repeated.

— For you, Uncle!

— I know that's right!

Already I'd spotted those four guys as the worst kind of audience plant. If they were in there to get us more excited their outbursts had the opposite effect. He hadn't actually done anything yet, so why the ecstasy?

— Awlraght, he muttered. At's enuff a dat.

After a pause the old man began again. — Iss not fo' me that youse heah. Iss fo yo lertle chilrens. Iss fo yo specel gurls. Yawl brung em roun our way fer de chance ta be a booty queen. Em ah raht? Well? Em ah?

Sure he was, but many of us needed time to translate his sentences. And I'm including most of the good people of Lumpkin. I don't want to say this man had a Southern accent, this guy's diction was warped well beyond questions of geography. Backwoods white folks used to be called hill apes by the wealthy planter class; this black man was making hill ape sound refined.

— Gurls. Wimens. Thas whut we talkin about. When ya had 'em dey was but so big, but nah dey is mow grown. An' ya want 'em ta start laff on de good foot. Ya come ta luvlee Lumpkeen hopin dey win dat Miss Inn-oh-sins booty contess an' take home scowlarships.

— Now folks fom Lumpkeen gon recanize me, but yawl out-ta-townas will nut. Jus' call me Uncle. Lahk we was blood.

Our Uncle raised his hands jubilantly and I wasn't the only one to gasp.

He was a small guy, I said that already. Could have been four foot eight; maybe he even had lifts in his shoes. Neither a midget or dwarf; a little person, but not clinically. Shrunk. But when he put his arms up they were as long as ski poles; that doesn't sound like much but remind yourself how tall he was. It had a freaky effect because when he put his arms straight up it looked as though he'd flung a pair of hands high enough to touch the ceiling, but his body remained in place.

—Now. Now. De reeson I struk up de tens an' invited yo' gurls an' famlees heah is cause I don' likes dat udda pagint. De Miss Inn-oh-sins. 'Cause ovah der dey's plannin on tellin yo gurls whut's wrong wit 'em. Dey gotta be dis tawl an' dis skinny an' if dey not, den fo-get it! Am I raht? Yes ah am.

—De peeple of Lumpkeen been seen muh contes' go on tree yeahs tuhday. But dis yeah we gots fotunate an' had all yawl famlees fum out-ta town comin fo' dat otha one an' I wanned yawl to come ta mine. I'm jus' glad ta know de flyas was put in yo rooms an' dat so many parens was willin' to bring yo gurls. Or was it yo gurls dat browght alla you?

Lots of the parents laughed at that and it was probably true. Some girls go for the enjoyment; Nabisase was one of those, but most were pre-teen professionals. If their parents wouldn't take them, I swear they'd charter planes.

—We gonna start bringin in dese gurls thas jus so lubbly, sweet an' fine. We not gon as' dem ta weah a church dress or bee-kee-nees in fronna you lahk dey wus sides hung up fah sellin. Dey gonna come up an' tawk. Tell whey dey frum an what dey been through cause hahd work make fo' bootiful souls.

I thought the crowd might be insulted, since he was telling them to forget the Miss Innocence format; that they'd feel he was chastising them in raising their daughters for beauty. But really he was making a deeper claim. That despite their splotchy skin or scrawny thighs this man, our Uncle, wanted to reward character.

The first few girls were Miss Innocence transplants and they did badly because they hadn't learned how to present themselves. Pageants were acting jobs, find the script and play that role. Most of them had the same heroine: pretty, firm, optimistic. That's what those first girls did wrong.

None were in gowns, but they wore cosmetics, hair made up all darling. Trussed up like this Uncle Arms (I heard others whisper the nickname) complimented the girls; he called them pretty, splendid, hellafine. Terms that earned tens on other judging sheets, but with Uncle Arms the wretched scored highest. The tenth girl was the first local to come along, wearing badly beaten Vans and a polyester sweatshirt.

The parents of Miss Innocence girls stifled laughs, en masse, looking at the pitiful uniform. But she received applause from half the room. Effusive praise from our Uncle when she recounted how her father had been fired from the apple orchard six months ago.

Soon as that act did well every out-of-towner changed strategies. Hair drawn into plain buns, blemishes displayed. And pitiful life stories for everyone. Those girls, the ones who'd traveled, were still in dresses (though not gowns), but they tried to compensate by slouching when they walked on stage.

— And it's ben hard to stay in school, said the nineteenth girl, because the factry closed and won't reopin.

— Well bless ya, said Uncle Arms to the teenage girl. Bless ya much. 'At's whut I say.

The young girl nodded then walked off the stage, out the tent and as the flap fell back I saw her go to the end of the line forming at that third tent, last point in the relay.

Another girl, fatter but more cheerful, walked onto the stage.

— Gi' yo' Uncle a peck!

The old man flirted, as old men are allowed to do. She touched his dessicated cheek lightly then pulled back up to smile.

— Now tayl yo' Uncle 'bout de misfortoon an' miseries.

— My Daddy and I are here this weekend for the pageant, but my Momma is not.

She paused as the tiny old man touched her hip. — Wha' couln' yer Momma be heah on such uh impotant weeken'?

The girl let her shoulders drop lower. — Well, you know we're just reglar folks from Tennessee.

— Go on an' tell it gurl, we all jus' good folks, we unnastan'.

— Well, my Momma was plannin' to come along, but then she was forced to work on the weekend. She already put in five days, but they told huh she had no choice.

Audience women nodded, familiar with tyranny.

— An' whut r dey makin her do? Dem people she wuk foh?

The girl dug her nails into her palm which might have been a tactic for producing tears.

— Momma had . . . she had . . . she had to go to Singapore to meet with the Minister of Trade and Industry.

The girl did cry at least. A third of the room felt compassion based on performance alone, but the rest of us held our applause. Even the old man looked at her crossly. He couldn't muster up some closing homily so he just pushed her out the tent. — Let's us git anutha gurl up heah.

You know who stepped out next, so why should I even say her name? It was going to happen, I knew this, but when my sister walked out I covered my face.

Nabisase still had Grandma on her back, but didn't look exhausted. Grandma weighed little and my sister was probably so excited she was strong. Nabisase could have untied her grandmother before now, but my sister must have wanted to win.

Nabisase undid the sheets from around them then Grandma

climbed off her grandchild gingerly. Already the gathered group was sucking the inside of their collective cheek with a curiosity that could be turned to sentimentality with a flick.

— Come ovah ta yer Uncle, said the man.

— Good afternoon everyone, Nabisase said.

Manners were smart.

— An' who's dis heah wif ya?

— This is my Grandma. She's ninety-three.

— R ya heah foe da pagint?

— Yes sir.

Sir! The only sir I'd ever heard Nabisase use before was the first syllable in the word service.

— An' where's de res' of yo kin? Yer Maw and Paw and sech?

— I don't have no other family, Nabisase whispered into the microphone. It's just my grandmuvver and me. We're orphans.

15

Even after Nabisase left the tent under a blush of hearty applause with Grandma hitched on her back again, even while the old man bent to pray for the poor child, I didn't move except to take the wallet out my pants and check the name on my driver's license.

The band came and left the block three times while other girls told their woes. Regardless of race, culture or where they'd come from, Ohio, Rhode Island, New York, Pennsylvania, the out-of-town girls really exaggerated their local accents, but still ended up using the same pitiful Southern-Fried pitch. As if suffering was in the nature of only one region.

Whereas Miss Innocence demanded beauty and virginity this little carnival was a desolation pageant; in the testifying tent sub-jugation brought about our rapture.

The winner got a modeling contract.

Girls were in competition for print work in local advertisements. Nothing national, the contest just wasn't that big. Maybe there'd be some catalogue work for the Grand Prizee.

Uncle Arms would announce the winner on Sunday afternoon to accommodate the many new participants who'd need the night free for that other, bigger pageant.

— Now I's so prowed tuh help dese gurls cause I know what de bad days is. Am I lyin? I am not. But lemme tell of sumpin good which is dis heah Oonited Stetes dat we lib in.

— I know der ben tubles, look at me an tel who know dat betta. But I ben to Aingland. Iss funny ta tink about, ain't in? Me. Uncle Allen, in Aingland and Frans too.

— An ova der dey got de rish peeple an po', but you know dey poor peeple cain't neva get rish? Not neva? Dey got class ova deah, dat's whut some peeple say. Well dey got class ova deah awlraght! Po class, workin class an uppa class.

— Den I come back to Amerrca an eben dough I seed us fightin wif eash otha I know dat if one a y'all git money den yous livin rich. We got no classes in de States an I'm prowed of it. We got dem peeple borned rish an dem othas dat becum it, but boff gets ta buy a fahn house. Am I lyin? No I am not.

Even I was feeling proud as Uncle Arms went on. I believed him because I could see him. Uncle Arms was his own billboard for striving.

— We not gonna hab just one oh two winnas an pack up dem otha gurls. Naw. We gonna hab many gurls workin cause I wan plenny of 'em ta git a chans. Dis heah is abou oppoitunitee.

The people applauded happily but nobody gave up their ghost; if you think he sounds like a preacher then you've just never met a man who works on commission.

Like most others I left the tent. Those who remained only wanted to speak with Uncle Arms. At first he obliged them from the stage, but even with that extra foot he was shorter than a number of the men and some of the women. When he finally stepped down for handshakes he disappeared.

I walked over to the third tent although I wasn't looking for my sister anymore. Is it fair for me to have been insulted? I was a wart that been dissolved. Good that I didn't see Nabisase or Grandma because I would have thrown my last two malapees at those foundlings. I would have screamed that my sister had lied. I would have ruined her chances. That's how angry I was.

In the third tent blue or yellow tickets had been distributed to the teenage girls, but I'll bet it didn't take long for the women with the yellow ones to realize they might as well be in the deli line at a supermarket. When I left the second tent it was five o'clock and the third tent already looked like an OTB at closing, with losing tickets covering the floor.

When he walked outside I tried to bump into old Uncle Arms myself, but kept missing him. Misjudged the angle of his head versus my elbow. When my sister publically crossed me out of her record book it made me wonder why they'd wanted me to come down here at all. I thought I'd be needed during the pageant, but I guess I really was only the driver. And they didn't want to leave me in their Rosedale home in case I'd rub my dirty, naked buns across their pillows.

After the third try to bump him I just introduced myself. —I'm a reporter, I said.

His first reaction was to recoil. —No no, I promised, I'm here to write three thousand words about the other pageant.

This calmed him. —Where fum? he asked.

—When did they start calling you Uncle Arms?

He made a scouring face. —None eva do, ta ma face.

—I'm sorry.

He smiled showing two gold capped front teeth. —I saw ya in dat suit an' I taught dat you had mannas, Brass Ankles.

—I do.

—Well whut ye did wit 'um? Et 'um?

—Look, I don't want to get into an argument. My fault. I'm sorry.

I followed him past the third tent, where a woman swept the yellow tickets away.

—How long ya ben in town?

—Since yesterday night.

—Fine anythin' ta tern yer nickel yet?

—Only that some of your girls have been lying about their circumstances.

We went off Braddock, right on Louden. A pawnshop one block away advertised a sale on weapons. This meant handguns as much as knives. Rifles more than nun-chucks.

Along the wall of this corner pawnshop there hung a white banner showing Uncle Arms's grinning picture. Not a painting, but a professionally digitized photograph. The caption read: Your Uncle has got just the place for you. For home loans call.

—Mm hmm, Uncle Arms replied.

—I've got proof of one contestant in particular who's falsified her family history. My editor says it's a much better story. The depths to which people will sink just to win. I'm very excited about it.

—Wha paypa it wuz you workin wit?

—*The New York Observer.* We're mean-spirited.

I expected him to question me. Maybe even yell. Instead old Uncle Arms pushed me into these bushes. He sacked me amid some Canadian Hemlock.

—What you claim to have heard you shall not speak again, he whispered.

He crouched on the balls of his feet. The back of my head was against the shaded earth.

I asked him, —Where'd your accent go?

16

By six o'clock that Saturday evening I was back outside the Hampton Inn next to vomiting from fear as I walked to the front desk. I poured myself coffee from a silver urn on a table.

The clerk was a pencil-shaped woman in green vest with a white long-sleeved shirt underneath. She waited for me to speak but my coffee was so hot that I was concentrating on keeping my mouth shut to keep from spitting it on the floor.

So she finally asked me, — Are you 603?

— 350 at the most!

She hesitated, but I wasn't trying to be cute.

— Did you leave your bath running when you went out today?

— No?

— Sure?

— I'll have you know that I haven't bathed once in twenty-four hours.

She believed me, which solved the problem of my guilt, but she stepped backward and covered her nose with one hand.

—The maid came to take up your sheets, she explained from her distance. The whole room was flooded up in there.

—I'm sorry about that.

She stepped forward quickly. —Why apologize?

—No one likes to see bad things happen to good hotels.

She didn't step away again, but did keep her hand over her face. I reminded myself to find time for soap this evening.

—You don't have to worry, the clerk said. The maid put down towels. It was about sixty of them. We'll find you another room.

Saved; not liable; excused from small-claims court; I should have felt lucky. Instead I stood in the lobby with dirt on the back of my neck and sweat stains darkening the inseam of my slacks, indignant.

—The maid did all that did she?

Room 414 and room 603 were like identical lamps. One lit, one unlit. I stood inside the new room.

Needing that shower I went to the bathroom but found I was scared of the nozzle. I turned the knob, but as soon as the water ran I imagined another mishap. Two ruined rooms would snuff the last of Hampton Inn's goodwill. I had a panic attack, that's all. Like a grief counselor I soothed myself, saying, —It's fine. Take a shower in a little while. Do something else. Not just yet. Soon. Turn off the water.

With the receiver of the hotel phone to my ear I listened to the dial tone stutter: a signal there were messages for me. They were transferred from room 603. Two were Nabisase's, at nine-thirty and eleven that morning. The first was the sound of annoyance, asking where was I. The second just dejection; —I guess you and Mom are busy.

The third message was from Mom, but hardly recognizable.

Her voice was a bouncy trill. I'd have thought it was a teenager, not a middle-aged woman. At three-eighteen PM she said. —I need to get the dogs from the car, but I'll send them to you later. Don't worry, Anthony. I will reach you in my own way.

—Walk over there, I said out loud to myself. Get up and find your folks.

I called our answering machine in Queens, but for what? Nabisase had more friends than the rest of us and she only had two. Checking home messages was just a way to avoid getting up.

To my surprise we had five. Five for Anthony. Which, I don't know why, made me feel handsome.

The first was one of the managers at Sparkle asking again if I'd like some weekend work. The other four were from the same man, one who clearly hadn't listened when I said we were leaving town:

—Hello, this is a message for Anthony. Give me a call. You know who this is?

—This is Ledric, I'm sorry if it's late and all.

—Nabisase, could you pick up and let me talk to Anthony?

—(groaning) I am the dumbest motherfucker on two feet.

17

The Dodge Neon's trunk was broken open. Its lock looked attacked by claws. Chips of white paint on the Hampton Inn parking lot. My duffel bag was still inside, but Mom's eighteen figurines were gone.

I forgot about Ledric like lickety-split, opened my bag to make sure my clean suits were there. It's possible that there was a gewgaw thief in Lumpkin, but I doubted it. I unfolded one suit, shook it out and changed in the backseat of the broken car. Though I tried a few times to slam the trunk closed, it wouldn't shut.

Stepped out then walked the eighty-five feet back to Comfort Inn. A girl in the employee uniform, jacket and smile, walked me back outside and pointed southwest to a huge carnation-red building where ceremonies were to be held.

The Blue Ridge Theatre.

— I think that's what you're looking for, sir.

Preliminary events, like casual and athletic wear, were going to run at eight o'clock.

—That's a half hour, I said.

—We have a bar inside, if you'd like to pass some time.

—I shouldn't start drinking, I told her. I've got to drive somewhere tonight.

—Is your daughter in it?

—My sister. Did you see that other contest this afternoon?

—Uncle Allen's? Oh sure. A lot bigger this year. My cousins were in it '93 and '94.

—Why not you?

—My life's been pretty good, she said.

I borrowed twine from the clerk to tie the trunk of our Dodge Neon closed. How sad the sight made me. Just a day before, on November 10th, Mom brought this car home; it made the block seem brighter because it was unspoiled. Now with the white string looped through the trunk this car looked like any of the duds double-parked up Hillside Avenue.

I started the car and left Lumpkin, Virginia, at seven-forty-five.

Miser's Wend was an even smaller town forty miles south of Lumpkin. The two were separated by the larger city of Winchester, Virginia. Miser's Wend would never have an exit on I-81 today if not for the Quakers who came in 1773. These facts, the year of founding and who did it, were stamped on plaques every eight feet within town limits. Declaring stones, curbs, cigarette butts as historic Quaker landmarks. But by 1995 the Quakers were aged right out of importance. When I drove into Miser's Wend I entered an extinct society.

Downtown was only four blocks long with one bookstore, a food market, a dry cleaner; their store fronts had all been built before the Civil War. I felt a mix of admiration and aching back. Sleeping in a car seat all morning still hurt me.

A Quaker meeting hall was in a large field, left to itself. Fifty feet by fifty, one story with a gabled roof. I wouldn't say it looked like a religious building except for the way it seemed to shine under direct focus from the moon. The wood became whiter. There was a porch on the right side of the meeting house with one small chair out there. It faced me; I drove by.

I touched the passenger seat where my sister had been on Friday. When I thought of her on stage with Grandma I regretted the mistakes I'd made today. Missing her phone calls and now, driving forty miles just because she'd hurt my feelings. When we came back to Rosedale from Ithaca on September 3rd, Nabisase helped me clean out the crowded basement so I'd have a neat place to sleep. If I was going to turn around and keep her orphan's secret there were still a few miles to decide.

Uncle Arms had written the driving directions on the back of a car loan application.

They were too damn specific for me.

Get up. Wipe off the dirt. Walk back to your hotel. Eventually get in your car. East on Jubal Early Drive. Take the on ramp for I-81 South. Merge onto I-81 South. Drive forty-six miles on I-81 South. Reach exit 303—Miser's Wend. Use exit 303—Miser's Wend. Follow off ramp to traffic light. Make right at traffic light onto Strop Street. Drive straight.

I entered the saccharine half of this community, where private homes were modest in size if not expense; their walls were limestone; their lights were out. Every house around. Beautiful, but forsaken. By eight o'clock the sun was well under the trees.

Turn right on McCutcheon. The house on the corner has an orange mailbox. Do not knock on any other doors. Drive slowly on this smaller road.

By now the directions were insulting. Maybe Uncle Arms acted the asshole with everyone. Was there a way I spoke or looked that made people think they needed to carry me with tongs? I'd thought I hid my confused state expertly.

After driving McCutcheon for ten minutes there was a private way to my right; thin as typewriter ribbon and it had no sign. His last direction read:

My road is nameless. Watch for lights in the woods. Come to them.

18

Uncle Arms stood on the front steps of his limestone home and waved. Even though it was two-and-a-half stories the house seemed small because it was narrow. There were three small chimney stacks on the long, pitched roof, one at either end of the house and the third in the middle. The place was fixed onto a plain but well-maintained field. In fact it was beautiful. The thin road became a driveway that continued around behind the house.

I wanted to drive back to the rear just so I could see the whole property, but he gestured for me to pull onto the front grass.

There really isn't any comfort in a rural night for me. I'm happy to see a traffic copter overhead. I decided that the cloudless star-filled sky looked like a busy switchboard, and it relaxed me.

Uncle Arms was still short, but wasn't wearing the gold teeth. His brown suit was better than the one he'd worn in the tent that afternoon. I touched his shoulder and the fabric felt softer than cold cream.

As we walked into his house through the front door I peeked at the backyard. There was a wooden cabin, much smaller than the main house.

—You're no newspaper man.

Uncle Arms said this only after we'd climbed into the front hall of his home. It was narrow like the whole house and I thought Quakers must have been some pretty slim people.

—How'd you find out?

—I made one phone call.

There was a seven-foot wooden clock against the hallway wall, but it didn't seem to work anymore. A sturdy cooling bench, six feet long, sat across from the clock in the hall. Instead of four legs to support it there were ten. There wasn't much room for me between these heirlooms and the ceiling wasn't very high either. I touched the bench and the wood was so supple I thought it would bend. None of his furniture had much flash, but it was superb.

—Your family's been rich a long time, I said.

He walked ahead of me, showing none of that stoop from this afternoon's carnival. You know what he looked like now? A former dancer. With that mean hoofer's stride. I didn't know how old he was, exactly, but his body was used to being limber. He didn't drag his feet.

A flight of stairs led up to the second floor, but we stayed on the first, walking left at the steps into another narrow room with an upright piano and light blue walls.

As we went through his house the floorboards made a noise, -snap-, -snapsnap-, under me. I was embarrassed. What made it worse was that Uncle Arms weighed about sixteen ounces; the proof was in his soundless footfalls.

We passed through the narrow room, that had the upright piano on one end and a mahogany highboy at the other, into the east end of his home. The only room, thus far, large enough to let me breathe.

There was a dinner table, a dormant fireplace and lots of floor space. I could have camped out right there and still had room to hang my purple suit up to dry. It was wet with sweat already and limp from general exhaustion; it clung to me.

Six framed plaques were on the wall, but I didn't stop to read them since he'd left a door open to the backyard.

His property slanted downward so that from the back door I saw the small log cabin only fifteen yards away and behind it was the rest of his property, another plain field, one acre at most. I was surprised at how far I could see with only a three-quarter moon, but stars also brightened the room.

At the back end of his land there was a patch of small trees and past them a smaller, detached field. Two dozen tents were pitched in that one. Little domes strewn around in the far grass.

I thought Cub Scouts first, but then those soldier-boys from my hotel came to mind. How seriously would they take their roles? Would their chaperon really have them sleep outside a night and appear at the pageant sore, hungry, deprived? A war-weary approximation.

Past the tents, right behind them, parked and empty, was a giant yellow beast. There were shadows across its back and the nose was brushed up against a tree. Its black tires were camouflaged by the grass so the yellow bus seemed to hover in the distant field. There was a white banner tied to its side. Too dark to read the slogan, but I remembered it from the rest stop ruckus; Pretty Damn Mad was here.

How did they get near Lumpkin?

Had they followed us?

— I invited them, Uncle Arms explained.

But can we forget them for a while because Uncle Arms shut the door. He'd put together a great dinner.

The long pine top table was, like everything else, quiet about its quality. Wearing a table cloth with no frills around the edges and a Mariner's Compass pattern sewn checkerboard into the cloth. —How old are these? Are they worth a lot?

He asked, —Is that how you think of the past? A numbers game?

—It was just a question. You know what I mean.

—When all the others fail history is the religion of humanity. In which do you believe?

—Can we eat? I said.

—Of course. Sorry. I tried to have some foods you'd recognize, he said.

Uncle Arms spoke to me like I was a foreigner, but I didn't want to take this North-and-South-two-nations-within-a-nation folderol that seriously. Though he had. By preparing (or probably buying) a variety of Spanish foods.

Rice and pigeon peas, roasted pork, chicken stew and fried meat. The smell of onion, peppers, coriander came up from the pots when he removed their lids. An odor so good I got that high, itchy feeling in my nose like I was about to sneeze.

—Where do you think I'm from? I asked him after looking at it all.

—New York.

—So why Spanish food?

—Because you're Mexican! He was stymied by my questions.

—No one's ever thought I was Mexican before, I said. Puerto Rican. Dominican.

—That's what I meant. Puerto Rican.

—So why didn't you say Puerto Rican?

—I did.

—You said Mexican.

He put his left and right hand up but far apart in two unaggressive fists. —It's like saying United States and America. Mexican. Puerto Rican.

—They're two separate places.

—Oh come on. He acted like making this distinction was the worst kind of oversensitivity.

When eating I'm a silent hillside. Sometimes my hands don't even seem to move because I heap my fork with a crane's worth of food, feed myself and chew it slowly.

Uncle Arms was peckish; I could see a lot of the white of his plate because his portions were so small. —You're no newsman, he said again, but he wasn't angry.

—I clean houses.

—But you're really here for the pageant?

—Sure I am.

—I can't believe anyone would have a girl admitted into that debacle.

Who was this guy?! He had been doing his best Vardaman and Bilbo routine not ten hours ago and now he was some old-money Quaker gentleman with his morals in a high chair.

—My sister's in it.

—And your father entered her?

—If he had she would have been disqualified.

He let me enjoy my own joke until the room was quiet again. I felt silly; I said, —Our mother paid the entrance fee, but my sister wanted to compete.

—It's vulgar that the girls qualify because of their chastity.

—Better than pain! I yelled.

Did I mention that I had two beers? Or that I was drunk? Maybe I've kept it to myself because I'm ashamed to admit I was a lightweight.

—Haven't you begun to think that the whole beauty system is archaic? he asked.

—Aww what does it matter, I sighed. No one's ugly anymore.

What a good feeling when dinner's over and there's only the gruel left on the plate. This time it was a mix of gravy, grains of rice, oil and bits of shredded pork. I tilted the dish to my lips. That slop was fine as port wine.

When there were only bones on our plates Uncle Arms served a light green liqueur in a dark green bottle. The taste was paprika and peppermint at once.

He said, —We were Quakers until my great grandfather was read out of meeting. He split with them over the question of servitude. He was for it and they were not.

Servitude was the politest euphemism for slavery I'd heard in a long while.

—He was the first black Quaker ever expelled.

—Were there any others?

—No.

—So he was the only black Quaker ever expelled.

—He'll be remembered as something else.

—As a slave owner.

—My great-grandfather Otis started three technical colleges. One in Mississippi and two in Tennessee.

Uncle Arms told me the schools used to offer courses in horse grooming, 'domestic science,' and had developed into computer engineering, business administration, even paralegal work. Thousands of graduates lived better because of Otis, the black excommunicated Quaker slave owner. Uncle Arms insisted. I listened but with only one eye open at a time. Because of the liqueur my mind wasn't worth one puka shell right then.

—How come you get up there like Old Remus then? If you're so proud of your ancestors?

—People can't imagine a black aristocrat. They've invested too much into a past filled with only one narrative. Whites and blacks would believe I was a devil more easily. So I appear as the raggedy, noble cottonpluck. In Colorado I've been Uncle Iron, of the

Southern Ute Indian tribe. I am the best businessman you ever saw. I promise you that.

Above the fireplace there were those six framed documents. One was a list of furniture either bought or sold in 1884. I did what everyone does, marveling that I could have bought a four-poster bed with the money in my pocket.

Among them was a framed newspaper clipping accounting a man's purchase of one hundred acres of Frederick County land. I should restate that. One hundred acres more. (Otis Allen, free man, purchases plot, livestock.)

Along with the text was a sketch of the man; he was slim and bald as a monk. The eyes were far apart and his nose drifted to the left; I hoped the illustrator was just untalented.

Uncle Arms walked next to me with two glasses of that green elixir. The top of his head only came up to my sternum. He said, —The Quakers thought Otis would perish without their help, but he flourished.

I've read that some of the first English settlers in Jamestown resorted to a sort of cannibalism; so frantic from starvation they dug out fresh graves and ate the dead to survive. I collect those kinds of true stories. They were all just horrible.

—The Quakers said he'd perish, Uncle Arms repeated. But what's become of them?

—If I had been a reporter what were you going to do?

—See if some of our girls were truly lying about their backgrounds.

—And then?

—If it could be proven I'd have to disqualify them. No luck.

—I need some air, I said. The wine with dinner, the emerald potion now, if we didn't get outside I'd vomit toward his fireplace. We stood on the back steps of his home with breezes arranged around us.

I wanted to see the cabin, but Uncle Arms walked me past that.

It was empty anyway, or at least the door was closed. We walked through his field; sometimes he was next to me and other times ahead. It wasn't long. Only ten minutes before we reached the stiff, sparse woods at the rear.

A faint dirt path waited. He was silent and so was I. It was darkest when we were in the middle of the trees. Still too far from the small field with pitched tents. There were leaves and brown thistles underfoot. Even Uncle Arms made noise walking across them. This brief forest trapped the coldest air along its floor. My legs and my head were in different temperate zones; my knees were chilly, but my face started sweating. I was having fun.

When we stepped out into the smaller field I covered my eyes because the nylon tents reflected light back at me. Twenty-five small domes zipped shut. I had a vision of Ledric stumbling, sick, out of each one. Hands on his stomach, phlegm in his hair.

The protestor's yellow bus wasn't totally empty. A thin woman was taking down their banner.

— Did you pay them to come? I whispered.

— You can't pay these kinds of people to act outraged, but they'll do it for free if the cause is just.

— And what did you tell them?

— That girls are being exploited.

— Do you know a man named Ishkabibble?

The tents weren't in rows or anything so when we walked through them it was a winding trail. I'd thought they were sleeping, but as Uncle Arms and I walked along I heard people talking inside.

As I moved through I brushed too hard against a tent I guess, it unzipped and a groggy twenty year old looked out to see. His beard was patchy, but already fuller than anything I could grow. Since I'd woken him, he climbed out to smoke.

Portable radios sat outside two different tents, unguarded; their owners must have trusted the elements.

Uncle Arms brought me to the woman folding the sign. She was older than I thought. Not nineteen, but thirty-nine. In jeans and a sweatshirt, but her feet were bare.

—Don't your toes get cold? I asked her.

She laughed loudly. It surprised me because Uncle Arms and I had been speaking in the quietest tones. She shook hands with Uncle Arms then me.

—Where are Jerry and his cameras?

She pointed at the bus. —They said it was too chilly in the tents.

—That bus can't be warm, I said.

—I don't know why they said no. It's toastier with two people in a tent than one on a vinyl seat.

—Jerry's inside? Uncle Arms asked and when she nodded he went in.

That left us there. I kicked a tire just to do something.

There were actually a lot of cigarette butts on the ground. Not thrown about, but in a neat pile.

—Take off your shoes, she said.

—What for?

She put one foot in the air. It was long and slim, the toenails were a lively red.

—I thought you people wouldn't wear makeup.

—Which people?

—You're with the protestors, right?

—That doesn't mean I'm dead! Take off your shoes and let me see your feet. Just put them in the dirt.

Uncle Arms stepped off the bus with two videotapes in his hand. He shook them in front of me. There was a diesel smell coming from beneath the truck.

—I'm going to take him back up to the house.

—This is your last chance, she said to me. It'll feel good.

—I'd feel silly barefoot, I admitted. I'm wearing a suit, I said.

She sighed. —Just once you ought to find out how it feels to be free from all those clothes.

—I'll consider that, I said.

Uncle Arms led me away, back through the trees and into his yard. Before we had walked five feet of his property, I asked, —Why are you doing all this?

Uncle Arms said, —Those students sleeping there are the descendants of conscientious objectors everywhere. Nowadays the enemy is this way of life that tells young girls they're beautiful because of their bodies.

—But you're running a modeling contest!

—My ladies win because of hardships. Fortitude is probably the only way teenagers can show character anymore.

—You'll never know how it feels to suffer generations of shame, he said. I mean to have your parent's mistakes continue on and affect you. I don't like what my great-grandfather did, but I'm not giving the money back.

We weren't far from the main house, but we were right next to the cabin. Even without lights it gave a ginger glow. The cabin was run through with an animate silence that reached out and cupped my ears. The shingled roof sunk low in the middle like it was being sucked down from the inside.

I still heard Uncle Arms, but from farther away. He said, —If I can try to make the lives of a few girls better now, that's one way to balance out Otis Allen's fortune.

I don't want to say I was scared. I was thrilled.

If not for Uncle Arms my night would have consisted of television and hotel food. Right now Nabisase was probably back in her room, the preliminary night over, polishing the shoes she'd be wearing with a formal gown tomorrow. Muttering about the failures of Mom and me. Why would I rush to hear that? I'd have the

rest of my life to get berated. Going to see my sister would have
been the right thing to do, but tonight I felt like a little fun.

—I want to help you, I whispered.

—What?

—Uncle Arms, I want to be your friend.

When I was eating dinner in the house the cabin had looked
quaint, but now it was much older. I thought it was a replica, the
kind they sell in miniature at Home Depot, a pretty place to keep
useful things like a lawnmower, rock salt.

—It's handmade, Anthony. More than two hundred years ago.

There was a window, but were there chairs inside? A bed? An
occupant?

—What can I do? I asked.

—This is quite a surprise.

I couldn't see Uncle Arms because I wouldn't stop watching
the cabin. Tricks of lights against the window; when I tilted my
head long shapes squatted.

—You wouldn't find it hard to open a door, would you?

—I want to do something better than that.

—You don't understand me, Anthony. This one gesture would
help me a lot.

—How much?

He said, —I wouldn't have to plant any of the protestors inside.
I can't trust them. They won't wait until the right time. The second one gets in he'll start chanting and throwing flyers. They're
too energetic.

—Are you going to hurt the people inside?

—I told you I wasn't a monster.

Fierce loyalty is a boy's game best played at night when the
imagination can transform every shadow into a foe. Uncle Arms
went back in the house and returned; he was as thin as a cane. He
brought out two small glasses, the green bottle.

—At a certain time during the evening's pageant you'll hear a knock at the back of the auditorium. Then you'll open the emergency door.

Here I'd thought the whole world was telling my story only to find myself stumbled into his.

While he'd gone into the house I hadn't stepped away from the cabin. We drank five feet away from it. I didn't want to get closer, but I didn't run.

Uncle Arms asked, —Does your sister win a lot of these things?

—No, I said. She never has.

—Maybe this would be her year.

—Could you do that?

—Winner's name means nothing to me. If it assures your cooperation and a few years of silence I'll give her quite a bit.

—She was the girl with the old woman tied to her back.

—The orphan! Uncle Arms laughed. I like the blood you come from, he said.

I was glad to do something for my sister, but also to feel like a grown man. I entered the cosmos of backroom economies on November 11th. Her professionalism aside, Nabisase's victory was rigged by an endomoprh and a goblin standing in crabgrass, and she would never know it. There are so many lives decided in this way.

After finishing the bottle of green liqueur I could barely stagger and I fell forward against the cabin walls. Once I was closer the silhouettes inside were easier to recognize. The backs of two wood chairs and iron pots hanging over the fireplace. A low slim bed in the corner. There was a form, wide as an oven and twice as tall, pressed up against the right side of the window pane like it was looking out. When I stumbled closer it moved away.

The door was made of three wide slats of wood joined together. They weren't decorated. There wasn't even a handle, only a hole in the door about level with the lower end of my stomach. Hanging through that hole was a leather string, like a bootlace. The hole in the shape of a heart.

Uncle Arms whispered from behind me.

— All the Quakers had to lock this door was a wooden board on the inside of the cabin. That leather string hanging out the hole is tied around it. When visitors are welcome the string dangles out. A visitor pulls on it, the board lifts and you walk inside.

He said, —That's where the saying comes from. A hole in my heart. When the string wasn't hanging out it meant that company wasn't welcome.

—Who's in there now?

—Open the door.

—What will I find inside?

—The unseen hand, he said.

My whole body was eager to find out. I touched the door and the wood was cold. I grabbed for the string, but it moved without me. Curling away slowly. It disappeared. Pulled backward from within.

19

Nabisase, thirteen years old, not safe, ossified, looked out the window of Grandma's room; so stiff she might have been there for eighty years and continue for eighty more.

Grandma lay on her back on her bed on her best behavior in the Comfort Inn room.

Nabisase turned away from the low hills outside to sit on the bed and touch Grandma's hip. Grandma made little gasps not only from pain, but in anticipation of more. She flinched. My sister pressed on Grandma's thigh, asking, —Does it hurt here? Here? Where?

I'd driven over from Miser's Wend at ten that morning. A Sunday. November 12th.

Mom's bed, the one farther from the window, was tucked so professionally that it couldn't have been slept in.

Rather than call ahead, as I'd tried the day before, I got on the elevator, pressed third floor and nobody stopped me. Walked the

152

hall and right into Grandma's room. I could've done that on Saturday, but I'd assumed there were guards posted.

Grandma skittered, sat up quickly, when she noticed me inside the room. The move made her squint with pain and she yelled, —How did you get in?

—Through the door.

—Wasn't it locked?

—Mom's gone. Nabisase spoke to me, but I didn't recognize the voice. Not frantic or angry, even irate; the tones I was used to.

—Did you hear me? my sister asked.

Grandma rose to her elbows. —We haven't seen your mother except Friday.

—We should tell the police.

Nabisase only repeated herself. —Mom's gone.

—I thought she stopped doing this, I said.

Grandma said. —She did. For some time.

I felt fevered, but not them. Now I wondered if her message had sounded more despondent than I recognized. —What did she tell you the last time you saw her?

Grandma said, —She left as my eyes closed.

—We can call the cops from here.

—Forget the police, Nabisase said.

—Why do you sound so grown? I asked her.

My sister sat down next to Grandma. Their postures were the same, but Grandma had reason to hunch over. She was ninety-three and her hip might be broken. While my sister was soon to be awarded Uncle Arms's gold prize. She didn't know and I couldn't tell her because I didn't think she'd believe me. But soon.

Even as they sat there confused, I was happy. I'd never felt like an oracle before.

—Were there any notes?

Grandma said, —Do you believe she gives a thought as she waves out the door?

Grandma was tired. Uncle Isaac. Mom. Me. How does a parent go on living, really pretty healthy, while watching her children decompose gradually?

— She'll be back by this afternoon, I said. I was optimistic. Sometimes Mom forgot her life and it lasted for a few weeks, but most often she got confused, wandered for five hours then came back to us.

— I'm not waiting to see, Nabisase said.

— We can't let her run around town getting in trouble, I pleaded.

— Can't we?! Grandma yelled.

This isn't the start of things I'm telling about. It's not the middle, too.

I stood, surprised that I'd become the paladin of compassion. — I'm going to get her back.

Nabisase and Grandma, both, touched their hands to their eyes.

— You'll have to take Grandma, Anthony. They have a woman who can help me with my hair backstage, but it's only me who's going to steam my dress. And I have to go find some glitter to put on my shoes.

— Will you miss the announcements? Grandma asked her. Of the winner? With the tiny man's contest?

Nabisase punched her own thigh. — Forget about that. It's not important. I have to be ready for tonight. Uncle Allen wasn't looking for pretty girls anyway.

I should have urged her to get the fuck downtown, right now, and collect her prize, but the offhand way she described herself made me angry. More than angry. Just a blubbery bitter boy. Petty because I wasn't good-looking.

— We may help? Grandma offered her. To prepare yourself.

— I need to get used to doing things on my own, my sister said. I want you both to go.

I felt like the appointed manservant of some young caliph, but did as the young girl commanded. Nabisase tied my grandmother to my back with a few sheets. I carried her that way to the parking lot and put her in the passenger seat.

In the wounded Dodge Neon we drove through Lumpkin, Virginia. There was the chance we'd sight Mom from the car, but not likely. So the new method was to travel, park, tie Grandma on my back and walk around a few blocks looking in stores or driveways.

In 1981 Uncle Isaac tracked Mom to a duck farm in Providence.

Grandma had a recent picture that we showed to clerks, people waiting to cross at red lights. Pedestrians and passengers stared at Grandma and me with patterns of bemusement on their faces as I carried her around. Most were nice enough to listen, but none recognized our dear.

Just like Southeast Queens the city of Lumpkin, away from the phalanx of tourist restaurants and hotels, was the Lord's territory.

Calvary Baptist, Grace Brethren Church, Sacred Heart Catholic, First Church of Christ Scientist, Mountainview Church of Christ, Christ Episcopal Church, Dormition of the Virgin Mary Greek Orthodox, Grace Lutheran, First Presbyterian, Seventh Day Adventist, Centenary United Church of Christ, Braddock St. United Methodist, Market St. Methodist, St. Paul the Redeemer, Beth El Congregation Synagogue Reform. In a pretty small town. With twenty-five houses of worship what's the gamble that, on a Sunday, marriage bloomed.

At an A.M.E. church the jubilant congregation stood outside. Women in pink dresses, men in red suits. The front lawn looked like a taffy shop.

The one-story wooden church was just another white house on a residential block, except for the wheelchair ramp leading to the front door.

Soon as I walked onto the lawn a short, wide man approached. He was one of those small guys with a rib cage large enough to store a car engine. —Hey now, he said.

He put his hand out to me.

—Yes, I said.

—Out strolling.

This sounds like a question, but he wasn't really asking. With his right hand on my shoulder he turned me away from the church so that Grandma and I faced the street once more.

Grandma said, —We are looking for someone.

—Yes, he agreed, but the face showed his unconcern.

He put one hand in his red vest pocket which matched his red shoes, his red jacket and tusk-colored shirt. I tried to show him Mom's picture, but there wasn't time.

—You both have a good day now, he said. You go on from here because we've got a whole mess of cars about to come up the road for a wedding. It's going to get crowded. Go on. Go on.

In a pantomime of friendliness he smiled.

A woman, his wife I bet, walked closer to us and she smiled.

The whole hill of people, hell-yeah fifty-five if I counted, walked closer to us and they smiled, too.

The guy pushed me without making it obvious. Maybe he bounced at bars. With his hand against my right arm he sent Grandma and I going. I had to walk because the momentum would've tripped me if I didn't move. I waved cheerfully until Grandma slapped my face.

—Why would you wave? She asked. They were not friendly. When she scowled her eyebrows covered her eyes, so that her face lost its light.

—They were nice. I was indignant for them because they'd smiled.

—They were disgusted.

— By you?

She pinched my ear.

— By me? I asked. They didn't like me? How?

— Because you are a stinker. One thin, mottled hand waved not across her own nose, but under mine.

— How could they know just by looking at me?

She hooked her thumb into the sheet where it passed under my armpit. — He smelled you.

— It's that bad?

— Terrible, she admitted.

I unbuttoned two of the buttons on my shirt and put my nose in. — What do I smell like?

Grandma wasn't going to detail the offense. I really hadn't noticed. It was three days by now. That is a while.

— I'm sorry, I said to Grandma.

The car was parked downtown; as I walked she reached over my shoulder, rubbed my cheek. Before we got back in the car we stopped in a little pharmacy with aisles so tight that when I tried to slide into the personal hygiene lane I knocked Grandma into a whole display of brightly tinted coolers. I wanted to find some cologne to spritz myself.

CVS was bigger; a chain store with plenty of floor space. There were perfumes in a glass case, but the case only opened with a key. I could've cracked it with my elbow, but who becomes a crook for such a dumb reason.

— I'm going to have to buy one, I told Grandma.

— These are too expensive. Try something else. She pulled my face away, to the right, not gently.

Some perfumes were twenty dollars, but I understood what Grandma really meant. It wasn't that she thought people shouldn't spend twenty dollars on cologne, but that they should bathe before it became an issue.

Opposite the perfumes there were bath gels so I went along opening many, putting them to Grandma's nose until she decided which one she liked. As she sniffed she pursed her lips close to the bottle. If I couldn't be trusted to soap up I didn't trust myself to choose.

What a finicky woman. On the twenty-third try, a hand lotion, she said, —This.

It didn't smell like flowers; not candle wax or ocean water. Worst of the lot. It was dank. It smelled like dirt really. Hearth Scented Body Gel by Mennen.

—If you take one that's too sweet, people will still smell you underneath. This one is strong, but not perfume. It will hide what you have done.

Flipping the plastic tube I squeezed too much on my hands. Rubbed them together until the green paste covered my palms and fingers. First I reached into my shirt to rub up my stomach. I put it on my neck and face then massaged it in long enough that the green color disappeared; only the scent remained. Man of the soil, that's me.

There was a small glass case near the lotion end of the store. There was jewelry in it; the pieces were pretty but sure to have brief lives. On a few I could see the glue that had been used to affix red or purple stones to the gold-plated rings.

—How about a necklace? I said to Grandma. There was a fine thin one with an orange stone.

—I don't wear, she said. She scratched behind one ear, gently.

And I realized she was right. Never bracelets, medallions, rope chain or earrings.

—How about a three-finger ring? I offered.

—Not anything.

—Are you allergic?

—I am not.

—Then let me get you one. You can wear it tonight.

I was about to call the man at the counter over to unlock the case, but she slapped my shoulder. I dropped my hand.

—You don't trust my taste, I said.

—I don't wear any, Grandma said firmly.

—Is it an African custom?

—African custom? You fool. I stopped wearing them for Isaac when he died.

—Did he wear a lot of jewelry?

—No.

—Was he allergic to jewelry?

—No.

—Then why jewelry?!

—I cannot be pretty since my dear son died.

We found Mom.

But it took two hours.

Sixty minutes of that wasted because Grandma wouldn't let me ask after Mom in bars. After Grandma did let me Mom's path lit right on up. Five of them had met her. Dick's, Dell's and the Doughboy. Happy Rabbit. Pretty Sue's.

We had a snapshot of her taken last month, in a department store. Mom stood beside a mannequin at the Macy's in Roosevelt Field Mall on Long Island. Both wore long coats with fur collars. Both were just trying them on. Mom's head was back and she looked at the camera with a predatory gaze. Her tongue stuck half-an-inch from one corner of her mouth. My sister had taken the picture.

When I showed this photo to the bartenders they recognized Mom, but not by the name we gave. That's your mother? each asked, laughed, smiled, winced then answered. She left here but was going to Dell's. To the Doughboy. And so forth.

Until we got to the sixth bar, Right Not Left. Where the woman serving drinks hopped on one foot, saying, — She just left. Right out the back door. With an Indian.

— Southern Ute? I asked.

— From Uttar Pradesh.

We found her outside holding hands with an Indian guy who had a twiny mustache so thick he could have been a Bollywood porn star; a brown Harry Reems had his arm over her shoulder. The trunk of his car was open so I could see black plastic bags in there piled a foot high. I wondered what was in them; probably just groceries.

It's true my mother had become magnetic. The Indian looked at her almost as intensely as Grandma and I did. He wouldn't step more than five inches far. Without seeing her face I'd have thought this whole scene was criminal because he looked fifty, but Mom was a summery sixteen.

She wore tan capri pants to exhibit her calves. Her cotton long-sleeved jersey was vacuum-wrapped around her torso; this made her look sporty. Forget heels or even shoes, she wore plain green sneakers that reduced her feet to snow peas.

— You really won't say, will you? He had one of those deep voices that make men who have them always need to be talking.

She said, — If I told you I was a bank robber you might turn me in.

— But first I'd let you tie me up at your hideout. He smiled, it wasn't even lecherous.

Maybe the plastic bags had the dog figurines; why would she need them if not for me? To decorate a new home? They shut the trunk together; a move that looked cute no matter who the couple was. I stepped back to hide, but if Mom was indeed having another episode she wouldn't recognize us even if I climbed right in their car.

—Doonay, she said to him. Doonay. I like your name, but it's not the one your parents gave you, is it?

—Doonay is what everyone here calls me. It's a nickname.

What if he was a serial killer; this is how that kind of things happens, yes? The scene could have come from *Murder Makes Me Writhe* or a thousand others. The overtly sexual woman in need of riding. Driven off by a stranger who dismembers. They were always doing that, the young women; being punished I mean.

—Hey, you can't be angry at me, Doonay said lightly. We met two hours ago and you haven't said your name at all.

—Mine? It's like yours. Too hard to pronounce, she said. You just call me Yummy.

They made into the car. My fingers smelled like dirt; I'd put my hands to my face.

He drove a black Monte Carlo, a very fast attraction. He might have had the nitrous oxide cannister attachment in the trunk; it makes the car go even faster for short bursts.

Mom laughed with him; the window was down. Grandma and I had been very close to them, but I walked us even closer. Casually Mom looked out at us.

As we stared she showed surprise, but no recognition. Frightened by this ambling creature to her right, Mom rolled her window up halfway. She stopped when we didn't attack her. Also Doonay was pulling out. After her shock passed she only gawked at us and started to laugh in an uncomfortable way, turning her whole body in the seat.

She looked back at us again. Doonay looked, too. Mom's life before this moment had been erased. Unaware that she would ever or had ever done anyone wrong, my mother was like a newborn. My mother was innocent.

—I could go stop her, Grandma.

—You could not.

20

The Blue Ridge Theatre was splendid from all sides. Windows scrubbed and its lights on. With skinny young Marines on duty as ushers; they were nervous boys but the uniforms composed them. And toward the back of a large crowd of parents, siblings and friends was a couple; one standing, one sitting; they promenaded.

The man on his feet, washed and oiled, was me; the woman was Grandma in a wheelchair borrowed from the Hampton Inn. I thought the hotel would charge me extra, but as long as I was registered, apparently, I was trustworthy. Pushing my grandmother instead of carrying her on my back made me respectable. Normal. Which is all I hoped to be. Three different people held doors for us.

I wasn't rancid anymore. Grandma wore a lumber-colored dress with a black cloche that was loose on her small head. Backstage Nabisase was wearing an orange gown and three brass bracelets on her left wrist. I had seen the outfit in the car trunk, but not on her. There were enough black girls in the contest that at least one of the backstage-beauticians would know how to do my sister's hair.

We were happy. Grandma, Nabisase and even me.

Of course she would come back, maybe even get to Queens before us. Until that time there was relief. An unfortunate word to use when talking about the loss of a family member, but Mom wasn't deceased, only departed.

Will you feel this way about me? I wondered. I wanted to ask Grandma, but what could she say that wouldn't sound patronizing. I wouldn't have wanted her to be honest.

The Blue Ridge Theatre had two grand auditoriums and seven smaller ones on the second floor. It was a strapping building. On the walkway outside there were these fire-hydrant-size lamp-posts every five feet. The white lights normally in them had been replaced so that there was a multi-colored gumball procession of bulbs.

Who felt better than me? I belonged like an alligator in the Everglades.

My green suit would be a shamrock-shame in tasteful places, but hardly anyone was dressed well. The fine designers at Bugle Boy outfitted most fathers and brothers. The best of them wore boat shoes. Those flat plastic slippers you get with a tuxedo rental would have stood out as much too worldly here.

One man, carrying his baby to his stomach, wore a denim shirt with the masonic symbol stitched on the back. Prince Hall it was huge: the compass, that capital letter G. This was a man in a secret society and he wanted everyone to know it.

Grandma's wheelchair bestowed influence. Wherever I pushed her the crowd cleared away. I made it a game, seeing how many times people would move, but Grandma stopped me because she wanted to get inside.

The lobby's walls were yellow. The floor was gray with occasional large maroon painted squares; young kids stood in those boxes playing games of endurance—who could stay inside the lines the longest.

One boy was winning over everyone; a few adults even cheered him on. He had red hair and black jeans tucked into his white boots. His father walked over, ignored the game, touched his son on the back of the head and said, —I'm missing you.

Then led his son away.

There were a pair of potted rubber plants in the lobby eight foot high. Two young Marines stood next to them asking people to walk inside. One was lucky, but his partner wasn't.

—Ma'am, would you please continue to walk, the unlucky one told an obstinate woman with hairy forearms. She was determined not to move until she'd examined everything in her purse.

—Ma'am, I've asked you three times.

—Well then stop, she said.

Grandma gave our tickets to yet another Marine inside the auditorium. They were everywhere. They were dignified.

When the boy who'd taken tickets from Grandma noticed that I wasn't following, just looking around, he came back and took my arm.

—Hello sir. My name is Ahab. Please let me help you to your seat.

I tried to pull free, but he had an intimidating grip.

Grandma laughed at me when the kid went away. —He was going to strike you, she said.

—I wouldn't have wanted that.

Grandma agreed. She pressed one thin finger on the very top of my round head. —I don't think you would.

When Grandma started coughing I went and bought water; when she was ready to move I pulled her soles from the heel loops of the wheelchair then flipped the footrests up. Helped her out of the aisle into the auditorium seat.

There were so many women! I don't mean that in a horny way. It just seemed like people had stopped having sons.

In the aisle in front of ours five women sat together in different dresses, but the same strange smiles. A few generations of lopsided grins. The youngest, on the aisle, chewed gum loudly and swallowed it even louder. Making a satisfied, -huhhh-, each time. Then went back into her small handbag, unwrapped another stick from its foil, and smacked again. I only hoped she wouldn't do it during the show or I wouldn't be able to hear.

In twenty minutes every row had filled except ours. Grandma was in the aisle seat with her wheelchair folded beside her. Then me next to her.

White masking tape had been pulled across the ten chairs next to me. 'Reserved' was written on plain white sheets of paper and left on each place.

It was Grandma, me, ten open seats, and free access to these double doors. An emergency exit. The only one not decorated with servicemen.

I stood up. I went over. I touched the doors expecting to hear an alarm, but none came. They'd open easily. I pressed my hand to one.

—Not yet, a voice whispered from the other side.

It was a big auditorium. This stage wasn't like the one in the testifying tent. It had red curtains that made a heavy thump when they were pulled together. I heard the noise from my seat and I was seventy-five feet away. A stage crew practiced opening and closing them a few times.

The stage had two sets of red curtains, one in the rear as a backdrop and one to the fore that would part during the show. When both sets were open we could see far back into the lungs of the theater.

Where a band of four boys with longish hair down over their

shoulders wore dungarees with black jackets. Kids who'd rather play *Bark at the Moon* than *Some Enchanted Evening.*

Perfume floated up from the audience. The air above our heads was a pinkish-purple mist.

The lights went out and I wasn't prepared. I thought they'd make an announcement. But the show just began without warning. I wondered how Uncle Arms was going to get in touch with my sister. Send her a sceptor in the mail?

For fifty seconds we sank into the gloom. I heard the curtains squeak as they closed in the dark. Hiding musicians and wires. The band, invisible now, dragged into a peppy tune. A doo-wop beat.

Small spotlights appeared, one then the next, each the circumference of a tea cup. A hundred of them twirled against the red curtain.

Our MC entered from the left even while the lights kept mulling around the far right. He cleared his throat, then the unseen techie swung his brights over. Once lit, the MC smiled.

—Family and friends! he said.

He wore a tuxedo and sang some awkward lyrics.

> *Miss Innocence, Eastern United States, 1995*
> *You darling star*
> *No mere happenstance or perfect chance*
> *Have saved you until tonight.*

He was very good, crooning these words so seriously that they seemed to make sense. His talent was like sausage, filling and familiar. A rich, deep voice. Reasonably tall and just barely stocky. Not handsome so much as pleasant.

The MC said, —We are here tonight because of some very talented and wonderful young ladies, aren't we? Let's hear it! He was so excited that he hopped.

—Yes folks, we've brought ladies from Florida to Nantucket to compete for the chance to represent the Eastern seaboard of the United States in the National Miss Innocence America next year.

He was a motivational speaker with top-shelf bombast. Introduced himself as Maximilian Duvet. —Tonight we've got a whole lot going on, don't we?

The crowd responded, but without vim.

So he asked again. —Come on folks. Don't we?!

He had no time for passive audiences, so he gave us a certain practiced grin followed by a handful of simple dance moves. He didn't seem expert, only excited. Giving us license to be happy. When he did that it was as if he'd cracked our atomic bonds. We, and I include myself, whistled, clapped, emitted energy.

He grinned, punched his hand in the air. —Yes! he yelled.

The small spotlights hadn't stopped fluttering across Maximilian's face since he'd started speaking. More than a distraction they were making him dizzy. —Okay. He waved his hands. Fellas. Guys. Lights!

The audience laughed.

—They're more excited than I am!

From the ether a dirgy song began, mostly bass and faint guitar.

—Let's take a moment to remember, Maximilian said. Never forget, he told us. Never forget.

Here came my battalion of ghosts from Friday night; the boys who'd been so kind to clean up after me. The Confederates dressed and wooden sabers drawn. Serious little toys. One of them walked out of formation to stand at Maximilian's side.

Maximilian asked, —Who might you be?

—My name is Lewis Tilgham Moore, Colonel of the 31st Virginia Militia of Frederick County.

Max kneeled because the boy looked foolish standing on his

toes, off balance with the heavy scabbard at his right hip. —And where are you going?

—We are off to Harper's Ferry, the boy said.

—And do you think there's trouble?

—Some trouble, but nothing that can't be fixed, I expect!

The kid was a natural actor; easy with his lines, serious without being a boob. His voice was high-pitched, but he spoke slowly and that made him seem mature. The boy rejoined the others and they marched slowly to the middle of the stage, where they turned from profile to face the crowd straight.

I wondered about this volunteer militia; not as a force, but the young men who took a rail one October afternoon in 1859 expecting nothing more than a skirmish. I'd read the newsletter their chaperone gave me. The boys went off to Jefferson County then to the federal armory at Harper's Ferry where John Brown, with a piddling force of eighteen, hoped to spark a slave revolt; within two years there was this Civil War.

It's only after a hundred years that crusades seem inevitable; after all that time the unjust are easily named. But in the midst of history who knows his role?

—You know folks, I'd like to take a minute to be a bit candid with you.

Maximilian was of the crowd now; he had walked down from the stage. Portable microphone held, he stood at the first row. One big but not bright light rested on his shoulder.

—Lately, he said, there have been terrible things happening to our industry. Little Pepper Miller accusing her father of wrongdoing on that *Current Affair* TV show.

Hearing the name Pepper Miller the whole crowd swayed backward in their seats. One unwelcome wind had come from behind the curtains to blow across us plains.

—But I want to tell you, he said, all of you. That I've been working pageants for thirty-five years. He smiled. That's right, three-five. I know I don't look it. At least I hope I don't. Do I?

Who could resist? I wanted to applaud. We liked him.

—Yes!

—But seriously. I've been on this train a very long time and I want you to understand something. Tabloids and television shows come around to film us. They ridicule the efforts these young ladies make. Of the time and expense not just to them, but to the entire family. Some groups even say these young women are being taken advantage of, but let me point out that no privately run organization in the world gives more girls college scholarships than the pageants of this country.

He paused for five seconds of nodding.

—Miss Innocence has been criticized for only accepting girls who have kept their chastity. I was there yesterday, on Braddock Street. And so were a lot of you. These ladies are tired from working twice on Saturday!

Less comfortable now. Even I shifted in my seat.

He scratched his head, pulled on his bow tie.

—I'm not saying there's anything wrong with it. We all go to hundreds of pageants. It's a good system. I respect that other one. Girls should be applauded for surviving hard times, but what makes Miss Innocence special is that we honor the girls who chose to keep living good lives. Being a virgin is hard. There's a lot of handsome young men out there. I know, because I used to be one!

He laughed and I did with him. Most of the audience, too.

—But even with the pressure in school and advertisements the forty-two girls backstage have decided not to be indulgent. There are so many things in this world that makes us feel powerless. Tonight we celebrate some young women who've proven just how powerful they are. That's right. You should applaud. I will.

He tucked the black microphone under an armpit and clapped. —Yes! he yelled.

I took off my glasses because I had an itch in my ear like a riot. It was bad enough that I had to use one of the arms of my glasses to dig in there right at the drum.

My glasses back on I looked over at Grandma who was interested, but confused. She might have liked this more if she understood the words.

Maximilian motioned for the first contestant who walked out quickly, lifting her feet. She stood beside him, he put his arm around her and then let her advertise.

—Hello and greetings. My name is Karen Tiffany Haynes and I represent the lovely town of Knuckleswipe, Rhode Island.

I wondered how Ms. Haynes would look sitting next to me. As a couple. Her hand on my thigh. My arm around her shoulders. Later we'd have a lot of sex. I was sure of it.

—Good evening. My name is Barretta Watkins and I'm here from beautiful East Orange, New Jersey. Come see us!

For Barretta I imagined a beach. Her in a thong and me wearing a gray sweat suit. Even in a daydream I was embarrassed by my body. I couldn't even imagine owning a buffer one.

Barretta coming out of the water, rubbing her eyes and then hugging me. We rolled around together. In my fantasy her little frame could support much weight. When we had sex it was everywhere. In the sand. On a rock. Standing up.

—Greetings and God bless, my name is Sareen Amber Follows. From myself and all of Tennessee, from the Natchez State Parkway to the Fort Donelson National Battlefield, we'd like to welcome you over for dinner anytime!

As each girl finished introducing herself she joined those who'd come out before her in a line at the right end of the stage. My fantasies lost focus as more young women appeared. I couldn't make up new kinds of sex that quickly and started repeating. Demetria Shavers was also sitting next to me in an empty theater. Tiffany Murdock in the sand.

When nine or ten stood around, smiling, I just started picturing getting them pregnant. The whole row bearing my children. I wasn't even thinking of the fucking at that point; just that very sexy time, about five months in, when the belly can't be ignored. A hard hump that precedes her; the skin a pleasure to lick.

After Uncle Arms's jubilee, to see the same girls on a finer platform was strange. Sareen Follows wore long gold gloves so that her skinny arms were concealed, but on Saturday afternoon she'd exposed them.

Whether or not I heard the knock I won't know, but I thought I did. As Maximilian awaited the next girl, I crept to the double doors.

I couldn't just stand up. I didn't want to be noticed, remembered, described to the police.

To Maximilian's surprise the lights went out, but not the power. His microphone still worked. In the suddenly dark auditorium, he yelped, — Spit!

Once there, I pressed the long metal bars on the double doors and heard the lock give.

A raiding party was outside, expecting me.

A road flare should be used outdoors.

This seems like practical instruction, like who needs it said, but common sense escapes some folks.

Auditorium illumination had sworn down to nothing, even Maximilian had dimmed. He needed someone else's cue. — Hello? he asked into the microphone. What part is this?

The audience was largely oblivious. This didn't take a very long time. One minute of darkness.

Then the road flares.

They have to be snapped before they start burning so first there were half a dozen cracking sounds.

I saw the protestors go in carrying the flares. The hallway, where they'd been waiting, was as dark as the auditorium.

The sallow woman came in first; she still looked nineteen, but she was thirty-nine. I recognized her even with boots on. Wearing a black leotard and a black thermal underwear top, but nothing to cover her face. Did she expect to be seen? Want it? I wondered where the film crew was positioned.

She dashed her flare down the aisles. So did the six that followed her.

They ran past me. I pulled the doors closed. I was still inside. We were in a room, but it felt big as the world.

After flares the protestors pulled can-horns from their coats and pumped them. The honks helped to orient people: Yes, you should be scared.

Some women in the audience screamed and others ducked their heads. The men did just about the same. Less yelling, more tucking.

The middle-aged woman, their leader in here, yelled, —No more beauty, just more art!

They'd been in a group, but then the demonstrators ran the aisles chaotically. Playing their can-horns whenever it seemed the audience might get their bearings enough to get up and slap these kids down.

Every two minutes. Horn! Horn!

This was supposed to have been fun. Except for the flares there was no light and I'd let seven imps in the room.

One problem was getting my eyes to focus.

As if the bleating cans wasn't enough, there were audience members screaming. Then the rusty ring of auditorium seats flipping up as people stood and slamming down as they sat again.

—Less beauty, more art!

The protestors were yelling, lecturing us, but who was listening? I heard the words, but didn't understand. It was loud enough in here that even Grandma covered her ears. When I scooted back to her, she'd pulled her cloche down over her eyes.

The rear curtains on stage pulled back, but the band was gone. There was a drum kit, but no one playing it.

With the backstage area exposed there was some light other than the hot-pink road flares. The lamps back there must have been on another circuit. They didn't do much more than illuminate the contestants, all of them on the stage now. A crowd of forty-two crying girls.

They were confused. So were we. Forty-two of them. I tried to pick my sister out so I could go up there and get her, but I didn't see Nabisase. A few of the girls climbed off the stage and tried to find their families. Many of them screamed, — Mommy! Mommy!

It sounded like they'd all lost one.

Maximilian started making noise. I wouldn't even have noticed his voice among so many others, but he was holding that working microphone. He muttered, — I'll be so glad when I get home.

Somebody should have turned the speakers off but in the commotion they'd spun the dial up to one hundred and thirty.

— I'll be so glad when I get home.

My eyes remained half in focus, half in the basement.

I saw many more of the Miss Innocence girls climb offstage. A few jumped. You might have thought they were on fire. We were beneath them, but they joined us. A magnanimous act.

Once the stage cleared the thirty-nine-year-old guerrilla hurled balloons up there. She was right at the front, but no one bothered her. Afraid to tackle the saboteur.

Her friends joined. Four throwing balloons and three facing the audience, waving their can-horns threateningly. They didn't have to. Everyone was scared of them. Even me.

The balloons wobbled heavily. When they hit they splattered greenish grease across the stage. Five balloons. Then fifteen. Great globs of oil stained the boards.

I tried to comfort Grandma, but she didn't want it. I wondered if she'd seen me open the double doors. It was her hearing, not her sight, that sucked. I touched her shoulder and she pushed my hand away. Head forward, screaming, —Nabisase! into her lap.

Around us whole families stood to run and sat again. They didn't know what to do.

I wished I had Uncle Arms in my hands so I could squeeze his lying neck. This was monstrous. I regretted helping.

When I went to the door a second time it was because I knew that I heard knocking.

It wasn't forceful and I thought of Uncle Arms's rapping from the other side.

My lightest touch made the doors move. I said, —Uncle Arms, I want to talk to you.

But he wouldn't have heard me over the echoing chorus in the room. I was surprised the can-horns weren't hoarse by now. If anyone but Maximilian was speaking I couldn't hear it. All other voices became traffic in the auditorium. A long vowel sound; a cloud of despair; or one ecstatic outburst from the mouths of God.

One door slipped back three inches. A light was on in that service hallway now. 10,000 watts. It was a clear, vivid, luminous, incandescent, flaring flaming fucking corridor now. I covered my eyes. Twenty-five more anarchists ran past me, into the auditorium.

We should have stayed in Rosedale. I could have cheated fate. It was November 12th. I remember.

Nabisase found Grandma.

I heard my sister calling a name, but hardly recognized it as my own.

Grandma and Nabisase were to my left, twenty feet. I held the door open with my hand; I was framed by the hallway light. Easy to see me. And to see them. Grandma in her seat. Nabisase kneeling in the aisle. Both of them looking at me. Misunderstanding.

My eyes began to flutter as I let go of the door. It shut. My family was in the auditorium, but I was stuck outside. Not alone. There was one last figure here, wide as an oven and twice as tall. It wouldn't let me in its cabin, but had come to take me now. It touched both sides of my face with its very small hands. The taste of salt water was on my tongue from crying. I opened my mouth, tried to talk, but there was a lion's egg in my throat. Two of us, in the service hall, became entangled.

3 HOUNDS.

Ledric Mayo could go ahead and die because I wasn't going to help him. I was saying that to myself the whole seven-hour drive from Lumpkin, Virginia. If Nabisase and Grandma had been speaking to me I'd have told them that very same thing.

It's what I told myself as I called in sick at Sparkle on Monday morning.

Then again at noon when I went outside to do yard work because I just couldn't sleep. To illustrate the mood of my family: I hid the kitchen knives and that's no joke.

— Aye nigga.

    — Get that nigga!

    — Get that nigga to stop cutting them bushes!

Three times Pinch yelled at me and three times I ignored him. He was with a few other guys in the yard next to mine, on the front steps of Candan's house.

Pinch stood up when I didn't heed his command to stop chopping at my hedge and he walked out then around into my driveway. Now I couldn't ignore him because his beefy hand was on my shoulder. I let go of the trigger of the hedge clipper and the high –chip– –chip– noise faded away.

—Those bushes never did anything to you.

He and I surveyed the hedge, which ran the length of my driveway. Twenty-five feet before it reached the backyard, where we had a less formal row of shrubs.

I was proud of myself because I'd really gone hell with the cutting. It wasn't fair that in the summer this bramble was going to bloom into one impossible green afro which would have to be trimmed every two weeks and yet it wasn't even really our property. The damn thing was growing from Candan's side. The President was the one who'd planted it, so why did I have to tend one half of its features.

—That's called being neighbors, said Pinch.

There were plenty of other reasons to be agitated, but the one that irked me most was Mr. Ledric Mayo. I really didn't see how I could go administer to an idiot who'd poisoned his own stupid self.

The two other guys, Candan one of them, stood in Candan's yard but came closer to disapprove of me from fewer feet away. Through the tindersticks of this bare winter hedge I watched them shake their heads.

Candan said, —Now that's too much, Anthony. Next time you don't have to cut a lot.

Who knows. Maybe the guy spoke to me that way because he truly meant to be kind, but it was the tone one takes with a guy who separates clear and colored glass for a living.

—You took the top two feet off that thing, Pinch said. The President's not going to be to happy about it.

—He's no one's boss, Candan said quickly.

Even I was surprised to hear him sound so ferocious.

Then the President came round the corner in his Lincoln Town Car.

His Town Car was a big mess; not even old; a '94 model, but damn that front end was battered. The headlights were held by gray duct tape. One of the rear-door windows was veiny from having half-shattered.

Pinch smiled. — Candan, you tell the President what you just told us.

The guy next to Candan was as fat as me. Out in Queens this wasn't as rare as the Surgeon General would wish. It was like, say, semi-rural Pennsylvania. I am the unattractive America.

The President didn't make it easy on his car, weaving like he did. He bumped against curbs a couple of times.

Going twenty-five miles an hour and without once tapping a brake the President spun that black car to the right just as he reached home. As the car entered the driveway it bumped one of the poles of their fence, making it shake rattlesnake-loud.

The President was not a drunk. It wasn't alcohol making him weave. — Youngbloods! The President yelled happily. He rolled down the electric passenger-side window, but still sat in the Town Car. Candan and the fat guy were on one side of the hedge, Pinch with me on the other.

Candan spat.

The car was turned off.

Out stepped the President in a turquoise track suit.

It was his eyes that were wrecked. I had never seen them this close before. They went in two directions and neither was straight ahead. His driver's license had gone out of style three years ago, but try telling him to renew it. Men never believe their powers will fail.

— Youngbloods, he said again.

Pinch smiled first. — How you, Mr. Jerome?

He shrugged. The President was that kind of man who meant

to be weary, no matter. If he was in bed he'd say his back hurt from being prone then when on his feet he'd swear the most he wanted was to spread out on a board to sleep. The President said, —They got me on the run, Chester. They got me out of breath.

Candan walked toward the car without greeting his father.

—I got the damn car keys! C.D. Come back over here. Where you been hiding? the President asked me.

—Took my family away for the weekend.

—How far? he asked.

—Viriginia. Seven hours' drive. We got back at four this morning.

—Are you all here? Candan asked.

—Where else would we be?

—Four of you came in this morning? Candan asked. One, two, three, four?

—Damn Candan, the President said. I think the man can still count!

I looked at his son, at Candan, wondering how people had spoken about me in the weeks since I'd returned.

The President joked around instead of letting his son press. He pointed at me and the other Jell-O-fellow beside Candan. —You two look like the bookends at a cookie factory.

Guys giggled, even the other big boy, but the joke didn't make sense to me.

—Why would a cookie factory have bookends? I asked.

But too late for that because the President noticed my work. He walked the length of the hedge while still in his yard then scratched his gray mustache. He wore a black leather baseball cap with an adjustable strap on the back. —You sure made a mess of this, he said.

I wondered why he had to accuse me, but remembered the big orange clipper in my hand.

The others waited for angrier words, but the nice thing about the President was that he was never going to get his gun from in the house. Most he'd do is crack an egg on your forehead.

— If I ever need a haircut I won't call you, the President said.

Before there could be any more jokes Candan's red dog came from their backyard and crouched at the President's feet. A lithe Doberman, missing one of its ears. I thought it was playing with the older man, but it snarled at the President until Candan walked over, slapped its side and yelled, — Shut up!

— Get back! Candan yelled.

The President bowed his head, but I didn't know if the gesture was in deference to his son or his son's emissary, the Doberman.

After Candan commanded it the mutt popped up, trotted off, thin body bouncing so high above the ground it seemed about to float off like some long, useless balloon. It barked a few times, which caused a few other nearby dogs to rev up so then there were pockets of howling in the neighborhood for close to thirty minutes.

One day; so far; no mother; not bad.

When the President went inside their house Candan paced casually to the Lincoln then removed keys the President had forgotten in the driver's side door. He shook them in front of us like Candan needed people to see that he was right to assume his father doddered, but we looked away, ashamed for him to show it.

22

When I walked back inside with bits of hedge drit still on my hair Grandma was in the living room with Nabisase. The younger was talking while combing the old woman's hair into braids, but they stopped when I came in.

Fatigue twists the tongue until it turns blue. —I think you're overreacting, I told them. Mom's the one who cut out on you, not me.

For the first time in years I felt like a child. A horrible time compared with adulthood.

—Did you hear what I said?

Nabisase and Grandma continued to play Easter Island; in the living room I stood three feet from a civilization unwilling to answer me.

Stupidly, I went and tried Mom's door. It was locked when we left so why would it be any different now. I got down on my knees and pressed my nose to the space at the bottom. Then my ear. I was waiting for a sign that she was back in there.

She wasn't.

I went to get the mail and that's when I realized I never sent Ahmed Abdel his note. It was in my jacket pocket, forgotten when I chased my sister and grandmother to Uncle Arms's charade.

As I got the letter, walked to the door, my sister finally said something.

— Are you going to see about Ledric?

— How'd you know about that?

— I played the answering machine.

— I was only going to mail a letter.

Grandma didn't look at me, but she said. — He sounds terrible and sick.

— You two have Ledric Mayo on the brain.

I tapped the letter to Ahmed Abdel against the door. They waited.

— I don't have the energy, I complained. This is the only thing you all can talk to me about?

Nabisase stood up. — I called him already and got the address. I said we were going over.

— Why'd you do that?

— Because we're going to.

I didn't want to bring Nabisase with me to Jamaica and luckily it was four o'clock so my sister's church was having its second Monday prayer meeting. She was willing to miss school, but not devotions. Christ had really impressed my sister with his Bible that you've heard so much about. The first morning back from Lumpkin she read Scripture while eating cereal.

But you know, I'm not even going to say Christ when I refer to Nabisase's faith because I still didn't believe she meant it. I'll say Selwyn because Nabisase wouldn't know the difference.

Nabisase walked with me, though not for the comraderie. I was on the sidewalk and she stayed at the lip of the street. She thought I'd betrayed her. On the drive up from Lumpkin I filled the car with gas and didn't make one stop; she and Grandma didn't speak.

Except when we were finally home and I got out, ran around to Nabisase's side.

Then my sister said, — Don't you hold any more doors open in front of me.

It's harder to stay close when someone watches you betray them. She thought she understood me perfectly and I just couldn't explain.

I smiled as we reached the corner of 229th Street and 147th Avenue. Nabisase went to hear sermons at the Apostolic Temple of Selwyn. A Church with Old Time Powers.

Watching her, I wondered how, exactly, a person finds religion.

After ten minutes a brown van stopped about a half-block past me. I waited for it to come back but the driver wouldn't rewind so I had to walk over.

There are two kinds of vans used for this small-business public transportation. The difference is in the size of the passenger door. One has a great big hatch while the other's got a portal the size of an airplane window. I will let you guess which this van had; it shouldn't take long to figure. When I opened the tiny entrance the crowd inside muttered. I distinctly heard one man whisper, — Oh god damn, at the sight of me.

Ten passengers watched me struggle in. The inside of the cabin smelled like sweaty feet and cocoa butter. Each row of seats fit three people, but those were to capacity so I had to get past them, to the last back ass end where there was the longer seat that fits four.

I knocked a woman's hat off her head with my big shoulder.

A teenager got so jostled as I passed that his whole damn magazine fell between his knees to the floor.

— Sorry, I whispered. Sorry.

Even the other fat people cursed me or rolled their eyes.

The driver was a fifty-year-old lady with a face like a betel nut. She waited until I was almost in the seat properly then pedal down, pedal hard.

There was dance hall music coming from the radio and the van's CB spattered conversation or static. The driver's name was Lorna Tintree and she picked up the microphone whenever her dispatcher called for her. They always used her full name. She yelled responses as she drove too fast.

Her voice had a thick island accent. I could imagine mango trees, but not any particular island. Slow down was the only message I wished her dispatcher would send. Her hair was a big loose spray of black semi-curls emanating from her skull like the sound waves of her rollicking conversation.

Each time she stopped talking there was a moment before the guy on the other end responded and the fuzz through the microphone sounded like a name:

-ledric- -ledric-.

Please understand how dangerous a van trip is. Lorna Tintree took curves doing fifty.

When we hit bumps and dips in the road eleven people tossed in the air. Only our driver wore a seat belt.

My sister might have thought I was going to help Mr. Mayo, but I was not. I'd go apply for a library card at the Jamaica branch, have some lunch and then come home. I'd tell her that I lost the address.

But after each leap, as the van banged back to the ground, the gnash of chassis against roadway was a familiar proper noun: -ledric- -ledric-.

My conscience sounded like my sister, her voice a guide in my head. Leading me past Rufus King Park. To Sutphin Boulevard and 88th Avenue where a certain fat bastard rented a room. Shit if I hadn't been avoiding saving his life.

23

Ledric's building was owned by a Nigerian woman who wouldn't let me into her home until I said his name a couple times. When I did she looked at me closely, asked, — You are the brother?

— Of course, I said. Let me see him?

This was a private home that the woman owned. One of three on the block between a pair of six-story apartment buildings. — Go round the back, she said.

The lady rented single-occupancy spaces out of her basement. Three rooms at $400 each. Probably covered the mortgage so that her own paycheck might afford the large-screen television I'd seen through her front window.

When I knocked politely and heard no response she kicked the door to Ledric's room so hard that it rumbled from the force of her boot. Eventually Ledric made a noise, but not for three minutes. In that time I watched the lady as she ran one finger across her gums then fed on a few remnant strands of beef.

Ledric was able to pull open the door to his room without getting up because he was lying on the ground. —Hey Ant. Nabisase just called me to see if you came yet, he whispered.

The Nigerian said, —I want money for getting Ledric's vomit out of my carpet.

I'm not a creature. There are human feelings in me. I got down, set my arms around his waist, and helped Ledric onto the bed. That wasn't actually a good thing because the whole mattress was wet through the sheets.

The Nigerian woman said, —And he's going to have to pay for the mattress if it's ruin.

Ledric's room was only big enough for a bed and desk. The window was open, which helped relieve the moist smell of yuke, but this was November and pretty cold.

—You should keep the window shut, I said to him.

The landlord covered her nose. —He shouldn't.

I helped him dress, but he couldn't get his arms through shirt sleeves. —I'm seeing in two's, he whispered.

His desk had nothing on it but work materials: envelopes, pre-printed labels and form letters from SunTrust, a bank in Washington, D.C. I went through them like they were my own. Offers for unsecured credit cards, all applicants considered.

—This is your job? I asked.

—I've got to complete a hundred-fifty more this week.

—I'm not going to do it for you, I said.

On any subway seat in Queens there are these little red cards with phone numbers and bold offers: Lose Weight—30 Lbs in 30 Days. Make Money—Assemble Products in Your Home. I never thought anyone was foolish enough to call the swindlers back.

I was angry at him, but he could hardly breathe. I sat him up while I filled a gym bag with his least grimy clothes. The boy just wasn't neat, even before the tapeworms I bet. Where was that jar?

—I threw it out, Ledric said. I don't know what I was thinking.

I helped him to his feet, but that was a losing proposition. He was having a bad time standing, but when he leaned against me we managed a kind of run that was basically the two of us falling forward under the combined weight. Six hundred pounds. Okay seven.

He was shorter than me and he had an enormous belly; the kind that suffocates genitals when the bearer sits down. But he had no tits at all and his legs were skinny.

Before we could leave the Nigerian woman said, —He still owes me for the last week. Your brother pays me last Wednesday.

—He's sick, I said.

—One 'undred.

I paid her with the bills in my pocket. Ten ten-dollar bills and she counted them in front of me three times. I had no bank account only some paper money in my wallet and the rest hidden in one box of my books.

Getting to Jamaica Avenue took half an hour, though it was just three blocks. Ledric had been slurring his words for twenty minutes and each time he opened his mouth a little drool played down his chin. It got so disgusting that I tied one of his T-shirts, bandit-style, around the lower half of his face to absorb the saliva.

This made it harder to get a gypsy car; outfitted as he was and me with Ledric's duffel bag on my shoulder taxi drivers probably thought we'd robbed a White Castle of its patties and buns.

—Call your mother to pick us up, he begged.

—She's not with us anymore.

—Is she alright?

I didn't feel like answering him. Eventually we were picked up. I gave the driver my address, and this is how Ledric Mayo came into my home.

24

I joined Clean Up that evening because even after bringing Ledric back, after explaining his predicament to Grandma then arguing with her over allowing him inside, after setting him on the living room couch and going to the grocery store for items Nabisase expected Ledric would need, I still wasn't tired.

Anyway, I couldn't ask Nabisase to get a job. She'd already missed school one day and I wasn't planning to let her pass another. Grandma had some savings, but we'd need income. I didn't mind any of this. It's not that I wanted to discover my manhood, I was going to invent it.

Clean Up was a twilight shift that paid twice as much as day cleaning. It was clandestinely run by Sparkle's assistant manager, Claire. She told me not to bring any identification when meeting her in front of the office at nine. Thought I'd be alone, but there were twenty people waiting. Carrying no green cards, visas, credit cards; we weren't even allowed to use last names.

At nine-thirty Claire drove up in her green van. It wasn't even as nice as the gypsy vans, which have four rows of padded seats. She had two long benches soldered down in the cargo hold so some sat on them. When those filled we sat on the floor between the benches. Like all Queens drivers Claire stood on the accelerator and the rocking in the back made for bruised butts. I'm too educated for this, I thought each time my tailbone banged.

The factory was only one floor, but very wide. We had crossed from the mall in Long Island back to Laurelton. Metal grates were closed over loading bays. A man in the shape of an ostrich egg was waiting at the only open door. He didn't let us in until Claire returned from parking the van blocks away. Once she took us in he locked the door from outside.

We were led through the staff offices, more cubicles than closed rooms. Through a rectangular area with table, tea bags, coffee machines. We couldn't walk fast enough for Claire who had on hiking boots and baby-blue jeans. She didn't speak with us except to yell, —Let's go! Do you people know how much I've got to do tonight?

Then we came to a room where boxes of furniture were in stages of being packed or unpacked. Lights hung from the ceiling. Seven red hand trucks against a wall. Claire took off her coat to reveal one of those thin upper bodies that is the opposite of good nutrition. Her arms were as stiff as the chicken wings I'll bet she bought through bulletproof Chinese restaurant glass. She was running a nefarious, illegal labor scheme wearing a white Old Navy T-shirt.

—The important thing for you to understand about Clean Up is that I'm always busier than you. While you're clearing a room I'm doing four or five other jobs. So don't bother me. If you see me smoking a cigarette don't come asking for more hours, because I'm doing inventory in my head.

She expected some reaction, maybe an ovation.

She said, —I'd give anything for one American. Then she yelled, If any one of you spoke English I'd pay $100 an hour.

—I speak it pretty well, I said.

She was surprised. —How did you get in here?

—You called me. We spoke on the phone.

Claire had a notepad in her back pocket and opened it. —You're not Esmeralda. Anthony?

—Yes.

—Anthony, I'm a very busy woman. I don't want you interrupting me again.

With that Claire led us to our workroom. I'd thought this was just going to be a bigger sweeping job. Gather factory dust, shine flanges and get twice my daytime Sparkle rate. You've got to realize how much energy I had; the coming work didn't daunt. I'd just driven for seven hours that morning, we'd been in Virginia twenty-four hours ago. I'd saved Ledric from his landlady and took him home to recuperate. Now what else, Clean Up? That's nothing. Six hours of work. I had the fuel.

We left the main floor by going through a thick door with four locks. There was an open dark stairway and I forgot where I was. For eleven seconds I had a waking dream that we were being taken to the basement so they could shoot us in the head and keep the blood. I know that seems stupid but besides me the other twenty women looked El Salvadorian so what child of the eighties wouldn't think of death squads? A feeling of nauseous exhilaration was in my sternum because I thought I was going to be killed, but then reality returned as I gripped the handrail and we were led downstairs by Claire.

The basement was twice as long as the factory space upstairs, but only half as high, eight feet maybe. Sometimes Claire covered her mouth down here. Like whenever she breathed.

She had a King Kullen bag full of white mouth guards. We put them on, but the rubber wire of the face masks scratched our cheeks so badly they left scuff marks. Claire walked to the top of the stairs leading to the first floor then addressed us.

—You grab those big pink sheets then put them in the barrels. When one is full you cover it tight. Jam those sheets down hard to fit plenty. If any dust comes up put on your air filtration units.

She shut the door then we listened to four locks click. I swung the surgeon's mask, was this the air filtrator? I'd seen sturdier toilet paper.

We rolled the long pink dry sheets; this worked for the top layer. Half the basement floor had stacks of these pink mats laid out.

Once we had mastered the right speed, one that kept the asbestos dust out of our air, the curling up was easy. We stacked the rolls on their sides next to the barrels.

A woman said, —We stop. We done too fast.

Two of the twenty women were sisters. They wore clean white sneakers that they'd been brushing with their open hands whenever a smudge appeared. Now on break they sat and took the shoes off, blew on them then used the bottoms of their shirts to wipe the heels. Pay Less sneakers probably, cheap, but I admired anyone who worked hard on her wardrobe. I rubbed at the dust stains on my purple suit.

Turning their shoes over both women cleared grains from the soles by running pens in the grooves. The green ink made the bottoms of their sneakers the dull color of an unripe olive. We rested for half an hour and watched the sisters maintain their beauty.

What a disappointment to find out later that this basement had flooded recently. It was obvious because the next layer of pink sheets were stiff but wrinkled like dried washcloth. These sections broke apart while being rolled so there was no way to avoid the dust. Below that was a layer still so wet it couldn't be curled. I paced the room looking for tin or flat steel to use as a shovel.

I found the lower end of a broom so I tried to sweep portions toward the barrels, but the pink molasses came apart under the bristles. Soon the whole room was a tableau of crouched figures scooping wads of asbestos into their arms, balancing the bundles as they walked across the long room to drop them into bins.

Every twenty minutes half a dozen people stopped to stretch their lumbar regions in the corner of the room not beset with pink dust devils. When the floor was clearer we tracked through puddles of grainy water as yet undried on the concrete floor.

The soles of those sisters' sneakers leaked ink into the puddles when they got wet. The pools were already cloudy, but they turned faintly green.

One woman pointed, saying, — It is the color of dollars bills.

We were punch drunk. We were half twisted off.

We'd been down there four hours so excuse our grogginess.

The general state was so bad that one of the sisters rashly splashed through the green puddle just because it was like money.

I did because it was like money.

The other ladies splashed in it and for a good reason, it was money.

The second sister even went through eventually, but only because she was a big follower.

We doused our shoes in the water more than twice because it was like money.

What a peppy crowd we became. Making friends and praising peace. Our pants stained with prosperity.

25

My long Monday finally ended at three AM Tuesday morning, November 14th, 1995.

The Clean Up shift was close enough to my home that Claire agreed to drop me at the corner, though the other women were only getting a ride to the 7 train.

She left me out on the corner of 229th and 145th Avenue where I had to hide behind a parked car because four loose mutts wrestled, yipped and yawned in front of Candan's home. His red Doberman barked then the four on the sidewalk whimpered. I was afraid of being snapped at like Ishkabibble at my cookout so I gave the dogs a few minutes to socialize. Soon, the quartet ran off, I thought they were done. But Candan's red dog was still there, nose pressed against its gate, watching me open mine.

Grandma hopped in from the living room as I took off my coat in the kitchen. Before I could ask why she was awake Grandma whispered, — He can't breathe. That boy.

I said, —Let him rest.

—Your sister sits with him the whole night.

I opened the basement door, but the lights were off. —They're down there now?

Grandma said, —We couldn't manage him down the stairs. He is as big as you. He is still in the living room.

He was in a sleeping bag on the ground with some couch cushions to prop him up. Between the sectional couch and the entertainment unit; his boots stood neatly with the other shoes in the kitchen.

Three in the morning and my sister was still awake kneeling by his side. She wasn't saying prayers, but playing Tetris on her Game Boy. She wore a long yellow nightdress that went down to her ankles. Her bare feet tucked under her butt so that the toes were pointing toward me in the hallway. There was a bowl of water with a face cloth soaking in it, and another wet one resting on Ledric's collarbone.

—What you'll need to do is take hot baths, Nabisase told him.

He responded slowly.

—I wish I met you someplace else, he said. I look kind of nice when I'm dressed up.

She was thirteen and he was nineteen, a huge age gap only to parents of teenagers. Those adults should shut their eyes, firmly, at malls.

—I don't care about that stuff, Nabisase said. Fat's not the worst thing you could be.

—Your brother tell you how I got sick?

—He said it was bad fish.

—I just got desperate. I don't want to look like this anymore.

She exchanged one wet cloth for the other; rubbing it on his face, his neck, his arms.

I didn't interrupt them. I went back to the kitchen's security door and slammed it as if this was my first time coming in. With that noise my sister rose and went right to bed. Ledric shut his eyes.

Grandma sat in the kitchen, waiting for me to carry her. — You need the hospital even more than he does, I said.

She told me, — I am fine.

This left the basement or my mother's locked room for my first sleep since Lumpkin. But I refused either.

I crept to Ledric's side and listened to him wheeze.

He slept for three hours while I never closed my eyes. I should have been exhausted.

At six I poked his ribs. — Get up, I said.

— Where?

— I guess we're going to Queens General, I said. If you're that sick.

Ledric whispered, — I'm not going to no hospital. His arms were above the covers, but he couldn't lift them. Only his puffy hands shifting proved his agitation.

— Listen to you. You can't inhale.

— No hospital.

— You still seeing double?

— I just won't open my eyes. To prove it he closed them, but couldn't even rally the energy to squeeze them theatrically. His big cheeks puffed out and he exhaled.

— My sister can't take care of you with aspirin and soup.

— No hospital, he stressed. They'll give me a disease.

His sentences were coming out between wheezes, murmurs really. I had to lean down close while on my knees. — I think you've got one already, I said.

He opened one eye to look at me. — Last year, this man went into Queens General to remove some warts and they took off both his legs. I'm telling you. I believe that shit.

I touched the top of Ledric's head, but that only made it slide backward until he was looking at the ceiling. The boy had very little muscle control.

— Okay Ledric. At nine we'll go over to the clinic on Brookville Boulevard.

The green-tiled one-story building at the southwest corner of 147th Avenue and Brookville Boulevard had been a Sons of Italy Lodge (Per Sempre) then changed to a cash-only medical clinic housing doctors from four continents, none of them North America.

It was shaped like a Cambodian pagoda, with a fenced lot next to it; I parked the Oldsmobile Firenza there. When I'd returned the Dodge Neon to the rental office I glued the trunk shut at the lock, hoping the people at National wouldn't notice—they hadn't.

I went into the clinic to borrow a wheelchair, but Ledric wouldn't fit so I came back with one of the carts used for unloading medical equipment. Just a wide flat tray on wheels. Ledric slid out of the Oldsmobile's backseat and flopped face-first on top of the cart. I had to push him through the delivery entrance.

We would have been in the waiting room three hours if Ledric hadn't started gasping. Once that happened an angry elf-owl of a nurse let me roll my brother to a small room where a stubble-necked Russian doctor asked a few questions, moved Ledric's head around. The doctor diagnosed this easily.

— Botulism, he said.

26

A condition that demands hospitalization.

The real torture to the Russian physician was that he'd have to release us from his highly profitable care there. He didn't have the equipment in this tiny clinic on the tri-corner hat border of Laurelton, Rosedale and Far Rockaway.

Though Ledric tried to protest again he was making no sense because he couldn't shape words; he might as well have been a manatee booing.

I wanted to take him to the hospital in the Oldsmobile, but the Russian doctor wouldn't let me. He was afraid I'd ignore his diagnosis and take Ledric home hoping he'd pull through. The Russian was already well acquainted with the rational paranoia of people without health insurance. — Botulism is not like a fever, he said.

— How am I going to pay for an ambulance?

— Your brother will die without it.

—Can you get them to come down on the price?

The Doctor huffed, but only a little; I doubt he'd been well off when practicing in St. Petersburg. He touched my shoulder. —Your brother goes to Queens General. It is reasonable and his care is precise.

Queens General hospital in north Jamaica is a choir of gray buildings taller than most in Southern Queens. I could say that it's run down but that would give the wrong impression, make you think the place was a quagmire. It was a decent operation and if money came into the coffers they spent it on equipment.

I followed the ambulance to the hospital the whole time wondering how I'd missed another day shift in the sticky mess of Ledric's life. I parked and walked the overpass of the Grand Central Parkway then down 163rd Road. Made a left on the slight incline that leads into the emergency room. The place was pretty empty because it was only 11 AM. There were two hundred grievously wounded people waiting to get medical attention instead of the usual twelve hundred of most evenings.

I had the good fortune of having a family member who'd been brought by ambulance and diagnosed with an illness rarely seen in America anymore. When I told the nurse at the front desk his name (she was behind Plexiglas so I had to shout) I was sent up to Ledric's room immediately. In the elevator I wondered how much a private room cost. I hoped they had him bunking with other people.

He might as well have had a Barcalounger near his bed for the excess space they'd given. How about a wide-screen television with a host of private movies and a masseur on call, since we're spending Anthony's money? I would've felt better, maybe nonchalant, if I believed that Ledric had even collected loose change in a jar. The penniless creep. He couldn't have asked for the room, too weak to say it, so some clerk had assigned this manse.

I left when the doctors finally came. They asked me to leave. There were two of them. When I returned in twenty minutes they'd written down Ledric's many symptoms but had done nothing to repair his health.

—What are you going to do for him?

The physicians nodded, but without looking up from their papers. They didn't seem wealthy, either one. For instance, their watches were cheap. Digital faces with plastic bands. One wore black while the flashy one's was orange.

—It's not botulism, said the first one. He told me like he was solving an illusionist's trick.

The second one agreed and laughed to prove it. —It is not botulism.

—But the Russian doctor was so sure, I said.

The first put his hand up. —There's a good chance your friend over there spent too long in a gulag.

—You should take his diagnosis with a tranquilizer.

—We'll probably end up giving Mr. Mayo a purgative, that's all.

—Oh that's good, I said.

—He'll get the runs, the doctor with an orange watch clarified. He pointed at things a lot just to show that gaudy colorful band. We're going to let Mr. Mayo sleep a while and check on him tomorrow.

—But he's not asleep. I don't even think he's breathing, I said.

—He's breathing under his own power.

—The next time you want to get well, come to us. I'll bet this Russian would amputate your foot if you came in with whooping cough. They laughed at the doctor and it seemed, in his absence, at me.

I thanked them anyway as they left. Sitting next to Ledric in a chair I kicked my feet. Hospitals are quiet when you need them to be.

I couldn't sleep, but I was exhausted. I took off my shoes, so that helped. Ledric was as big as the bed. The nurses had dropped the metal guards from the sides of the mattress because he wouldn't have fit on it otherwise.

I walked around the room in my socks to see him from all angles. Even crouching at the foot of the bed, staring up from his feet to the rise of his belly. I pulled the sheets above his ankles while I was down there just to see those five-pound potatoes he called feet.

It was like I had an audience with my own body; a chance to see how I'd look laid out on a bed. Except for his face we were enough alike. I walked to the window, blocking daylight, and Ledric's figure worried me. I don't mean his weight; the lonesomeness. Other than myself no one else was going to visit.

When I sat next to him again, heard his fuzzy breathing, I forgot sympathy and only remembered the burden. How had he become my responsibility? Nabisase and Grandma expected me at home. Was this how my mother felt before we went to Virginia?

To pass the next hour, since Ledric wasn't going to tell any jokes, I tore off the cover of the hospital phone book and wrote a few more quick movie entries. *Night of the Hatchet, Bet They Die, Easily Eaten.* Why did the one-eyed drifter take his hatchet to the people of Tarpenny, Florida? In a surprise twist, they were a town of warlocks and witches and the drifter was a righteous man.

I looked at the words and felt guilty because I wasn't going to give Ishkabibble a film. Only summaries of them. Not a movie, just letters.

After an hour and a half I left the room to call Grandma and yelled when I heard that Nabisase had skipped school a second day. They were happy to know Ledric was safe.

At home we ate dinner in the living room. We watched television awhile, sitting on the same sectional couch watching the same show, it was actually pleasant enough.

The nice thing about working as a house cleaner is that there's some room allowed for personal crisis. The Third World isn't running out of reserves to fill the posts.

Between a short day shift at Sparkle then another night at Clean Up I went to visit Ledric on November 15th. He didn't seem to have moved since I'd left the afternoon before. It was a good sign, though, that he was still breathing without equipment. I guess that was a good sign.

While I waited I touched his hand. I picked lint out of his hair. There was even some on his eyebrows. What a dummy. I hoped he was alright.

The general practitioners returned after I'd waited an hour, both smiling, holding Ledric's many medical forms. I thought they were going to discharge him and these were the bills.

Instead each guy tried to outkind the other. If one shook my hand, the other put his hand on my shoulder. The first offered me a stick of gum and the second gave me a whole pack. I thought they were preparing me for an outrageous invoice.

—We looked at the results and had a neurologist in to see Mr. Mayo. We feel very confident now in our opinion that Mr. Mayo has contracted botulism.

From his bed Ledric raised a pointed finger. He struggled to direct that mini-carrot at me. If he could speak, Ledric would be gloating: No hospitals I said. He would have, but couldn't because the physicians pulled his arm back down then pulled the covers over his belly, right up to his sweaty neck. They snugly tucked him in and grinned.

27

A problem with dogs is that they can't be reasonable. I don't mean just the wild ones.

When I came back from the hospital on Wednesday afternoon my reserves were tapped; a two-day snooze was in order. I wanted to try and get one, at least.

Near my home I stopped at the old white house on the corner to rest against its low fence. My vision was spotty, and I realized that I hadn't eaten since plucking Ledric from the room he rented.

You did that, I crowed to myself. You saved the boy's life.

But forget five minutes of pride because Candan's red Doberman chased me half a block home. It had been out wandering, I suppose.

It could have caught up. It should have. Instead it paced me, staying about an eighth of an inch behind. Not snapping its jaws so much as clicking its teeth. I got so confused that I tripped. When I fell, just two houses from my own, the red Doberman stopped and waited for me to stand.

Soon as I did it sparked again; snarling; going on until I was inside my yard with the gate closed.

The dog then ran past my place, past Candan's to the one-family home of Henry and Althea Blankets. Older folks with a fat German Shepherd. The red Doberman stopped there to bark hysterically at their yard until the German Shepherd inside the compound answered.

After the German Shepherd started the red Doberman ran to the next house and did the same thing until an Irish Setter completed the quorum.

28

As I came in the house my sister apologized. —Not another day, she said, before I could.

—You'll go back to school tomorrow, I told her. Did you see those dogs outside?

She pointed to her bedroom. —I packed my bookbag already. So how did Ledric look?

—Big. Am I that size?

—Did he seem any better though?

—They hadn't even started treating him yet.

—That's Anthony? Grandma yelled from the sectional couch. She stamped her good foot on the carpet, summoning me.

She was covered in gossip magazines. Nabisase had walked to the store to buy soda and reading material. Grandma was turned on the couch so her right leg was up.

—Put some rub on my leg.

Grandma meant the mentholated gel, but that was for colds not fractured bones. — It's not going to stop the pain, I told her.

— I don't want to talk of hospitals.

—They helped Ledric, I told her. Eventually.

— Sure. Just please rub. Just please rub. Your mother used to do it, but now.

After I was done I rolled her gown back over the right leg and washed my hands in the bathroom. After that I bashed in my mother's bedroom door.

The lock held, but not the cheap wood around it. The door popped from its hinges after nine good kicks and then it was easy to get inside.

The room still smelled like Ghost Mist, a perfume sold in stationery stores. Usually just beside the *South Queens Tattler,* a local version of the tabloid news. You were as likely to read about 6th District Representative Floyd Flake's legislative agenda as the goat in Cambria Heights that looked like Billy Dee Williams.

A streak the size of an otter had dried into one wall where a perfume bottle had shattered. Glass fragments stuck in the carpet hairs.

Mom's dresser sagged on its little legs because all four drawers had been pulled out, flung around, and without them the cheap wooden frame was weak from years of beatings.

Some of her clothes were still on the ground. A shirt with the arms spread in an explosive diving pose. A pair of pants with the legs crossed over themselves in a sprint.

My mother had never left a sloppy room in her adult life. Where do you think I learned to clean a house with such aplomb? How many weeks had she slept in this mess, preparing herself to leave?

If I'd put the door back up, blocked the opening, Nabisase wouldn't have seen. It was disconcerting to think about how many times we'd passed Mom's room and didn't fathom her life inside. Or felt too tired to ask.

Nabisase went off when she saw the chaotic room. I guess it was unsettling. Down the hall, into the living room, where she didn't scream but made a smashing sound. She broke the little Sidney Poitier statuette.

She could have kicked in windows, but my mother hadn't made them. Nabisase picked the small head up, then threw it down again. Once the piece broke she took off her sneaker to crack the rest precisely.

Grandma watched from her convalescence on the couch.

I went to my mother's bedroom and overturned the bed.

29

—You got French fried, I told Ishkabibble, because he looked worse today than he had a week before. I couldn't stay home while my sister broke Sidney Poitier's chips into bits of dust. After tossing Mom's mattress around I needed to get out.

Ishkabibble pulled the collar of his button-down shirt away from his skin; took out a plastic bottle wide as two fingers then rubbed lotion on various parts of his reddened neck.

He was planning to meet me because I had a mortgage check for him signed by my grandmother, but she didn't want him invited home. We agreed to meet on 147th Avenue and 223rd, though I bet if I'd let the scent of Grandma's draft out to the wind the man would have found me in Sierra Leone.

Before the money I gave him a large envelope.

Ishkabibble's enthusiasm went to rubble when he found it was no movie script.

—That's not what I wanted to do. This is it.

—A book? he yelped after I explained.

—A book. He was doused.

—A book! He threw it to the ground.

No worry though, I'd bound the sheets of paper in a gray plastic expandable folder. They were all in there: on the backs of Uncle Arms's flyers, napkins from the coffee shop in Lumpkin. The torn-off front cover of a hospital phone book and many sheets of legal paper I'd found at home.

—You don't like it?

—Tell me where the movie went.

—Why worry about one when you've got two hundred of them here?

Ishkabibble must have been used to this kind of disappointment. He thinks a woman should buy a Jeep Wrangler, but she wants an Acura. A guy borrows money to open a business and decides to burn it on a boat instead. No one wanted his advice, just his funding.

—I can't hardly read these. What's this say?

—*The Dead Reserved a Room,* I read. 1974. When a woman in her fifties, Dorie, inherits the old motel her grandfather once ran she travels there, to Michigan, in the hopes of making it a profitable business again. When she arrives a number of women from the local college are lodging there. At first there's little to disturb their lives and the older woman befriends the college students. Eventually the girls are killed off. Each time it's Dorie who finds them. She discovers that her grandfather is killing them from beyond the grave. He doesn't want Dorie taking their advice: sell his hotel and move to Chicago where she'd always hoped to be in a band. A quieter version of *The Texas Chainsaw Massacre,* tales of family businesses gone awry.

—You have got to be kidding, Ishkabibble said.

—Should I read another one?

—I got it. I'll take that. No problem. I'll think of something. He tapped the collected pages. I never heard of any of these though.

—And I'm sure you know the banking laws better than I ever will.

—That suit makes you look like a football player, he said. Big Man. Feel like helping me out now that I'm going to help you?

He asked politely, and that made the difference.

We didn't walk far, still on 147th, but right before it reaches Farmer's Boulevard. On one side of the street there were private homes, but across from those a hive of warehouses that saw local and long-distance deliveries fifteen hours a day.

Next to a red weathered matchbox of a deli was a yellow home so humble its back was to the public road. The front windows and porch faced an abandoned yard not the street. Ishkabibble posed me right on the grass. He really told me how to stand; with my arms crossed and not to speak even if the guy inside said something to me. Ishkabibble knocked on the side door, which was actually the one that faced the street.

There were no security bars over the windows. This didn't create an air of freedom as much as implied there was nothing valuable inside.

That side door opened then Ishkabibble stepped aside so that the man could come out. Bald, but with a fastidiously maintained long beard. More gray than black. A real mantle of righteousness. He shut the house door behind himself. They spoke a bit.

Ishkabibble pointed backward, toward me. I thought he was bragging about my film encyclopedia. Getting a few advance sales. He was smiling if the homeowner wasn't. I waved at the bald man and he pointed at me, a response I mistook for friendly.

—You don't threaten me, he yelled. Hear?

I said, — Zuh?

It was just surprise that made me stutter, but he heard what he wanted to.

— Fight? he said to me. I'll fight you, you ras . . .

Before he could finish the curse Ishkabibble said, — I don't want it to come to that and neither does he.

This was me Ishkabibble referred to. I'm the 'he' at the end of that sentence.

The homeowner, despite respectable flustering, looked summarily defeated; as if street boxing was actually a question of weight classes. I leaned back against the man's fence and it made some noise, sure.

— You going to bust my fence now too?!

Ishkabibble looked at me, — He's going to pay, Anthony. Don't worry. Stand straight. Relax.

The man walked into his home and two of his children came to the only window on this side of the house. A bathroom I'll bet because there was fog on the pane. Two girls, younger than Nabisase, who stared like it was me who'd come to collect their daddy's soul.

But let me refrain from acting po-faced for too long. Once I realized that Ishkabibble had propped me up to play his muscle, a hired lug, I loved it. The man actually believed I was menacing just because my upper arms were as big as some people's thighs.

When he came back out with a folded envelope for Ishkabibble he looked my way but I remained impassive. Looked at his home rather than him. He came to me. Stood one foot away. Then I was afraid. Those wiry guys are the toughest meat in the world. If he'd actually starting hitting me my best defense would've been to fall forward, hoping to crush his thorax.

— You lay down with a man like Ishkabibble and you going to have hell.

I had shut my eyes, but opened them when he stopped speaking. The man's thick beard looked softer from here. For no reason I wondered how many pens he could store in it.

—Who is this boy? he asked Ishkabibble.

But my buddy was already walking off. —Anthony come on, he said.

—Are you that one, then? From down over 229th Street way.

The man touched my neck so tenderly that I wasn't agitated anymore. I felt like an animal that knows, instinctively, when it meets a decent human. He yelled at Ishkabibble. —You're wrong for using a boy like this. He's big, but don't know better. Doesn't matter Anthony, he said. Anthony, yes? I'm not mad. I heard about you. I'm always sorry for people with troubles.

I walked far behind Ishkabibble; he wouldn't slow down for me. At every corner I expected him to throw out my manilla envelope, but he kept it. How far he expected me to escort him I'm not sure, but passersby stopped me more than once. Couples mostly. In the middle range; forties, fifties and sixties.

Mr. and Mrs. Blankets said hello and asked about my day. They were walking that husky German Shepherd. It pulled at the leash; it pulled at the leash; so they weren't able to stay.

Mr. Rumtower and Mr. Brace patted my arm and said, —Alright Anthony, when I passed.

Ms. Tandyamara, who drove a tractor for New York City, gave me five dollars. Popularity never felt so bad.

I said thanks to her. I said it to everyone. They shrugged or laughed; some friendly and some uncomfortable. Don't believe it when you hear that everyone mistreats the mentally ill and that they always have. Compassion smashes up against confusion, unease. The pileups make messy scenes.

I forgot about Ishkabibble until he had almost disappeared. A long, thin doodle ahead of me.

30

For days now I'd begged Grandma to let me help her. I was sleeping twenty minutes a night, that's all. I'd lie down, but the eyes wouldn't shut; I lay flat until that got boring then rolled onto my side. I tried to find the cool spots on my pillow. With Mom still gone I stayed in her room, the one that seemed to expel its occupants.

On the 17th of November, a Friday, Grandma finally let me pack her up. Of course she could have waited until Saturday because I didn't have to work, but then most people find the exact wrong time to accept help. I called in to Sparkle to miss a day and the receptionist only grunted.

I had to drive Nabisase to school because she'd skipped on Thursday to visit Ledric in the hospital. I found out because the school called me. He could speak well enough already to give my sister a phone number for his parents in Chicago. They said they were going to send some money; it was that or have them visit.

I vetoed a plane trip because I'd be the one getting them at Kennedy Airport, driving them to Queens General and back. And I didn't even like this guy! My sister was his sympathetic bet.

After I watched Nabisase walk inside her school I came back for Grandma.

— Bring the mail, she said as she dressed. We'll be waiting a while.

From the clinic's parking lot there was a view of Brookville Park; a parcel of spare woodland that divided Rosedale into halves, one mostly white and the other mostly black.

I'd wheeled Ledric through the service entrance, but I carried Grandma to the front. The clinic's waiting room was still small, but it serviced a tiny clientele. Immigrants fed this practice. Carribean, West African, East Indian and some Irish. Black Americans, yes, and Chinese from Valley Stream. If a job or Medicare wasn't covering hospital charges, then you went here.

The waiting area was occupied by rows of chairs that were soldered down in groups of seven; they were orange. Twenty people sat around already. I took a number from a red dispenser that looked like a canteen. Our number, A44, was called so quickly I expected to be home fast.

This first walk to the receptionist was only to register, though. We were allowed to request a doctor so I chose the apparatchik. Now the disinterested woman behind the Plexiglas gave me another ticket, a new number, and told me to sit some more.

— One is yours, Grandma said when I sat again. She pushed the piece of mail into my chest.

I would have liked to peel the stamp off as a souvenir, but there wasn't one. Only that faded red punch of machine postage. The left-hand corner of the envelope showed the group's name and return address in Boston.

Free Ahmed Foundation.

Dear Conscientious Supporter (this was printed on the page, the rest he wrote by hand),

Thank you for the letter. You will be added to our growing mailing list.

You are correct, I do have a lot of friends. The number grows more each day as my case gains more attention. God is good.

I did quote a comic book in my interview. Would you have respected me more if it was Diderot? They are both just entertainments in the end, don't you agree?

Many people have asked about my name, but I do not understand their confusion. I have found friends in here who introduced me to the virtues of Islam. Faith is important in prison. I think you see religion as a child's toy, but it's a weapon. The schemes of powerful, treacherous men fall before it.

In your letter you seemed quite angry. I hope I am incorrect and that you rest at peace. You ask if I wish that I was black. I do not. I am not crazy. Have you ever wished to be a woman?

Some people write asking that I tell them how to be productive. Often they sound like you. Misguided. Let me sign off by telling you what I've told many of them. Be active. Activate!

Ahmed Abdel

At two-thirty they called Grandma's name.

I carried her to an examination room then propped her on an examination table. I stayed in there with her, watching the clock go. The windows were opaque so the sunlight that came in turned a buttery yellow.

Grandma said, —Thank you for bringing me.

—Do you have to say it like we're strangers?

She turned her head away. —Why did you let those people in? Your sister might have won.

—Miss Innocence? What was her talent going to be? Punching out the MC?

—But you even stopped her fun.

The Russian shook my hand quickly when he walked in, but no more. He hardly looked up. Just said, —Hello. Hello. I'm going to close this curtain so she and I have privacy.

I was actually hurt that he didn't recognize me as the botulism brother.

From outside the beige plastic curtain shell I heard Grandma undress as the doctor put on rubber gloves. I recognized the snap as he pulled them down to his wrists from the times I'd used those same gloves to clean ovens.

—We will x-ray the hip, the doctor said to me when he eventually stepped out.

—Do I take her?

—We have a wheelchair. Come back in ten minutes.

—What about her purse?

—Take it with you if you're worried.

Being outside in the cold was nice until I noticed that I'd become a focus of the waiting room audience. The television was broken and I was there in the large window. Just another screen.

I didn't want to stand there carrying Grandma's handbag while people watched me so I patted my suit jacket and pants as if I'd bought cigarettes, but couldn't find them. I tapped myself harder. I almost hurt myself because the more I acted this way the more people inside the clinic looked at me. That only made me more frantic to seem normal as I slapped myself around looking for a cigarette I never even had in the first place.

I thought of going to the park for a walk to get away a minute, but with my good fortune Grandma would finish up with the doctor, come out to try and find me, wander into the street and get hit by garbage truck.

A woman in white pants and nurse's shoes came outside.
— Why you jumping around out here?

— I was looking for a cigarette.

She had one. A plastic aquamarine lighter too. Coming out to check on me was a good excuse to have some herself.

I didn't actually know how to use a cigarette.

When I put it in my mouth I put it in too far, choked up on it and got half the thing wet. Then the lady had to give me another. The next one I left hanging so far off my lips that the wind snatched it from me and carried down the block.

— This is the last one, she said.

She brought the lighter close. She had big hands. We were standing outside the clinic on the wheelchair ramp.

— Activate, I said.

I tried hard and pulled properly. A successful blaze. Since this was only my fourth cigarette in twenty-three years I didn't inhale correctly, but the action itself was well carried out. The woman stubbed out her own cigarette against the railing I leaned on.

I must have looked awful because she treated me so nicely.

She said, — I'm going to tell you, okay? Because I bet you'll need to know. Don't ever go to St. Luke's. If you're in Manhattan and they pick you up one day. Not St. Luke's. They'll strap you down for three days in their psych ward and never let you stand even for a shit.

I was surprised and couldn't hide it.

— What do I look like to you?

She said, — Sympathy.

While I smoked and coughed with her, five dogs trotted out from the park then ran along 147th Avenue ignoring cars, buses and vans. Their mouths were open. A smug furry procession.

After passing by the nurse and I, the dogs ran across the busy intersection at the corner of Brookville Boulevard. Every driver managed to use the brakes. Lots of people witnessed this, not just me. When the hounds had crossed against the light safely, stopping traffic, they howled. Then went farther down 147th Avenue untethered.

31

Soft in the middle, queasy from the cigarettes, I walked inside the clinic holding my belly. The people sitting and waiting tried to smile at me, but stared. If you're ever trying not to seem mentally unstable, avoid carrying an old woman's large pocketbook while taking your first tobacco hit in front of a jury.

I had to knock at the Russian doctor's office door because it was locked when I got there.

—You came back, Grandma stammered when he let me in. She squinted.

—Of course. I touched her shoulder. I'm not leaving.

She was lying on the examining table with both legs bent at the knees so that her soles were flat and her shins faced the back of the room.

—The hip is fine, he said as he went around the examination table. Deep bruises takes longer to heal at her age.

If he had been speaking with her before I got there he wasn't doing so anymore. Now I was the authority in the room. —But now we find another problem, he said. I am cutting it off.

—Cutting where?

—From my leg, Grandma muttered.

He had a silver tool that looked like a cookie cutter stubbed into her shin. Blood came out from where the silver plunger hid. Dribbling down my grandmother's leg.

—Shit! I screamed.

He pulled the cutter out; it had a small cylinder of her flesh in the once-hollow core now. —I will do stitches, he said.

Grandma held her face like she was trying to pull it off.

—Can you feel it through the anesthesia? I asked.

—There is none, the surgeon said.

—Where did it go?

—I didn't have any, the doctor said. Many people here don't get any. It is expensive for all sides.

He carried some thin black thread in his palm. —She wanted none, he added.

Grandma rubbed her two thin bent arms together at the elbows, inches above her face.

—How come you're not screaming? I'll get the police! There's blood, Grandma.

She told me, —I had him do it this way.

The Russian stitched the site. Explained that after giving Grandma this punch biopsy he'd send the flesh to test for cancer.

I fell back into a chair clutching my own leg.

—I am sorry, Grandma whispered. To all of you. Many nights I wonder how I brought this sickness to my children.

Instead of running away I pulled the chair closer. The doctor's needle made no sounds entering her skin except for Grandma's rasping. She said, —What did I do to you?

—You'll never be able to move around on that leg, Grandma.

—Why should I be spared?

The doctor must have wanted to be charming. He thought he was making a joke.

The Russian said, —Now your children will have to carry you.

32

I was part of a *Current Affair* family. The *Hard Copy* demographic. *Rescue 911; Real Life Stories of the Highway Patrol; Unsolved Mysteries* starring Mr. Robert Stack. Beginning on November 14th television news and the reputable papers explained that the entire U.S. Government was shutting down due to budgetary squabbling between Democrats and Republicans, but the effect on us was minimal.

Looming cuts to our national budget were advertised as either a prelude to the Rapture or Satan taking control, depending on your political affiliations. Even atheists and the spare Marxist agreed when allowed a few minutes of punditry on cable stations. The way politicians yelled I expected warlord-supported gangs to commandeer our homes and daughters. Federal Government deadlock was on every major network which meant, of course, that many of us changed the channel.

To programs that were more entertaining. I was a fan of the Morton Downey Jr. show just like Nabisase. When Grandma had finished with the *Star* I took it to the bathroom and read quietly. One of us was watching television at all times.

Besides, serious news only reported on small lives like ours when they'd been caught in the trajectory of someone's gun. Other than that it was war crimes, statewide fires and unctuous assemblymen; famine in the hot belt of the planet. More important, I'll agree.

Call ours minor items then. The shooting of Mary Jo Buttafuoco. A priest who had a sex change. One Hartford man who'd faked more on-the-job injuries than anyone in America. Ordinary epics. Legends are still to be created.

Into that stewpot add a beauty pageant for virgins. No national scandal, but a five-minute item for sure.

The revised *Norton Anthology of Poetry* was on my sleeping bag open to the bottom of page 1249. I'd opened it while feeling particularly distant from college one evening; actually pretending I'd enjoyed my Survey of American Poetry seminar freshman year. I plowed it from the bottom of one of my book boxes and read awhile, but turned it down when Grandma called to me from the living room.

—Anthony! Come on, Anthony!

Even my sister said my name as she hadn't done since the 12th, and it was the 20th already; hearing Nabisase speak to me really was a miracle worth thanking Selwyn for.

When I got upstairs they were on the couch. Grandma leaned forward, left elbow on her good thigh, resting her chin in that left hand, tapping the tip of her nose with her pointer finger.

Nabisase said, —Anthony, look at this.

The TV was speaking.

A cabbage-headed man hosted the show, but he wore a suit for dignity. His Australian accent made him sound smarter. Out of those clothes he'd look like any alcohol-pounded, red-faced, bartender, but not behind a desk.

—Beauty pageants built this country, he said.

—They're one of America's sacred institutions. Women make more money, have more power, now than ever before in human history, but let's hope we never forget to appreciate the precious faces of the ladies who compete in the pageant system year after year. Here's our Jerry Ganz with a story we call, Pretty as a Picture.

His face dispersed into pixilated dust on the screen, which refocused on the image of a shaded runway. It was footage of a contest, but not Miss Innocence. Women in their twenties wearing gowns; this passed quickly. To teenagers in a similar promenade.

A new deep voice began; Jerry Ganz.

—Beauty, he began. Pageants, he finished.

—Every state in the nation hosts dozens each year. Fitness America, Cracker Jacks Bikini Contest, Miss Italia, The Black Mother and Daughter Pageant. Even Manhunt International, for gentlemen.

—While most of us can see that these institutions celebrate competition, excellence and, yes, good looks, not everyone agrees. The weekend of November the 10th found over forty families traveling to a small town named Lumpkin on the border between Virginia and West Virginia. A place where crime of any kind is rare.

—You can see the local temperament at the annual Apple Picking Festival, where families from every part of Frederick County come to enjoy apple cider, apple pie and apple fries.

The shots of sunny orchards were replaced by flashbright footage of college-aged men and women, skinny and sanguine, surrounding a Wendy's restaurant.

—Film obtained recently shows this band of college students taunting helpless travelers a year ago. The old women you see trapped in this circle of belligerent twenty year olds were only buying copies of *The Rescuers Down Under,* a Disney film, for their nephews and nieces. When they were accosted, in 1994, at a Parsipany, New Jersey, rest stop.

—The Miss Innocence pageant was different from many others because they only accepted contestants who had held onto their virtue. A contest for girls from ages eleven to seventeen who'd done what few will nowadays—remain a virgin.

—Here you can see the Blue Ridge Theatre. Where musicals such as *Oklahoma* and *The Music Man* are regularly run. Gospel choirs practice on the second floor. And on Saturday, the 11th, these girls staged one of the most enjoyable shows in years.

The tabloid show had film of the night of the blowout: the protestors walking around outside the Blue Ridge, of them opening the door to the service hall. A camera man had perched himself at an auditorium window and there was footage of people inside running, spasming, crying as the flares burned. You could hear the horns, but the glass muffled it some. They had shots from inside the protestor's yellow bus, but none of Uncle Arms.

Jerry Ganz was the gigantic man I'd seen taking notes at the McDonald's foofaraw. He wore very small glasses, the frames strained to reach both ears.

—Rumors were circulating that the students had a bomb planted somewhere in the audience. If it had gone off who knows how many lives would have been destroyed?

Jerry Ganz was standing in front of the marble Lumpkin library as a man in frayed jeans and tatty T-shirt cleaned the steps behind the reporter.

—But we wouldn't even bring this news to you if it was just one long sad story. There are enough disappointments in the world. It's true that Miss Innocence was ruined. But there were actually two pageants that weekend. The second, a local event in its third year. It was conceived by one very special man.

— Ah neva hade it easeh, nut fo' one minut ov ma lahf.

— His name is Uncle Allen. That's what he likes to be called. Most of the year he's in his office in downtown Lumpkin helping people of all incomes to buy a home. Uncle Allen is a mortgage broker. And how did he get started?

— Ah wish yawl cood see mah back, ah tell ya. Gots enuf bruis- uss fo a fooball team. I dun hahd woik an' ah buhleev dat good peeples awlwuss comes out on top.

— Uncle Allen, the son of men and women who had to work on their knees, now has the money to help others stand. And how does he do it? With his own contest. One that rewards girls for their character. He's only got one question when they come on stage: Have you suffered?

— Because Uncle Allen knows, maybe better than most of us, just what rewards suffering can bring.

— Ah calls 'em mah Goodness Girls. Da winnas.

— And what good fortune really for Uncle Allen and his Goodness Girls. If the Miss Innocence pageant had gone on without incident we may never have known about Uncle Allen, whose pageant brings modeling contracts to girls of all sizes and shapes.

As proof they scrolled a few of the past winners and their advertisements across the screen. I couldn't disagree about his standards. Only about a third of the girls had waistlines. They modeled ponchos, long jackets, overalls, serapes. Circulars for Good Will, an Army & Navy shop.

— This ends with a mystery though. One of the Goodness Girls is missing. As we speak.

— She left a picture, but not her name. Maybe she didn't expect to win. A child who, Uncle Allen says, stole the show when she stepped on stage. We have only the Polaroid, taken when she reg- istered, carrying her sick grandmother on her back.

—Uncle Allen hopes she'll contact his office if she sees this, and the number is at the bottom of our screen.

—But maybe it's fitting that she went off without a trace. A beautiful girl is just a daydream. We'll end with her snapshot on the screen so you can see, as Uncle Allen put it, what an angel looks like.

33

Nabisase didn't want to celebrate with me. When I reached over the couch and rubbed the top of her head with my sweet fine knuckles, she jumped away.

Grandma even stood up, painful work, and said, —Anthony, don't do that!

—I was congratulating her!

My sister touched up against the entertainment center, one hand on the television screen as if it brought her more warmth than me.

She didn't want to celebrate at all.

Nabisase put on her coat and left the house. She didn't even tell Grandma that she was going. To the Apostolic Church of so-and-so. That's where she called Uncle Arms. Same evening that the program showed.

After she left I told Grandma, —She shouldn't be scared of me.

—It should be the other way round? My grandmother laughed.

At least her award package came to the house. Nabisase still used it as her mailing address.

When the Federal Express guy asked for a signature I was the only one home. Let me correct that. Grandma was home, but if I'd called her over she'd have taken thirty minutes to shamble from her room.

I took the envelope. Overnight Delivery. It arrived early on the 22nd. Closed the door.

I didn't open it though I dropped it a few times on the chance it would pop open and let me inside.

Candan rang the front doorbell and when I answered it he said, —I saw the FedEx man.

I didn't invite him inside, but stepped out there. He was taller than me by a head. I wanted to press his minuscule ears; they were the size of buttons.

—I wondered if it was something about your mother.

—That letter was for Nabisase.

—From your Mom?

—Uncle Allen, I said.

—I thought your Uncle was dead.

—Then it's a message from the grave. I walked down the steps just to make him follow me. You have any reason to be expecting her? I asked him.

He shrugged. —I'm not her family. You would know.

—I know she's not coming back for you, Candan.

I was standing by my Oldsmobile, looking at my reflection, but he'd stayed by the front steps. Candan snapped his fingers. I thought he was commanding me to come over to him, but it was the dog, that Doberman, pressing its face against the hedge. It wanted to push the way through, maybe to eat me, but when Candan snapped the animal returned to the backyard.

—Did she say something about me? he asked.

I didn't even turn around. — She was too busy driving off with some Indian guy, I said.

— She didn't.

— She did.

He opened my gate, shut it and walked back to his house.

34

I left the house after Candan went away because I couldn't sit for hours, alone with Nabisase's letter, and not open it. Not for hours.

I brought a small pot of tea and two sandwiches to Grandma's room. Changed her socks and helped her to the bathroom before going out. I wanted to get in a van and ride the way up to Queens General so I could find out about the attraction between that bacterial-bozo and Nabisase. I should have gone and pulled the tubes out his veins, but I was too tired. I felt like I hadn't slept even one night my whole life.

Ishkabibble is who I wanted to see, but I had no home phone number. He called you, but couldn't be reached. If I tried to find him whose home would I check? Nearly everyone was indebted to him so he told no one his address.

Finally I ended up in Brookville Park because I knew he liked it there. Quiet. Empty. No one angry because he wants the check.

Its small ponds had sprouted tan reeds that tossed dryly against themselves.

The most distinct landmark in Brookville Park was the rigid purple monument at its east entrance. An abandoned semitrailer that had been scratched, cut, spray-painted, signed. It was specked with spots of orange rust.

Its support legs had fallen off a long time before so that the semitrailer leaned forward, a Muslim kissing soil for the third time in a day.

I was happy for my sister, but jealous too. She was ten years younger and already poised for something spectacular. Fun, at least. I wondered if my bitterness was only going to get stronger until the time when I stopped remembering my name and how to care for myself. Maybe one good side-effect to flipping out was that I could forget how little I'd done.

—Hide me!

Ishkabibble came out from the trees, running. His overcoat snapped behind him and one of his dress shoes had come off. He ran so fast I almost missed him; attache case in his right hand knocking the back of his right thigh.

—I'll take you home, I said.

—You're not fast enough. He looked over his shoulder. Hide me now!

I pulled at the door to the semitrailer. He was fast, but I could be strong. Not strength, but power. Grabbed the handle and simply leaned back.

The door opened and it was like night time in there. He was tentative. It smelled of mildew; there were small plants growing in the standing water. When I opened the door both our shoes were splashed.

—You can always dry your feet, I said.

I pushed it closed and walked away. Not far—thirty feet—to

one of the baseball diamonds. I stamped on the mound, but it was already gone. An indent instead of a hill. As I kicked around out there a military outfit shot from the trees.

Black boys on mopeds. Ten bikes and twenty kids. Friends shared the padded seats. Two even rode the handlebars, dangerous as that was. They drove quickly, dangerously, screaming Ishkabibble's name.

When I let him out he owed me a favor.

I waited there, he went home and came back in fifteen minutes.

While he was gone I opened the door to the semitrailer again. I was wearing boots, not shoes, so I didn't worry about the inch of water. I went in, shut it. The incline was pretty minor. There was grass and weeds growing in here. I couldn't see them too well, but felt them against my pants. Some were as tall as my shins. A marsh inside the semitrailer; the semitrailer in a park; the park in my suburban neighborhood. I never understand what people mean when they say, getting back to nature. As if they ever left.

Ishkabibble came back, calling for me. When I stepped out he said, — I know you were praying for this.

I didn't look at the book, just held it.

It was hardback, 184 pages. I wanted to hammer nails with it. That's how strong I felt. I swung it around in one hand a few times just to know the weight. Page numbers were at the bottom, centered under the text. The paper was thin and there were some smudged pages, but I recognized every line. It had striking red endpapers. The first page listed my name, the publisher (Rahsaan Robinson Press; Tattleback, Connecticut) and the title, *Killing Is My Business.*

It didn't have a dust jacket, but that was no problem to me. I always lose those plastic wraps anyway.

— What happened here?

—That was a printer's error, Ishkabibble said. Sorry about that.

There was no title on the turquoise cover, only my name in gold. All capital letters. Anthony James.

I pointed at both words. —This is going to give people the wrong idea of what's inside.

Still, how could I get angry? With this talisman in my hands.

Most pages had two entries, sometimes three. They were broken up like any dictionary. Alphabetical sections. A. G. J. There were even a few in Q. *Quiet or He'll Hear You, Quarrel with Fear, Quetzalcoatl Craves Blood.*

—Why don't we sit down for a minute? he asked me.

—You want to?

He laughed as we walked to a bench. I read to him when we sat. Just a few short ones. *It Woke One Night. How She Bled. Eviscerate Steve.*

He asked, —How did you turn out to be my best friend?

35

I had a book. And what did my sister win?

A book of coupons, 40 percent off at most of Lumpkin's stores. One round-trip bus ticket to Lumpkin. And an appointment to pose for two color photos on the weekend of January 5th–7th next year. They'd appear in the Hoddman's Sunday Circular soon after and pay $600 upon publication.

Uncle Arms benefited more. By 1997 prospective Goodness Girls came to compete from every county in Virginia.

But an encyclopedia was better than any of that. As soon as I had it I bounced around.

Soon as I got home from the park I asked Nabisase to go out with me to the movies. We both had accomplishments to celebrate. She refused and called Ledric at the hospital. Spoke with him the rest of the night.

I asked her again the next day, the 23rd, in the evening, after work. On Friday, the 24th, too. Nabisase adamantly opposed me until Saturday, around one o'clock. I was in Mom's old room. Mine now.

—Ledric says I should be nicer.

I lay on the bed I'd brought up from the basement by myself. —Why did you ask him?

—'Cause I talk to him every day, she said. He's getting released tomorrow.

—Did his family ever send us that money they promised?

—I haven't seen it yet.

It was the 25th of November. Nabisase and I walked instead of using the car. She was thirteen and I was twenty-three.

We crossed Brookville Park and entered Town, a three-block strip of shops: Key Food, two corner stores, a Korean market and four hair salons. There was a minor branch of the public library, used mostly for the free toilet. I pulled my sister across the street, pinched the fleshy lobes of her ears. —Let's get these pierced, I said.

Nabisase clutched a parking meter. —You said we were just going to a movie.

—I figured that since we were out, we might as well. She wasn't smiling, but I was. I had an encyclopedia of horror films, have I mentioned that?

Nabisase looked down the block. —I always thought I'd do this with Mom.

—How long do you plan to wait?

My sister rested her chin on the top of the parking meter. —I miss her.

I pulled Nabisase into this jewelry store that also sold pets. It was situated between a laundromat and a pizzeria. She was aghast because the place had no dignity.

—How about the Piercing Pagoda in Green Acres Mall? she asked.

—The mall is as far as the movies. That's twenty minutes from here. This is where we are.

Nabisase tugged her ears hard like she wished they would come off. —I saw you let those people into Miss Innocence, she said.

—But look how things turned out.

—You going to try and take credit for Goodness Girls now?

They sold animals toward the front of the store and gold from a glass counter in the back. Why try to make money in only one way? If not for space limitations they'd have sold 50 cent bags of cookies too.

The woman who owned the store was in back, by the jewelry, her head wrapped in bright green cloth. Another woman was back there too, tall and as yet unimpressed by the jewelry choices. The customer switched her purse from one shoulder to the other, making no motion to unzip and spend. —You all right? she called suddenly.

I was going to answer, but a child's voice came. —Yeah Momma, come look at fishes!

Against the walls of the store were cages of lizards and snakes, some green, some brown or black. Two rows of fish tanks, eight feet high and fifteen feet long, split the center of the store into aisles.

The sun was up, but we were still dressed heavy for winter. The store itself was humid. It smelled like wet, mossy stones. I stuck my gut out to see it stretch my shirt so far that the buttons might burst. I did that to make my sister laugh, but my imperfections had lost their funny side for her.

Nabisase and I looked into a tank of ten baby lizards. They

tumbled over one another. They stood on one another's heads. As a unit they turned and watched us.

That kid who'd demanded her mother come watch fish appeared wearing black jeans, a black sweatshirt, blue cap, no holes punched in her ears.

—That's bearded dragons, she said.

I thumped my belly like the old man she'd say I was.

— Is that right? my sister asked.

— Snakes is better though. Lizards and fish are boring.

— Maybe they think you're boring, I told the girl.

Nabisase said, — Shut up, Anthony!

— I'm sorry, but who is she to criticize them?

The girl smiled like I'd said something nice because I'd used a kind tone. Then she pointed her thumb.

—That's your thumb, I said dismissively.

— And this is my pinky.

Her stern mother looked at us. — How you doing over there Samarra?

— Good, Momma.

The little girl looked at me as though she had done me a service, perhaps spared my life.

Sam took Pop-Rocks from her pants pocket, snapped the small pack in the air. Her little belly stuck out under her sweatshirt, over her jeans. — Pop-Rocks! she yelled.

— Samarra Kroon you stop that screaming!

Sam ate a handful of the purple candy then opened her mouth to show the science fomenting.

— You put all that in your mouth at once? Nabisase asked. She knelt between the girl and me, but the kid could not be mesmerized by kindness. It was with me that Sam spoke. — You know which finger this is?

— Do you? I asked back.

She shyly peeked at her mother then turned to Nabisase, who was tapping a turtle tank to get the conversation away from me.

—That's the longest finger, I answered for her.

Sam grinned widely. —Nah-uh. That's not the word.

—You tell me what it is then, I dared.

—It's the fuck-you finger, she whispered.

—You saying that to me? I asked.

Sam laughed.

Nabisase did not. —Let's go. Anthony.

—No, I said to Samarra Kroon loudly. Fuck you.

Then here the girl's mother came. A blue flame surrounded her.

—You get back! she screamed. I don't give a damn, you get back from my daughter!

Little Samarra began to cry. The store owner reached under the counter while her husband came out from a closed office door. My sister could have helped by explaining that I always joke around with kids, but the only thing my sister did was step away. I had to run outside by myself and wait for her around the corner.

Outside the movies I fumed. I also panted. We walked fast from the lizard store to here. I was afraid Sam's mother would be looking for me.

—I really thought you'd help me, I said again.

Nabisase wouldn't discuss this anymore. I stood behind her, in line to enter Sunrise Cinemas Multiplex, pressing my thumb into her back. Either I'd annoy her or she'd answer me, but I wouldn't be ignored. Getting into the movies was a slow process ever since they'd put up metal detectors. My sister wouldn't look at me like I wanted her to.

—Which movie do you want to see? I asked.

She was distracted, holding a small cork to her nose. I was too annoyed to take notice.

—Why did you come with me if you're not going to talk!

When she heard my voice raise she turned to me. —Whatever you want to see.

Then she looked around or through me again, sniffing the little stopper with her back to me.

—What is it? I asked while the ticket line stalled ahead of us.

—Uncle Allen sent it to me, she said. It was in my award envelope, but I don't know why. It has a funny smell.

She gave it to me. A move so casual that she must have really wanted an answer and hoped I could provide it. If she hadn't wanted my help she wouldn't have explained anything to me.

Even after holding it under my nose a full minute I didn't recognize the scent, so I put the top in my mouth.

—Oh Anthony, my sister said.

—It's spicy and sweet at the same time. Paprika and peppermint.

—You've had it before? She seemed encouraged.

—Never have, I lied.

It was a soggy cork now. I held it out to her. —Can I keep it?

She shrugged —You act like it's a Christmas card.

The film was being shown in the smallest theater to the far, far left. I walked behind my sister. I passed the concession stand so easily that everyone at Halfway House would have applauded. The only sign that I noticed the snacks was a sheen of sweat on my upper lip as we went by.

I had trouble with the chair. They're only cut to accommodate so much. My body was pinched. I strained to get myself in. I yelped a few times in the process.

—Please, Nabisase said quietly. Can't you just try to relax.

—The seat's too small and I'm too big, but forget that. I want to talk about what a girl like you should know.

But she was easily distracted, by couples, a family, a strong breeze, anything that came through those doors. Anyone besides me. Faint tunes played through the room's speakers and the lights were up.

—Do you know about Toxic Shock Syndrome? I asked.

The previews began so the room was only half as bright as before. We were still visible. I saw her rub her forehead.
—Anthony, please.

—Toxic Shock Syndrome, I said loud. No one hushed us; we were in the right theater for conversations. There were other couples talking nearby.

—I found this when I was cleaning out Mom's room.

It was the instructions from a box of Playtex tampons. Along with TSS, it described how to insert one.

To her credit, my sister acted maturely. She stood up. She walked away.

She sat a few rows down and on the opposite side of the aisle. I saw her slip into an empty seat. I sank lower in my own, feeling defeated. I took the cork out and tasted that night in Miser's Wend, Virginia. Uncle Arms, we're even.

Behind me. The theater doors opened. Both of them. Letting in light so I looked back. Annoyed enough right then that I might even pick a fight. And it was him. Ledric Mayo. Standing at the door.

He started to walk along, leading with his strawberry-shaped nose. As if he was sniffing out my sister.

I'd thought he was going to be discharged tomorrow, but he was at the movies with us on Saturday afternoon. He hadn't even dressed well. The guy was in his hospital gown. His front was covered, but it couldn't be tied, so the back was open to discovery.

He walked slowly because there was an IV in his arm and no one else in the movies noticed him. The IV was on a drip so Ledric was dragging it along beside him. A dirigible of a man pulling a long thin silver pole down the middle of a movie theater.

Ledric passed me and sat next to her. Nabisase acted so happy that it was like she'd expected him. He stuck one fat foot into the walkway.

The screen blew on, kindling our faces. A bonfire.

I leaned far back enough in my chair that I felt like I was falling. This made a terrible creaking noise in the theater. When I popped back up I tried to find my sister and him again.

There they were.

No.

There.

His arm already over her, her right hand on his lap.

She squeezed his thigh.

I wished I'd sat farther back.

I tried to leave, but had wedged so hard into the seat that I'd need a little help to get up.

So I stayed.

I tried to watch the film.

When I looked at my sister again she had less of her left hand out. It was in his pants. Through the zipper. Rummaging as though untangling a wire.

He dipped his head to try and kiss her, but her face was still down, watching to make sure she didn't fumble. Also his stomach made it hard for him to move around.

The screen seemed brighter because the music soundtrack was so loud.

Oh, what was that?

Was it out?

Why did my sister stroke it?

She bent his penis like a plastic straw and lucky for him it was still soft enough to twist.

Nabisase tried more. She did better. The screen lit them like I wished it wouldn't.

He leaned back.

There's never a good day to see your sister suck a dick.

I leaned forward less to vomit than to breathe. I couldn't look away. The dark silhouette of Nabisase's head moved slowly. Then Ledric pushed his toes forward and backward like he was pedaling a bicycle.

The more his leg kicked, the bigger his belly became. It grew to the size of a weather balloon, but neither of them floated. I couldn't see much of my sister's head after a point, just his inflatable belly swaying.

I wanted to tell her don't be like that. Don't be so nasty. Goodness Girl.

It was Saturday, November 25th, 5:00 PM. That's the first time I was ever thrown out of a movie. Because I wanted my sister to stop slurping I raised a ruckus, nearly broke the noisy chair.

Leaning forward and back, once and again, hoping the squeaks would distract my sister, but it didn't. She kept going. Ledric too. They were the only ones in the room not mad at me.

My waist felt sweaty and my feet were cold. I was so hyper that I finally had the strength to stand on up. I did and screamed my sister's name.

—Nabisase!

When I was a boy her birth had been the momentous event of my lifetime. My father visited us once, when I was ten. He drank beer with me one afternoon, out of cans and on a park bench. He made me think a man in glasses could be handsome. He spent the rest of the trip chasing my mother. He left after a few days. Nine months more and my sister was.

Having her around had been like a promotion; from only child, from little boy. I hadn't been so matured in one decade as that first evening I picked her up. Supporting the back of her head with one hand.

—Nabisase! I yelled again.

The doors in the back opened as an usher walked in, but I watched my sister stand up. Ledric had disappeared and I wondered how a fat man moved so fast. Nabisase ran to the other exit, below the screen. Her hands across her mouth and nose hiding her disgrace.

36

When I reached home, walking from the movies, my hands were so stiff it could have been a bone disorder. Our block, 229th Street, was subdued in the early evening. When I cleared my throat the sound was amplified.

—You out here, too? the President asked from his front steps. In silhouette that hedge looked the worse end of a knife fight.

—It's just us, I agreed, then leaned against the fence though this was a lousy move as it caused the red Doberman to stir. It came from the backyard.

—Quiet, the President commanded. Quiet! he tried again.

To no end. The man had to call his son. Candan took the leisurely route. When he appeared he only said, —Viper, quietly. The dog stopped watching me and went to Candan inside the house.

—Why would you name a dog after a snake? I asked once Candan had gone inside, taking Viper.

—He named it for the car, the President said.

I wouldn't say that this man enjoyed my company, but that his own son was no friend.

The President took off his glasses, which made the already awkward eyes go bobbling to the farthest reaches of each socket. I looked away so as not to laugh, because the man was alright.

—He works hard, the President admitted. Soon that boy's going to make a lot of money and his mother and I need the help. He pays half the mortgage right now, the President said.

—Is that right?

—Hell yes. So he's got to make some room for himself in the house. I can understand that. I tell myself to.

Candan came to the security door three times. I took this for jealousy, but then saw it as a territorial instinct. I had the feeling that Candan would keep his father in a jar if he could.

The President finished his beer. He had torn away the label. He plopped it down with two others on the stairs. I took those three to the recycling bin, and when I returned he said, —You have got to be the neatest nigga since Moses.

—He was neat?

—Who gives a fuck! I'm talking about you.

This didn't seem like it was going to be much of a year for snow; that was all right because it saved on shoveling.

—You keep some long hours, the President said. I see you come and go. Don't know if it's working or fucking.

—Last woman I got doesn't call me anymore.

—It happens. My wife stopped giving me the soft serve when our boy came home.

—How long's that been?

—I bet a year.

—I went longer than that without any, I gloated.

—But I married her behind!

—Stop making a fuss! Candan commanded from inside.

The President licked his lips a few times before putting his mouth to a new bottle of beer.

—Lost your mother, I see.

—How'd you know?

—Four people leave and only three come back, so what would I think? And C.D. was crying in the house last night.

I tapped my thighs because I wasn't going to feel sad for Candan.

—I had a lot of hope when you moved in, the President said. Thought you were going to straighten your family out.

—And how's your home life?

—You can't guess how me and him got to acting like this. It's not like you all.

Candan called his father inside, but I told him not to go.

—He probably needs help getting his mother from in front of the TV. Horse racing took more money from us than taxes this year.

—Sounds like there's all types of problems you need fixed, I said.

—Well who doesn't, Flapjack? You got a solution?

—Sometimes one word can kick-start your day, I said.

The President shook his head. —You tell me you love me and we're going to have a fight.

—Dad! Candan demanded. The President went inside.

I stood on their stairs and looked at the doorway. It wouldn't matter if I screamed or whispered so long as I said it.

—Activate.

37

I left the President's yard not when the father and son began yelling inside, but once Candan let the Doberman out through the side door. I heard its nails clip along the concrete driveway and I rose.

A genuine Volkswagon Jetta was parked in our driveway behind my Oldsmobile Firenza and I knew Grandma hadn't bought a new car while Nabisase and I were at the movies. It was impossible to see into the house from our yard because the front window was eight feet off the ground. I crossed the street to stand in the yard of the couple who owned an RV and the lights were on in our living room. With a glow coming through our one front window.

Inside I saw my sister with two, frankly, enormous figures. Men or women I couldn't say, but each was an airship. They were inside, moving slow, talking with my little sister; it was as if I could see clearly the nightmares in a monster's head.

I wanted to avoid walking into the house directly in case she'd hired two hooligans to beat me raw after the debacle in Sunrise Cinemas. But why get mad at me?

Into my yard and to the back where the honey-scent of laundry detergent dimmed the air around me. A line of clothes had been left out in the yard of the house next door; not the President's, but the high-school teacher's on the other side. The smell of clean clothes made me nostalgic for housekeeping work.

Our basement door, the third entrance to our home, opened to me so easily that I felt a nuclear charge. I put my hand to the sturdy door and it swayed for me.

On top of feeling brawny I also had the house key.

It was dark but I had the basement's floor plan memorized. I was in the house, but the others didn't know. I felt great again. Quiet. Invulnerable.

Only fifteen feet away from my book; it was lying on my bed in the dark.

The door at the top of the basement stairs was open four inches, enough to see into the living room. Stairs didn't creak; suddenly I wasn't heavy.

Those two bigger figures were women; they seemed attached by an invisible chain. Both carried black bags; not leather, but plastic. They set these on the living room table at the same time then sat. Without a cloth the white top made the purses seem darker and brighter simultaneously.

Nabisase made tea for them.

Merril and Devona introduced themselves to Grandma. I heard them. Then they helped my grandmother from the living room back to her bed.

Maybe they were cops. Could Nabisase have me arrested for making a scene in the movies that day? We'd never had my mother committed, but I'd heard it could be done.

Merril and Devona both wore their hair short, flat and close to the scalp. While they waited for my sister they played with anything near their hands. A few photos. The PennySaver. Pens. My book. My book. My book had been moved from my room.

This made me want to dash out there and take it back, but again, what if they were detectives?

Nabisase took a pot, boiled water in it then added the tea grounds. Not in a kettle, but a small open topped pot which is the way Grandma and Mom taught us. Next she poured in the milk. After that Nabisase added wedges of ginger. She cut the flame out as the tea bubbled to the rim then it settled to a flat formula. Steam rose as the drink breathed. She poured the tea through a strainer to collect the grains.

They were from her church, but who knew. Neither spoke of their Lord for half an hour. Eventually the conversation came around to Nabisase's television appearance. They took so long to bring it up that they must have planned exactly how to talk about it.

— And when we realized that was you we almost fell over.

Merril, the bigger of the two said, —That's right. She's not lying. Mrs. Hubbard told us. She had you on tape! You looked so nice.

— I want to get a copy, my sister said.

— We could do that for you.

Devona said, — So many people at the church wanted to meet you after we told them.

My sister asked, — Really?

— I'm talking about the kids your age. They wanted to listen to you. I mean, you've been on television. You could reach so many people.

Of the pair Merril was more serious-minded. Devona kept getting up to look at framed family photos on the entertainment unit. She'd ask who each person was. When those explanations were exhausted she couldn't remain polite any longer. —What is that? she finally asked.

—Devona!

—I'm sorry, but I want to know.

—My mother made it, Nabisase said. It was a statue of Sidney Poitier that got broken.

—I wish we could have met her, Devona said.

Nabisase rubbed her solar plexus. —I don't know. You might still.

I stopped crouching, stood, behind the door. Like that I could see that Nabisase had collected all those pieces she'd smashed when I opened Mom's bedroom.

They were in a small orange flowerpot. Enough fragments to reach the rim. The only piece that had stayed recognizably facial was Mr. Poitier's flat round nose. She'd set the nostrils on top of the pebbles and then put it out on the living room table. She must have done it today, after the movie. From where I was it looked like she was growing a person.

Devona touched the pot at the bottom. —I can see the nose looks nice.

—It was so good-looking before it fell, my sister said.

Nice! As in well done. This almost made me flop backward down the stairs. I thought she was lying, joking, deranged, but my sister's wistful whisper suggested that she now remembered it that way. I imagined her telling Ledric: My mother was such a great artist. And believing.

After an hour of somber conversation Devona would have jumped through the big front window if she could have. As Merril and my sister were becoming even closer, Devona lost interest. She pushed her seat farther and farther from the table.

Merril said, —Let's be straight now, Nabisase. What made you call us tonight?

My sister cried into her chest. Tears brought Devona back.

—I don't want to hate anyone, my sister whispered. But I feel like I do.

Merril finished her tea, only a sip or two.

It gave Nabisase some time to shake before Merril went down the girl's throat with compassion. Grandma could be heard in her bedroom, but her actions sounded like small ones. I doubt she wanted to hop out here and talk.

Nabisase said, —I remember when the church helped Ms. Petit find a place to live when she wanted to take her kids and leave her husband.

Devona nodded.

Merril tapped the tabletop firmly. —People know who you are now. I bet it's them who would feel lucky to have a TV star staying in their places. They'd tell all their friends!

Nabisase laughed along as well.

—We want to help, Merril said.

Merril put on her glasses when they were reading Scripture; even Devona clowned less. I crouched on the other side of the door. Nabisase said, —I know a lot of people say this, but if I only ever got to ask Selwyn one question I would want to know why he made some of the people in my family get so sick.

—Is that the only question you've got for Him? Merril asked. If that's true then, baby-girl, you're lucky.

It was the only time I saw Merril get angry; it revealed her to me if not my sister. A woman in her fifties coming to aid a pretty teenage girl who, by some luck, had been featured on a national television show. A little wackiness in one's family probably didn't seem like much pain.

Merril said, —We learn to read the whole Bible, not just the parts that make us feel good.

—Selwyn had brothers, Nabisase said.

—Mark tells us so, Merril agreed.

—I was scared when I read that because I never thought of it before.

Merril said, —Maybe you heard of the Bible, but never really learned it.

—It's easier that way, my sister said.

—That's why so many people only come in on holidays.

—I don't want to be one of those. Nabisase had both hands open, faced down on the table. I want Jesus' protection.

Even now Devona was impatient and turned from their Bible to ask what is this? —A map of Uganda as a dinner mat, my sister explained.

And this?

—Look at it, Nabisase said.

Devona opened my book and read:

—Gather.

Wishing to return a long dead mystic to life Jimmy Larson begins raiding the local morgue because he's learned of a scientific process by which a fresh cerebral cortex can be siphoned of its vitality, which becomes a purple paste. Enough of it, when injected into a corpse, can bring back the dead.

Devona said, —What the fuck?

—Devona!

—I'm sorry Merril, but that's just odd.

Devona looked at a few other pages. —*Killing Is My Business*? I watch scary movies with both my boys and I never heard of these.

Merril slammed the book's cover closed so hard that I winced. —Can we get back to the important business? There's only one thing on this table that matters to me.

Devona said, —Okay Merril, don't act high post. You almost broke my finger.

Merril said, —There's a lot to learn, Nabisase. You should read the Word for moral guidance. It's the power of Jesus. But you'll see that when we read about Abraham of Ur. How he traveled to Canaan and in Egypt. You'll find out that this isn't just about one man, it's the development of a whole people. Their arms eventually stretched so wide that they found you and I. Today. Right here. They hold us close to their bosom. The book becomes a record of ourselves.

38

Wish that Ishkabibble had been my best friend when he quoted me the cost of publishing two hundred and ninety-nine more copies of my encyclopedia. Or that he'd named this price before sitting me down that day in Brookville Park with the formalized pages in my hands. Before my Thermite gladness. Previous to letting me walk around owning it for two days. In advance of my loving it.

— Five thousand dollars is the sweetheart price, he insisted on the phone.

It was November 26th and Nabisase had gone with Merril and Devona. Not permanently, just for Sunday morning service. They left the night before and came back at 8:00 AM. Then left again, together, at noon.

Have you ever held your own book? I'd like to pretend it's nothing, but I'm not in a self-deprecating mood.

— You've printed all three hundred copies already? As I asked I poured Grandma's tea, then brought it to the living room couch.

— And trust you to repay a bill that big? You pay, Anthony, and I print.

— How do I know you won't just make a few thousand copies of it first and get rich off of my work? Maybe you could sign an affidavit that you won't cheat me.

— Do me a solid and get your book. Now read one to me.

—*Homunculus,* I began. 1987. An unnamed fishing town in Maine is preyed upon by a presence that has impregnated its women. The wives speak of waking on different mornings to find a tiny man in bed with them. Climbing inside them. There is no pain. The fiend appears once to each woman and never again. The children they bear are malformed, give off noxious odors, and they mature rapidly. After a month they're as big as toddlers. The men of the town are horrified; they shun these mutant children. Even the mothers are ambivalent at first. Until they realize that these children can't be hurt. Completely indestructible. Faced with such an idea the mothers rejoice. Men leave town in disgust. The women age, and though they pass away they are glad; their babies will never feel pain. The film ends displaying an entire town of monsters intermarrying, persevering. Victorious. A horror movie with a happy ending. It's my favorite film.

Ishkabibble was on the line, but quiet besides breathing.

— I don't see your point, I said.

— Forget it. Look. I'm not giving you any affidavit because I don't even want to waste money on a notary public until I see cash from you.

— But I'm your boy!

— That's the only reason I didn't charge you for the copy in your hand.

— I don't have five thousand, but what if I take orders? Then you could see how many people want to buy it.

— Get money, not names on a sheet.

— How much would you charge?

—Don't ask for any hundred dollars, that's a bet. Ten would be cheap enough.

—Three hundred books at ten each is only three thousand.

—You come up with that much and I'll let you pay me the rest slowly.

—That's very generous. Must mean you don't think I can sell fifty.

—The possibility did come to mind.

—Want to buy a book? I asked him.

—Why would I?

—Since we're friends.

—No. Come up with a convincing pitch.

—Buy one because ten dollars doesn't mean much to a successful man like you.

—Poor people always think about how much they don't have. Everyone else thinks of how much they want to keep.

—To support a great artistic endeavor?

—Don't sell your aspirations to me.

—Encourage local talent?

—Forget about what you think you are and think of what other people see.

—You should buy a copy to get the neighborhood kookaburra off your stoop.

Ishkabibble chuckled. —Next time I see you I owe you a dime.

A neighborhood can seem like a nation when selling door to door; the enterprise is most fruitful when there's something sad to sell. Americans yield for tragedy, not altruism.

The hardest work, what got me into many living rooms, had already been done by people like Candan, Mr. and Mrs. Blankets, my own mother probably. Folks knew of unfortunate Anthony, that my brain wasn't worth a wheel of cheese. I had $90 after nine homes. A few thousand places were left. My confidence multiplied. Shame withers beside success.

So many people were at home; it was late afternoon on a Sunday with little else to do but welcome a guest.

I rang the doorbell of Mr. Goreen, who worked as a piano teacher out of his home.

He was mildly suspicious so he looked at every page before giving me his money. I let him watch as I wrote his title, address and dollar amount on the last few blank pages of my book.

—Your cursive is so neat, he said. Do you want some water? I can make a sandwich.

To get five thousand dollars only five hundred people had to fund me. I had a thousand bucks after only one hundred and eighty minutes. The only uncharitable homes were those where the owners had been out. My neighbors were kind. Many families fed me; a slice of banana bread at least.

The more money I took the less I looked at folks directly, but my embarrassment only made them more generous. They tried, in small ways, to take care of me.

A diplomat finds himself at the doorstep of important people as he travels through any country. Eventually, even the President must be met.

He asked, —How many other people gave you money?

—Everyone.

—I guess I'd be the first to say no then?

—Are you going to say no?

He was holding the book so now he actually looked at it. —You telling me so many people like these freaky-deak movies? How am I even going to rent them? I know I never seen any of these at Blockbuster.

—It's like owning a book about Madagascar. You'll probably never go, but you can get an idea of what the place is like.

—How much?

—Ten dollars.

—You want it right now?

—Yes I do.

He went into the house and almost as quickly he returned.
—Come back in a little bit, he said. I've got to see if I can borrow.

—Forget it Mr. Jerome. I'll put you down and you pay me later.

—You come back in half an hour and just hush.

I went on until I reached the homes that abutted Kennedy Airport. It was so loud out there that I yelled my introductions. Even the bald man with a beard, in the house without window guards, slid me money. By 7:00 PM I had fifteen hundred dollars and sore knees. With a car I could have done three times as many places.

I gave the President sixty minutes to rub together the money, but he hadn't been able. When I rang the bell it was Mrs. Jerome, the President's Wife, a beautiful fat woman with a Manhattan phone book balanced on one hand. The President came out when she called him; she patted her husband's stomach before going back down the hall.

—I can't buy none, he said. I'm having trouble getting the money. I told Candan what you were selling, but he's not interested.

—I'll write you down as paid, Mr. Jerome. It's fine.

He looked at the doorknob. —Candan won't even listen to me.

No one in Rosedale seemed more my twin than the President; robust once, but surrendering to a power that hemmed him in. There was no time for comradery because that red Doberman cantered from the back then growled behind the President until the old man went back in. After he'd gone off the dog sat on its haunches at the doorway and stared at me.

I stuck my tongue out at the dog. It didn't recognize the gesture. I pulled $1500 out of my back pocket, one hundred and twenty bills, ten and twenties, all of them. I flapped them around and Viper tilted its head up at the motion.

I went to the next yard having forgotten it was mine. In the kitchen Grandma was unpacking a suitcase while Nabisase was packing another.

—Ledric's coming, Nabisase said.

—You're letting him move here?! I asked Grandma. I slammed my book down on the kitchen table. As soon as I did I picked it up to make sure it was fine.

Grandma pulled pairs of Nabisase's very small panties out of a white suitcase.

—He's coming to take me to my friend Devona's. Grandma stop!

My grandmother was sitting in a chair, bent forward. She sat up and touched the wood cabinets behind her. —Will I be left here alone?

—I'm still around, Grandma.

She looked at me and said, —Yes.

Grandma moved to a smaller tan suitcase, pulling out pairs of folded jeans. As she did that Nabisase refolded her panties.

—Is it money? I asked. Is that why you're going?

I took my earnings from my pocket and put them on the table.

—I don't want to be bribed.

—You won't take money, but you will suck dick. Tell that to your church friends.

Nabisase stopped packing. Lights were on in the kitchen, the living room, the hallway, the bedrooms. —It would be better if you were just dead for a while, she said.

Grandma didn't get up, she pulled her chair a few feet across the white-tile kitchen floor. It was a way to get around without having to get up. To the table. To my money.

—Did you steal this? she asked.

—What do you think I am?

—Then where did you get so much?

—Mr. During. 143–44 227th Street. Ten dollars.

Nabisase held my encyclopedia.

—Give it.

—Mrs. Binni. 145–46 229th Street. Twenty dollars. All these people gave you?

—They paid me.

—For what? Grandma asked.

Nabisase shook my book while holding the spine waiting for the valuable item to fall loose. Dissatisfied, she threw it in the air, over my head. It landed on the floor with such a thump that I didn't know what to do. I'd been excited when I walked in, and I still was, but I became so angry, too.

—For that! I screamed, pointing at the wounded encyclopedia. For me.

My grandmother threw my money at me and it separated in the air. A shocking soft explosion. The spine of my book was broken. My sister's clothes were untidy on the floor.

Grandma picked up my hardcover and brought it to her nose.

She stood up and gave the pages a glance.

Grandma held it open with two hands and asked, sincerely, —For such nonsense?

So I hit her.

39

Ever seen a man smack a woman? Most of the time it's anti-climactic.

I punched my grandmother, but didn't knock her down.

It was a glancing blow, more on the shoulder than chin; I didn't aim correctly. She fell sideways, but not to the floor. Grandma leaned against the fridge.

My sister drove her forearm into my back as though it was my weight she hated, not me. Then she kicked me in the shin, so I was relieved of that idea. Grandma sat on the closest chair, reached under the kitchen table, got a boot and threw it at me. Then Nabisase, ever the showstopper, swept cups and bottles from the kitchen table. The glass didn't break, but landed softly in her scattered clothes.

I turned around and hit her too. With a bit more shoulder in the delivery.

My sister's nose opened.

Blood went down into her teeth.

Grandma stood, swung a broom against my back and fell into her seat again. When the broom handle broke she moved to a cheap thin flashlight, bashing that against my knees.

Nabisase hit me with the broken end of that broom handle; it popped against my shoulder, went from eight inches to four. She hit me with it again then jabbed the wood into my cheek. We tussled and Grandma stayed in the kitchen. Nabisase and I went to the living room.

Over by the TV Nabisase threw a ruler at my head. D-cell batteries. Celery sticks.

As Grandma hurled pretzel rods I put up my hands, screamed, —I get the point!

Nabisase picked up a pair of scissors which are deadly even when folks are calm so I used my best defense and fell on her. She was fast enough to turn and start running, but I caught her under my breaker, if not my wave. Nabisase fell forward, onto her stomach and let out a sound closer to a burp than a scream.

Then a siren rounded the corner, three cop cars a moment later.

I ran to the window. Grandma had wobbled into the living room, but she didn't have a phone in her hand.

—You have a panic button in the kitchen?! I yelled.

Then the ambulance, slowest of all emergency vehicles, parked in front of my home.

I ran past Grandma as she struggled toward my sister, grabbed my book off the floor, by the fridge. I imagined Mom calling the New York Police from a duplex in Virginia. Reaching us, protecting us, even now.

The four cars had stopped in the road, but still made noise. Their lights moved across an already gathering crowd.

My sister was on her belly and Grandma was on her knees and my neighbors emptied from their homes into the street. I could see them through the front window. I wanted to explain my situation before I was arrested. I opened my front door. The police stepped out of their squad cars. Three began crowd control, one spoke to the EMTs.

The last two touched their guns as they entered the President's yard.

The paramedics followed, inside the President's house with a gurney. From 144th Avenue to 145th folks had gathered on 229th Street and it wasn't my fault.

The police brought the President out. I'm glad to say he wasn't handcuffed.

—Mr. Jerome! the crowd yelled.

—Mr. Jerome, what happened?!

Ledric arrived, but couldn't drive his Rent-A-Wreck car onto 229th Street because it was full of people. It better have been a rented car, if he owned one I'd be upset. Since I was on my steps I saw him leave the gray-green car on the next block and walk to my home. He wasn't wearing the white hospital dress now.

Instead he'd had a haircut and wore a sleek, large leather coat. He'd finally washed his face, no more oily sheen. His ash-colored slacks still showed their creases. Ledric Mayo was styling.

He entered my yard, but stayed on the bottom step. I didn't move from the top.

Ledric looked at the police, the President and back at me. —When I saw those cops I thought I knew who was in trouble.

—You're the one that brought problems into my home.

He climbed nearer, but not right up to me. —I told her to be nicer to your ass, Anthony.

—You can't mess around with a thirteen year old. I'll call these cops on you myself.

He seemed afraid to walk past me, but he finally did it. —Not all families should stay together, he said.

Then he went into my home.

I went down the six front steps until I was with the crowd.

That must have been an old gurney the paramedics had, from the wheezing noise it made when dragged out of the President's house and along our uneven sidewalk. Actually, it sounded more like whimpers.

When the EMTs pushed past me I saw the red Doberman, Viper, on the gurney. It had a claw hammer lodged in its neck.

The dog looked longer stretched out on the white bedding. Viper was on its side so the one visible eye squeezed shut and opened again, slowly. The hammer was so far inside that only the wooden handle showed. The metal head, both blunt end and sharp, had gone deep into the muscles. Viper opened its mouth to bark, but such noises were obstructed. The most it could do was sigh through the nose.

There were two paramedics, a man and woman. The guy had a body like telephone cord; he stood at the foot of the gurney massaging the Doberman's lower paws. He was crying.

The woman didn't seem as deeply affected. She kept digging her nose.

—You pick up animals now? I asked the woman.

—The call was just about an attack, she said. Didn't know who was hurt until we got here.

—Oh damn it! Ledric came running from my front door, down the steps and to the EMTs.

—She's bleeding, he told them.

—Another damn dog? the woman asked.

—My beautiful girl, Ledric told her.

I could see where each paramedic's sympathies lay. The humanitarian ran into my house with her emergency kit, Ledric right behind, as the partner wheeled Viper to the ambulance. The crowd let him go, but slowly. They wanted to see.

The police went around taking witness statements for a few minutes. I wondered what they'd ask me.

The paramedic who'd helped my sister soon ran down the front stairs, carrying that heavy black box slapping on her left thigh. —Don't put that dog in my ambulance, Ricky! Shit!

Ricky was already loading Viper inside.

The President was propped against a squad car while two cops interviewed him. He was tired; they were tired. The President's wife walked out of the house with a third police officer, but Candan didn't.

—Ricky! Stop! We're calling Animal Control!

A heavy woman leaned against the ambulance and hadn't yet bothered to move. The other cars on the street had been converted into benches. Three boys climbed up two trees. As the crowd got louder the youngest kids covered their ears.

Nabisase came to the doorway with Ledric. Her face was almost gone behind white tape and bandage. She looked like a poison warning before me.

I waved at them from the sidewalk. Relieved, even happy.

—Hello, Anthony, Mrs. Blankets said and smiled at me. Is that your book I've heard about? she asked.

I showed it to her and she clapped twice, enthusiastically. Genuinely. A festive mood filtered through the crowd.

My sister and her boyfriend went back inside. As I greeted other people, Grandma stood at the front door. She opened it and left a bag outside, at the top of the stairs.

I walked up to it. Some of my clothes were inside. I didn't care about the jeans or T-shirts. Someone had packed my two other suits. I wore the purple one now. When I stood again, after touching through my belongings, Grandma locked the security door. She did that when I was watching.

—I could break this door open easily, I said.

She leaned against the handle. —Don't.

—Where's my money?

—It is with your clothes, she said. We apologize, Anthony, but there is no room for you.

—Who's going to take care of you?

—Your sister will stay.

—I thought she said she was moving.

Grandma nodded. —Her or you.

—You could let me have the basement. I won't come upstairs.

—I apologize, Anthony.

—You're overreacting, I insisted.

—I do no such thing.

Grandma closed the door.

Let her try to live on an envelope-stuffer's salary. He'd have to mail out 80,000 letters a month to cover the mortgage. I decided to be happy. A person can do that.

There really were worse situations than mine; like Viper had a hammer in its neck.

The crowd laughed, watched the paramedics wrestle the Doberman in and out of the ambulance. The woman screamed at Ricky as she pulled the gurney out and Ricky, refusing to lose, tugged the gurney back in. Even the President watched. I waved at him, but he didn't notice.

Standing on my front stairs I could see past the crowd, over their heads, behind them.

To 145th Avenue.

Where the old German Shepherd, once owned by the Blankets family, jogged by without a leash. Without an owner. It went along.

After the German Shepherd two Pit Bulls ran behind the crowd.

A Jack Russell Terrier.

One limping Basset Hound.

A Rottweiler. A Rottweiler. A Rottweiler. A Pug.

More Pit Bulls.

Soon so many dogs were shooting down 145th Avenue that cars couldn't pass. The dogs seemed to know what would happen. Traffic stopped.

A skittering, yippering Chihuahua went by. Eleven kinds of mutts.

The air took on that wet-sock smell of canine breath.

The EMTs stopped arguing. Both climbed on the ambulance's rear bumper. Children were lifted onto their parents' shoulders. Police put away their big, black notepads. Viper continued to breathe.

It was impossible to believe there were this many loose dogs in Rosedale. Even if they'd been imported from nearby Laurelton. It made no sense. Had to be two hundred now.

But I recognized the fat, haggard German Shepherd when it passed 229th Street a second time. Six minutes later it passed a third. Every one of them did. The Great Dane. The Mastiff. The Affenpinscher, too. They weren't running away. They were running laps.

Now there really are only two ways to react to the extraordinary. The first is to ponder the grand purpose until all the fun is sucked away, the second is to enjoy it. The President's Wife left his side and ran toward the breadbasket of the crowd. She screamed, —I got $80 on Mr. Frame's boxer! Somebody better take my personal check!

Then everyone started making bets.

The dogs sprinted along 145th Avenue until they reached 225th Street. There they made a right for one block, right again on 144th Avenue, down to Brookville Park, right once more to the corner of 145th and started again. A good-sized circuit. I thought some driver, at least one, would beep at the dogs and scatter them, but not one did.

Beers were passed around soon. Given away by any men or women with a few in their fridge. All gamblers paid out when their dogs lost a lap and then picked a new breed each time. The police had to put the President in a squad car, but they left his windows down and told him how much his wife was losing.

November 26th, 1995, was the last time I lived with my family but I didn't know it then. I'd thought our fight was just a mishap not a tragedy. Mom had put them through it one thousand times. Couldn't they endure one more? It was such a surprise the first night I tried to get back in and my sister called the law.

That evening, the hounds formed a barrier. Their vigorous bodies blocked us in. We were free to mill around here, but not beyond. A person could run from one corner to the other but never, really, away. We were together. We were bound.

And I was a grown man in my fine purple suit. My black shoes fit me snugly. I held the front cover of my book to my chest. Anthony James. I felt the raised capital letters through my shirt; it was like I was screaming my name back at my own heart. That made me laugh. That made me wiggle. I felt so powerful I could have torn the moon in two.

Acknowledgments

Chris Jackson. Hard editing from a kind man is any writer's dream. Literature needs fifty more of you. Friends.

Jenny Minton. Together from the start. Smart, exacting. You're wonderful.

Dr. Raymond Smith supplied much needed information on botulism and its treatment. And attested to the snobbery of American physicians for their foreign trained pets.

John McCarthy's *The Official Splatter Movie Guide* served as a model for Anthony's own horror encyclopedia.

Last, I'd like to express my affection for fat people and crazy people everywhere.